WHEN DEA'

~by~

Alan McDermott

Also by Alan McDermott

Gray Justice
Gray Resurrection
Gray Redemption
Gray Retribution
Gray Vengeance
Gray Salvation
Gray Genesis

Trojan

Run and Hide
Seek and Destroy
Fight to Survive

Motive
Fifteen Times a Killer

Prologue

Fernando Costa ran his fingers through his long black hair and took another pull on his cigarette. The streets of Tingo Maria were quiet, even for a Wednesday night, and of the few people he saw as his car cruised down Raymondi, none fit the profile.

Young, female and alone.

"Wanna try the bars?" Xavier Ramos suggested from the driver's seat, but Costa dismissed the idea with a wave of his huge paw.

"We're not looking for a toothless old *puta*."

The kind of girl he was looking for wouldn't frequent the local bars and nightclubs; school children rarely did. His job would be a lot easier if Jose Diaz weren't so fussy, but it wasn't his place to question his boss's preferences. That would only make his life a lot shorter.

The problem was, with a population of only 46,000 people, the choices in the town were limited.

"How about her?" Ramos said, looking out of the side window.

Costa leaned forward to see who the driver was referring to, and spotted a girl hurrying down the street, several books held close to her chest. She appeared to be the right age, but it was hard to tell in the failing light. "Let's take a closer look."

Ramos spun the wheel, despite being on a one-way street. There was little traffic, and most people in the town knew who the gleaming black four-by-four belonged to, so there was no audible objection to the maneuver. The car pulled up ten yards in front of the girl and Costa got out.

She looked to be about fourteen, which was how Diaz liked them: fourteen to sixteen, but no younger. Her long black hair hung around her shoulders, and big doe eyes radiated fear.

Costa was used to such a reaction. The huge Colombian planted himself in her path, his hands on his hips and his powerful chest puffed out. "Hey, chica."

The girl's eyes darted left and right, looking for an escape, but she seemed to realize that she had little chance of outrunning him. She began to tremble.

"Don't be frightened," Costa told her as he caressed her soft hair. "I just wanna be friends. What's your name?"

"S…Sara," she squeaked. "Sara Alvarez."

"A beautiful name for a beautiful girl."

"I…I have to get h…home," Sara stammered. "My father will be…angry if I am late."

"Then I shall tell your father that you were entertaining Señor Jose Diaz," Costa smiled. "I'm sure he will have no objections."

Fear seemed to grip her at the mention of the name, and Sara tried to run.

Costa was expecting it. His hand shot out and grabbed her arm. Her books tumbled to the ground as she bucked and twisted to escape his grasp. It was a futile attempt. Costa lifted her by the bicep and let her dangle in the air as he carried her to the Mercedes-Benz G-Class and threw her into the back seat. He got in beside her and tapped Ramos on the shoulder. "Vamanos."

Ramos put the vehicle in gear and they drove east, taking the familiar—and only—route back to the Diaz residence. The road was in the process of being paved at Diaz's expense, but the pavement gave way to a dirt track at the halfway point. It would be a few more months before it was completed, and then Diaz would be able to indulge in his other passion: expensive automobiles. By the end of the year, he'd be able to drive into town in his Lamborghini or Ferrari, but until then the only sensible way in and out of the villa was by off-roader.

The remaining couple of miles to the house was a bone-jarring ride, but one that Costa was used to. The girl didn't seem to enjoy it at all, but the short journey was going to be the least of her worries.

Two more of Diaz's men opened the gates, and then Ramos pulled up outside the house.

It was a huge place, eight bedrooms over three floors, with a magnolia-covered exterior and a roof topped with terracotta tiles. Two more armed guards looked down from the top-floor balcony as Costa pulled the girl from the back seat.

Sara was tearful. She wiped her nose with the back of her hand and sniffed loudly.

"Don't cry," Costa warned her. "I told you already, Señor Diaz doesn't like it. You don't want to anger him."

His words only added to her distress, and Sara began sobbing.

Costa pulled her toward the house. "This is your last warning. If you go into his room crying, you won't leave it. Understand?"

Sara's eyes widened, her mouth hanging open.

"Do you understand?" Costa repeated.

She gave him a nervous nod, and he hoped she was telling the truth. It wasn't just the girl who would be in trouble if she didn't stick to the script. Diaz liked things a certain way, and it was Costa's job to ensure the night went smoothly.

He led her up to the second floor, then along a corridor and into a small room with an en suite shower room. There was a dressing table with an assortment of make-up in front of a large mirror, and the only other furniture in the room was a wardrobe. Costa opened it and showed Sara the contents.

"One of these will fit you," he told her. Sara saw that the hangers were filled with red dresses. They all looked the same, just different sizes.

"Shower first," Costa said, 'then fix your face and get dressed. You have thirty minutes."

Sara just stood there, her body trembling.

"What are you waiting for?"

The girl averted her eyes. "I've never got undressed in front of a man before."

"You're going to do more than undress for Señor Diaz," Costa told her, his hands on his hips. "Get on with it."

Her eyes widened.

"What? Did you think you were here to sing and dance for him? He's going to make a woman of you, and you'd better enjoy it. If he thinks you are not pleased, you won't see your family again."

A single tear ran down her cheek, and she flinched when Costa raised his hand as if to slap her.

"I warned you about that! Now pull yourself together and get ready."

Costa took a seat and gestured for her to get on with it.

Sara turned her back and slowly stripped, putting her clothes in a neat pile on the dressing table.

"Turn and face me," Costa told her, and she did, her hands covering her modesty.

"Okay, take a shower."

He wasn't interested in her body. He just wanted to make sure she didn't have any unsightly marks that might draw Diaz's ire. He'd made that mistake before. Never again.

Twenty minutes later, Sara was dressed. Costa inspected her, and satisfied that she was up to Diaz's standards, he led her down the hallway to the master suite. He knocked and waited for his boss to call him in.

"Come."

Costa opened the door and saw Jose Diaz sitting in his armchair, wearing the silk robe he always favored for these moments. He was in his forties, his hair slicked back and a bushy mustache his only facial hair. If not for the pot belly, he would have been considered handsome by most. He had a neutral air about him, radiating neither warmth or malice, but those close to him knew him to be cruel and sadistic.

"Who do you have for me?" Diaz asked.

Costa nudged the girl forward. "Tell Señor Diaz your name," he instructed her.

"Sara Alvarez," she mumbled.

"And how old are you?" Diaz asked.

"Fifteen."

Diaz looked at Costa and inclined his head toward the door.

Costa understood. He left, closing the door behind him, then went downstairs to the kitchen to make himself a coffee while he waited.

Diaz would be done within the hour. If she was lucky, Sara would be dropped off in town with a warning not to speak to anyone of her experience.

If not, it would be Costa's job to dispose of the body.

Chapter 1

Simon "Sonny" Baines was glad to see the back of Lima.

It wasn't that there was much wrong with Peru's capital, but therein lay the problem. It was...nice. Pleasant, beautiful, good food, great architecture, warm and friendly people. It was just...lacking excitement.

Having spent most of his adult life in war zones in a variety of countries, he didn't sit well with the tourist life. It was okay in small doses, but he and Eva Driscoll had been doing it for over a year. What he really needed was something to get the adrenaline flowing. He'd done paragliding, bungee jumping, white water rafting. He'd even taken flying lessons in helicopters, but nothing came close to the ferocity of a firefight. The smell of battle, the knowledge that each passing second could be your last, that the next bullet could have your name on it.

Even now, as they drove inland toward majestic mountains and lush forests, Sonny failed to be impressed with the scenery.

"What's up?"

Sonny looked over at Eva in the driver's seat. "I miss the life," he said. He could have told her that nothing was wrong, but she would know it to be a lie. The bond between them was so strong that they could pick up on the tiniest incongruity.

"You don't think this is the life?" She smiled, a simple action that never failed to melt his heart.

She has a point, Sonny thought. They were rich beyond most peoples' dreams, with over fifty million dollars to their name. Most was in precious stones, spread out in deposit boxes in banks around the world, some in cash, with the remainder in cryptocurrency. On top of that, he was in love with the most intelligent and beautiful woman he'd ever known, and he knew she felt the same way about him. On face value, it *was* the life, and billions of men would have swapped with him in a heartbeat.

That didn't stop him pining for the old days.

"You know what I mean," Sonny said, resting his hand on her knee. "Don't you ever yearn for some action?"

"To be honest, no. I've seen enough death and lost too many friends." She put her hand on his thigh. "I don't want to lose you, too."

Her statement hit hard. She'd lost her lover, Carl Huff, a few years earlier. Sonny's best friend, Len, had been killed in the same incident. In fact, Sonny had lost everyone he knew, either killed in action or hiding from the same shadowy organization that would kill him and Eva on sight. The Executive Security Office, or ESO, were the most powerful people on the planet, controlling the media, banks, law enforcement agencies, even governments. Eva had crossed them a few years earlier, dragging Sonny, Len and Tom Gray into the fight, and they'd been on the run ever since.

It helped that the ESO thought that he and Eva were dead, but one mistake could put them back in the spotlight.

Perhaps it was better to stay anonymous, living an idle life with no financial worries. He might not have the action he craved, but at least he had Eva. He squeezed her leg. "I guess you're right."

"You know it."

The sun was already setting, and they'd put over two hundred miles between themselves and Lima. Their next stop was Tingo Maria, another three hours or so on the road.

They liked the small towns. The hotels were more inclined to offer rooms without requiring ID, and Sonny and Eva were less likely to come across anyone remotely connected to the ESO. If they visited large cities like Lima, they stayed on the outskirts, only venturing into town to eat or take in the sights. The downside was that they never got to stay in decent hotels. If they were lucky, they got air-conditioning, but little comforts such as room service and silk sheets were a thing of the past. Not that any of that bothered Sonny. He'd spent years in the army, sleeping in the open for days at a time. A flea-pit hotel was luxury in comparison.

The place they settled on looked promising from the outside, and the inside pleasantly surprised Sonny. It appeared clean, with a functioning en suite shower which he was eager to test.

"I'm famished," he said as he dried himself off a few minutes later. "I saw a place near here, a bar that looks like it does food. Wanna try it?"

Eva stripped off, and Sonny caught himself admiring her body once more, all thoughts of food suddenly gone.

An hour—and another shower—later, they were dressed in shirts and slacks.

The bar was just a couple of hundred yards from the hotel. A red neon sign announced the name of the place in Spanish, which Sonny was able to translate to the Dancing Bull. As soon as they walked in, the aroma that filled the space made his mouth water.

The lighting was dim, and smoke hung in the air. Sonny had learned that pretty much everyone in Peru ignored the ban on smoking in public buildings. As they couldn't cook for themselves, Sonny and Eva had to suffer the rank odor every time they ate.

An ancient oak bar ran almost the entire length of the right-hand wall, while tables and chairs filled the rest of the floorspace.

"Grab a table," he told Eva, "I'll get a couple of beers."

After ordering from a surly young figure behind the bar, Sonny found Eva sitting at a table at the back of the restaurant, near the washrooms. Her choice allowed her to keep an eye on the front door while being close enough to the rear exit to make a quick getaway if necessary. Despite being officially dead, neither of them had let their tradecraft slip.

"Two days to the Ecuadorian border, another to Quito," Sonny mused as he put a frosted bottle of beer and a menu in front of Eva. "If we're gonna be traveling so much, I think we should consider another form of transport."

"You wanna buy a plane?"

Sonny beamed. "That would be cool, wouldn't it?"

"Yeah," Eva grinned, "but it's not happening."

"I know. I was thinking more along the lines of a boat. Sail up the coast at our own pace, drop anchor wherever we want."

"Nice idea," Eva conceded, "but too dangerous. In a car, we can take a side street and lose a tail. At sea, there's nowhere to run. If the coast guard takes an interest in us, we're sitting ducks."

"There is that," Sonny said, and chugged his drink. He held up his bottle and licked his lips appreciatively. "I'll say one thing for the locals: they sure know how to make a decent beer."

Eva was studying the menu. "I'm gonna have the Lomo Saltado," she said.

"I'll have the same," Sonny told her. He was a big fan of the local marinated beef dish.

There didn't appear to be any table service, so Sonny returned to the bar to place their order. As he waited to get the bartender's attention, three men walked in. The first was huge, with shoulder-length black hair and a formidable build. The giant's two companions were smaller but looked equally menacing.

The young bartender acknowledged them with a nod of the head and popped the tops on three bottles of beer. He placed them on the bar and put three glasses and a bottle of whiskey next to them before returning to the person he'd been serving.

Sonny waited patiently for his turn, then ordered the food and a couple more beers. When he turned to take the drinks back to the table, he saw the giant and his friends hovering around Eva.

He was used to guys hitting on her, but this time it was different. The way the bartender had dropped everything and rushed to serve the trio suggested they had influence, and as they didn't look or dress like politicians or officials, that left only one explanation: they were trouble.

Most men walked away when they discovered that Eva was with him, but Sonny expected it would be different this time. The three newcomers looked like they could handle themselves, and he suspected they were used to getting what they wanted.

Sonny decided to use his two-stage approach to the problem. He'd hit them with the Baines charm, and if that didn't work, he'd resort to swift and extreme violence. Despite being outnumbered, he had the advantage of surprise. They wouldn't see him as a threat because of his size, and he figured he could take two out before the third knew what was happening.

He just hoped it wouldn't come to that. Though the idea of a bar room brawl was tempting, Sonny was starving.

"Hey, guys," Sonny smiled as he approached the table. "What's happening?"

The trio looked at him, but Sonny's eyes were on Eva. He saw her point a foot at one of the men, indicating which one she would take if things kicked off. That left Sonny with two targets, one of them being the big man. He was obviously the ringleader, and Sonny figured that if he took him out first, the others would soon cave in.

"We want to buy the lady a drink," the big one said.

Sonny knew he had more than that on his mind. He held up the two bottles. "She already has one."

One of the goons stepped between Sonny and Eva. "Go now, while you can."

The decision was made, and it was the outcome Sonny had expected.

Dinner would have to wait.

Sonny brought his left hand up and smashed the bottle against his opponent's teeth. Blood erupted from the mouth, and Sonny followed up with a punch to the throat. The man fell, clutching his neck, and Sonny turned to the next one, the leader of the trio.

He was a fraction slow.

A sledgehammer blow caught Sonny on the temple, knocking him off his feet. He went flying over a table and landed heavily on his back. Sonny had never been hit so hard in his life. He struggled to clear his head. His vision swam, but through the fog he could see Eva taking on her opponent. Sonny watched her deliver a roundhouse kick. The man parried, he stepped closer and launched a punch to her head. Eva stepped to the side, evading the fist, but the man followed through with his elbow. It struck her temple, and Sonny saw her stagger against a table. She managed to regain her balance, but her opponent kept coming. He swiped her legs from under her, and Eva had nowhere to go but down.

Seeing his lover lying winded, Sonny knew he had to get back in the fight, and quickly. He pushed off the floor, onto his knees, but as he tried to get to his feet, a black boot flew toward his head, striking him under the jaw and catapulting him into darkness.

Chapter 2

As Sonny slowly regained consciousness, the first thing that registered was the pain in his head. He was hot, his mouth parched, and when he tried to open it, his jaw screamed in protest. Sonny opened his eyes, but the darkness remained, and a humming sound reverberated inside his head.

Memories came flooding back. The bar, the fight, Eva going down…

Sonny tried to sit up, but he banged his forehead on an invisible barrier, sending a fresh wave of pain coursing through his skull.

What the hell…?

He felt around him and realized he was in a confined space. His first thought was that he'd been buried alive, but he soon deduced that the humming sound wasn't the result of his injuries. A sudden jolt threw him against an unseen ceiling. Sonny braced himself in case it happened again, as it became clear what was happening.

He was in the trunk of a vehicle, and that was never a good sign. He could think of no scenario where being transported this way would result in anything but trouble.

Sonny felt around him for some sort of weapon. His hand came to rest on cold steel, and he felt along its length to discover that it was a tire iron. That would have to do.

His thoughts turned to Eva.

What had they done with her? Was she in the back of the car, or had they taken her somewhere else? He would only discover the answer if he managed to extricate himself from his own dire situation.

The journey continued for what felt like another fifteen minutes, which Sonny used to think of a crude plan. It hinged on them not killing him the moment they popped the trunk lid.

The vehicle stopped and the engine died. Sonny was facing away from the rear, curled up with his weapon hidden up his shirt sleeve. He heard two car doors open and close, which told him how many people he'd be facing. Sonny felt a gust of fresh air as the trunk opened, and then something hard jab into his ribs. He'd expected it, and didn't flinch. Letting them think he was out cold would give him the upper hand.

Rough hands grabbed him under the armpits and dragged him out of the vehicle. Sonny knew that if they dropped him to the ground, he would be at an immediate disadvantage. The moment his feet cleared the trunk, he planted them on the ground and spun to face his two opponents, pulling the iron bar from his sleeve as he turned. He brought it around in an arc and it connected with a skull. There was a satisfying crack. Sonny didn't wait to watch him fall, but turned to find his next target three yards away. He was relieved to see it wasn't the giant from the bar, but the one he'd taken out with a beer bottle. One side of the man's face was puffed up, his top lip split and swollen.

And he was reaching for the gun in his waistband.

Sonny threw the tire iron. The man turned to protect his chest and it hit him on the elbow—not a serious blow, but enough to distract him while Sonny closed on him. Split Lip abandoned the attempt to draw his weapon and blocked Sonny's punch, then countered with one of his own. Sonny twisted and took it on the upper arm, then lashed out with his foot. He missed, but he kept advancing, never giving his opponent the chance to pull his weapon. Sonny aimed another punch and it connected with cheekbone, and Split Lip staggered backwards, desperate to stay on his feet. Sonny charged in, landing another right hand and felling the man. Split Lip fumbled once more for his gun, but as he got his hand on it, Sonny dropped on him knee-first. Sonny heard ribs crack as his weight forced the wind from the man's lungs and trapped his gun hand. Sonny reached for the pistol and snatched it free from Split Lip's waistband.

Sonny stood and held the pistol on Split Lip while he checked the other goon. It was the one who had fought with Eva, and he was out cold. Nevertheless, Sonny searched him and found another pistol, which he tucked into the back of his waistband.

He took the time to take in his surroundings. Though it was dark, he could tell they were no longer in town. They must have taken him out into the wilderness to kill and bury him.

"Where's my girlfriend?" Sonny asked Split Lip, who was curled up in a fetal position and struggling to breathe.

The response was a stream of grunted Spanish laced with most of the expletives Sonny had learned over the years. Sonny kicked him in the side and told him to get to his feet.

"Fuck you!" Split Lip spat.

16

"Suit yourself."

Sonny went over to the other goon and put a round in his head. When he looked back he saw a stunned expression on Split Lip's face.

"Ready to talk?" Sonny asked.

Split Lip looked from his buddy to the barrel of the pistol. "You don't know who you're messing with," he snarled.

"Enlighten me," Sonny said. When he was met with a blank expression, he dumbed it down. "Who am I messing with?"

Split Lip spat on the ground. "You're a dead man."

"Well, believe it or not, you're not the first person to try to kill me, yet here I am." Sonny took a step closer and aimed the pistol at Split Lip's head. "Now, one last time. Where is Eva?"

When Split Lip grinned, Sonny knew he was going to get nothing useful from him. He fired his second shot of the night, then went through the dead men's pockets. As well as plenty of cash, he found two phones. Both had driver's licenses, and he learned that their names were Xavier Ramos and Hector Pineda.

Someone in town would know who they were, and he decided to start with the bartender.

* * *

Sonny turned the car around and drove back down the dirt road until he reached what passed as a highway. There were no signs at the intersection, but to the right he could see distant lights. He turned in that direction. Fifteen minutes later, he was back in familiar surroundings.

His first stop was the hotel to see whether Eva had managed to escape. The long shot proved to be fruitless. There was no sign of Eva. No note, nothing. Sonny gathered their things and checked out, making an excuse about having to rush to visit a sick relative. With the bill paid, he dumped their gear in the trunk of their car and drove to the bar. It was almost closing time. Through the window, Sonny could see just a handful of customers left. The young bartender was helping to clean tables, cajoling the customers to go home to their beds. Sonny waited until the last one left, then went inside and locked the door.

"Cerrado," the bartender said without looking up from the table he was wiping.

"I know you're closed," Sonny said. "If you ever want to open again, tell me where my girlfriend is."

The bartender's jaw dropped when he looked up and saw Sonny. His eyes darted around looking for an escape route, but the pistol that appeared in Sonny's hand made him think twice.

"Sit!" Sonny barked, gesturing with the gun to reinforce the order.

The bartender did as he was told, his eyes never leaving the weapon.

A barmaid emerged from a storeroom, her eyes glued to her phone. She said something, and when there was no answer, she glanced up and took in the scene before her. A scream began to form, but Sonny turned the gun on her and put one finger to his lips. Her mouth closed, but the bottom lip trembled.

"Now, who speaks English?"

"A little," the bartender said.

"Good. I'll make this nice and quick and you can both go home. Where is my girlfriend?"

The bartender swallowed. "I don't know anything."

As lies went, it was one of the flimsiest Sonny had ever heard. "Then let me refresh your memory. I came in here earlier with my girlfriend. Three men attacked us—in here—and two of them put me in the boot of their car. They are now dead. Who was the other man, and where can I find him?"

The bartender looked pained, as if he wanted to say something but knew he shouldn't.

Sonny decided to help him make up his mind. He strode over to the girl and forced her head down on a table, then put the barrel of the gun to her temple. "I'm losing patience. First she dies, then you die. Someone in this town knows who they are, and I won't stop killing people until I find out."

The girl whimpered. She was looking at the bartender and pleading with him, but he just shook his head slowly as tears began to fall from his eyes.

Sonny tried one last approach. "I guess this man is powerful, and that's why you don't want to give his name. So let me tell you what's going to happen. I'm going to confront him and one of us is going to die. If it's me, he won't know you told me about him. If it's him, you won't need to worry. So, for the last time, *who's got my girlfriend?*"

The girl screamed as Sonny pushed the pistol harder into her temple. He could see the bartender was approaching a full-blown meltdown. Sonny didn't want to follow through with his threat to kill the pair, but he was fast running out of ideas.

"His name is Fernando Costa," the bartender babbled, and his head dropped.

"Where do I find him?" Sonny asked. When he got no reply, he shouted the question again. "*Where can I find him?*"

"He lives in the villa outside town. Jose Diaz's place."

"Who's Jose Diaz?" Sonny asked.

The bartender shook his head from side to side, and Sonny knew he was about to clam up again. He walked over, grabbed the boy's hair and pulled his head back, placing the pistol on his forehead. "Who is he?"

"He's a dangerous man."

"So am I," Sonny told him. "How do I get to his place?"

"Take Avenue Hipolito Tuesta east as far as you can. You can't miss it."

"How far?" Sonny pressed.

The boy shook his head. "I don't know. Maybe five miles. When it becomes a dirt road, you are halfway. Look for the big gold gate."

Sonny stood back but kept the gun on the boy. "Give me your ID," he said. "I want hers, too."

The kid said something in Spanish and the girl fumbled in her purse. She dropped a driver's license from her trembling fingers onto the table. Sonny snatched it up and took the card offered by the boy. He read them both, then dropped them in the bartender's lap.

"I know who you are. If I get to Diaz's place and they're expecting me, I'll come back for you. You don't want that."

Sonny unlocked the door and disappeared into the night.

Chapter 3

Eva came to with a start. She tried to straighten her leg to ease a cramp, but found she couldn't move. She was lying on her stomach with her hands and feet tied behind her back, her heels against her backside.

She instantly remembered the fight at the bar. She'd been knocked to the floor, and though she recalled getting up and hitting the local with a beer bottle, it was blank after that.

No, there was something else.

Sonny.

She had seen him fall.

Eva craned her head to look down the length of the seat, but she was alone in the back. In the driver's seat was the big guy from the bar, and the front passenger seat was empty. She had no idea where she was, but they were no longer in town, that was certain. Outside, she saw nothing but darkness.

She had to get out of there and find Sonny, but she would have to be patient. Right now, she was helpless, but they would untie her at some point. If the plan was to kill her, they would have done it by now, so they must have something else in mind.

Eva had a pretty good idea what it was.

She lay still, conserving her strength. Her opportunity would come.

A jolt almost threw her off the seat, and then the road went from smooth to bumpy. She felt like she was lying on an unbalanced washing machine on high spin, and she felt grateful that she'd never been prone to car sickness.

The constant vibration lasted twenty minutes, until the car came to a stop. Moments later, it began moving again, and through the window Eva could see huge gold gates pass by.

When the car stopped again, the driver got out and shouted something. The rear door opened and Eva was dragged backwards out of the vehicle.

"Where'd you find this one?" Eva heard in Spanish.

"A bar," the giant who had been driving said.

"She's a bit old for Jose."

"She's not for him," Giant said. "She's mine."

Between them, the two men carried Eva around the back of a huge, two-story Spanish-style house with terracotta roof tiles and clean stucco walls. It was set in an expansive, immaculate lawn with several concrete ornaments.

The two men carried Eva into a kitchen where they placed her on the floor. The giant took out a knife, sliced through the rope around her ankles and pulled Eva to her feet. Her hands were still bound behind her back, so she didn't struggle.

Her time would come.

The giant took her arm and pulled her toward a door. As they approached, it opened.

A man in his forties stood before them, wearing a silk dressing gown with *JD* embroidered on the chest. His black hair was cut short and greased back over his head, and he

22

sported the bushiest mustache Eva had ever seen. He was short, maybe five-seven, and his stomach was going to fat.

"Costa," the man said. "I see you have brought company."

"Señor Diaz," Fernando Costa said nervously." I thought you'd gone to bed."

Judging by Costa's reaction, Eva surmised that Diaz was the giant's boss, and he must be a powerful man for Costa to fear him. He didn't look particularly menacing to Eva, but if he scared his employees, even men like Costa, he was one to be wary of.

"I was hungry." Diaz said. He shifted his attention to Eva, looking her up and down appraisingly. "Who is this?"

Costa swallowed. "I found her in a bar in town."

Diaz's right hand crept to his groin. "She's a little older than I like."

"I know, that's why I—"

"—but there's something about her," Diaz interrupted. He walked over to Eva and ran his fingers through her hair. When he leaned in and smelled her, she recoiled in disgust. That earned her a slap around the head from Costa.

"I'm sorry, *Jefe*. She's feisty. I hoped to break her in over the next few days."

"No need," Diaz said with a wave of the hand. "I like her spirit. Have her prepared and sent to my room."

Diaz ended the conversation by walking past the trio and opening a refrigerator.

Costa grabbed Eva by the arm and dragged her out of the kitchen, cursing under his breath as he did so. "Once he's done with you, it's my turn," he growled in Eva's ear once they were in the hallway and heading for the stairs.

Eva said nothing. She hoped that by remaining passive, they would let their guard down at some point.

When they did, she would strike hard.

At the top of the stairs, Costa directed her to a small room and pushed her inside. He took his knife from his belt and sliced through her restraints, then shoved her onto a bed.

"Shower and get dressed," Costa said. He pointed to a wardrobe. "Pick a dress from in there."

Eva considered launching her attack now, but the six-inch blade in Costa's hand made her reconsider. She would have to choose her moment.

And find a weapon.

Eva went to the wardrobe and opened it. Inside she found several red dresses. She picked one off the rail and held it up against her body. It would do. She walked into the bathroom, but before she could close the door, Costa followed her inside.

"A little privacy?" Eva asked.

"No," Costa sneered. "I don't trust you."

Eva was pissed, not because her guard would see her naked, but because she intended to take the wooden hanger apart and use the metal hook as a crude weapon. With that opportunity gone, she had no reason to delay. She stripped off her shirt and pants, then discarded her underwear. She could feel Costa's eyes on her, but she ignored him and stepped into the shower.

As the water cascaded over her, she thought about Sonny. She doubted the trio would have just left him in the bar, which meant the two goons who had been with Costa would have taken him somewhere. The fact that she hadn't seen them since the bar was a good sign. If they showed up, Sonny would be dead. If not, there was always a chance…

Costa tapped on the glass and made a motion for her to hurry up. She ignored him, lathering herself slowly as she contemplated her escape. Her best chance probably lay with Diaz. It was unlikely that he would try to seduce her with a weapon in his hand, but if he did, she was confident she could take him. He was the same height as her, and she was in much better shape.

Another rap on the glass, this time harder. Eva rinsed herself and turned off the water. She stepped out of the cubicle and dried herself. Costa was sitting in a chair with a pistol in his hand, his eyes molesting her all the while. She saw that he had placed clean panties on top of the dress, but no bra. She slipped into them, then used a brush to fix her hair.

"Dry it," he said, pointing to a dryer.

Eva gave her hair a once-over, then stood before him for inspection.

"Okay," Costa said. He stood and gestured for Eva to leave the room.

Another man was waiting in the hallway. He took Eva's upper arm and led her to a set of double doors. He opened them and forced her inside. Costa followed.

The room was bare except for a dressing table, a solitary chair, and king-size bed. Any hopes of overpowering Diaz blew away when she saw the handcuffs lying on top of the silk sheets. She stopped dead, but an instant later she felt the barrel of Costa's gun in the back of her head.

"Don't even think about it," he warned her, as he pushed her up against a wall, pressing the side of her face against the plaster. "Hands behind you."

It was crunch time. If Eva let them put the cuffs on, they might never come off again. Not while she was alive. She decided to use Costa's fear of Diaz against him.

"No," she said in Spanish, pinning her arms between her chest and the wall. "And you can put that gun away. We both know you're not gonna shoot me. Your boss would kill you if you did."

"You're right," Costa said, "but we have other ways of making you compliant."

Eva felt a prick on her leg, followed by a searing pain as a liquid was injected into her thigh. She bucked to get free, but Costa had her pressed tightly up against the wall and her strength was already waning.

"It's just a muscle relaxant," Costa whispered in her ear. "It only lasts a couple of minutes, but that's all I need."

Eva tried to lash out, but her effort was feeble. Costa stepped back and she slumped to the floor. She felt her arms being pulled behind her back and the handcuffs closing, then Costa lifted her with ease and placed her on the bed.

Eva felt utterly helpless for the first time in her life. Well, perhaps the second time, after her experience in the torture chair at Camp 33 in North Korea. That time she'd managed to escape and punish those who had tried to kill her. She vowed to do the same to Costa and Diaz.

Costa looked at his watch, then stroked Eva's thigh with his huge paw. She recoiled, and Costa nodded to the second man.

"Fetch the boss."

The man disappeared, and Costa went over to the dressing table. He opened a drawer and took out a syringe with a plastic cap.

"Señor Diaz will want to…chat with you for a while," Costa said. "I'll wait here until he's ready for his fun, just in case you get any ideas."

26

Eva liked the idea of a conversation. It would give her time to formulate a plan while she regained her strength. Her legs still felt sluggish, but feeling was returning with every passing second. Whether she could take down two men, one of them the tall, powerful Costa, was debatable, but she had to try. The alternative was to lie back and accept death, and she wasn't ready to do that just yet. For one thing, she had to discover what had happened to Sonny. If he was still alive, she would find him. If not, she would make everyone in this house pay with their lives.

Diaz entered the room, and Eva knew that the rest of her life hinged on what happened in the next few minutes.

Chapter 4

Jose Diaz entered the room and looked appreciatively at the woman on the bed. She was a fine specimen, though a lot older than the company he usually preferred. Over the years, he'd shared his bed with many beautiful women in their twenties, even thirties, but the sex had soon become stale, repetitive. Most men wouldn't have complained, but Jose Diaz was no ordinary man.

Born in a ghetto in Colombia, he'd been orphaned at an early age. His mother was a whore, his father one of her endless string of tricks. When she'd died from a severe beating from one of her clients, Diaz had found himself on the harsh streets of Bogotá, where he literally had to fight to survive.

He was eight years old.

The young Diaz fell in with a group of fellow orphans, street waifs who did whatever was necessary to survive. They were led by a thirteen-year-old named Raul, who taught Diaz what he needed to know to survive on the street. That included theft. They had to eat, and no one was going to employ an uneducated urchin, so they stole what they could to fill their bellies. It wasn't just food, though.

Raul introduced Diaz to solvents and glue. Inhaling the vapors helped stave off the hunger pangs, for a while at least.

Diaz's early career as a pickpocket didn't go smoothly. More often than not, he was caught by his mark, and he suffered some terrible beatings as a result. Raul showed him how to fight dirty, how to gouge and bite his way out of trouble, and it was something Diaz picked up easily.

By the time he was twelve, Diaz was an accomplished thief and a fearsome fighter. He would gladly take on people twice his size, and once he got the upper hand he would show no mercy. Mercy was for fools, and though he lacked a formal education, Jose Diaz was by no means stupid. His reputation grew among the street folk, and it was enhanced three years later when Jose chalked up his first kill. He attempted to rob a businessman at knifepoint. Seeing the blade was usually enough to make them hand over the goods, but not this man. He was much taller than Diaz, and well-built, but Diaz stood his ground, demanding the man's wallet and watch. The mark lunged for the knife, and Diaz, reacting on instinct, buried it in his chest. The murder went unsolved. Those close to Diaz knew the truth, but none dared to share their knowledge with the police.

It was at this point in his life that his fortunes changed. Gang-leader Raul was recruited as a junior enforcer by Felix Hernandez, head of the Soldado cartel, and he convinced his new boss to let Diaz tag along. At first Jose was given menial tasks, like delivering messages and washing the fleet of vehicles, but it paid well. He had a warm place to sleep and three meals a day.

It was just before his seventeenth birthday when his stock rose. A rival cartel sent twenty men on a nighttime raid to kill the cartel boss. Diaz was still awake, and decided to go for a stroll in Hernandez's huge garden. As he opened the door to his accommodation, he saw blood spurt from the heads of Hernandez's two guards, and then their bodies drop to the ground. It had to have been some sort of silenced weapon. Diaz went back inside and quietly raised the alarm. The attacking force, thinking everyone was still asleep, had rushed the house, only to find ten heavily armed men waiting for them. Diaz picked up an automatic rifle and claimed three kills of his own. Hernandez tortured the sole survivor of the attack force until he gave the name of the man who had sent them.

Revenge had been swift and brutal.

As a reward for his quick thinking and calm actions, Hernandez gave Diaz his choice of assignment. Diaz opted for a place on his enforcement detail. From that day on, if a message needed to be sent to rivals or the authorities, Diaz was the one to deliver it.

"Where are you from?" Diaz asked Eva in Spanish.

She said nothing.

"She's American," Costa told his boss.

"Ah," Diaz said, switching to English. "And what are you doing here in Tingo Maria?"

"I'm on holiday," Eva said. "With my boyfriend. Where is he?"

Diaz looked at Costa, who just shook his head.

"It seems your boyfriend is no longer with us," Diaz said.

He watched anger distort the woman's good looks, but he wasn't concerned. In his time, he'd taken on many men, most of them bigger and stronger than himself. A diminutive woman wasn't about to cause him any anxiety.

"I'm sorry for your loss," Diaz continued, without sincerity, "but you should see this as an opportunity, not a catastrophe. I am one of the most powerful men in Peru. Hell, in all of South America! I can offer you riches beyond your wildest dreams. Could your man do as much for you?"

"At least Sonny was a real man," Eva growled. "He didn't have to kidnap me to get me into bed."

Diaz heard Costa chuckle and shot him a filthy look. "Does something amuse you?"

Costa looked shocked. "I'm sorry, *Jefe*. It's just...her boyfriend's name is Sonny. It sounds like something you would call a dog."

Diaz smiled. "It does!" He looked at Eva. "Maybe I'll get you a chihuahua. You can call it Sonny." The smile turned into a raucous laugh. "Whenever you miss him, you can cuddle the dog!"

Costa joined in, chortling with delight, but the woman didn't appear to be in such good spirits.

No matter. Diaz would break her eventually. He had time on his side, and he was a patient man.

Having been given a role of hit man by Felix Hernandez, Diaz had gone on to kill over forty men for his boss. He was well-paid for his work, but he had ambitions beyond executioner. He wanted to be where the real money was, and that meant becoming a *celeno*.

Hernandez didn't run his empire like most other drug cartels, which tended to have a strict hierarchy and a centralized structure. Hernandez preferred to have cells that worked independently but reported to one manager, or *celeno*. These men ran operations in many different locations across South America. Coca was grown not only in Colombia, but also Bolivia and Peru, and each country had a *celeno*. The one running the Peruvian operation was Juan Carlos Cabrera, a close friend of Hernandez but a man with a guilty secret.

He loved the product he was creating.

Hernandez made it known that no one in his employ should ever use drugs. They were for the weak, the feeble of mind. They clouded judgement and led to rash decisions, and that jeopardized the entire operation. When Hernandez heard rumors that Cabrera was using, he dispatched Diaz to investigate.

"If you simply confront him, he will deny it," Hernandez had said. "You must be creative. Bring me back definitive proof, one way or another."

Diaz had arrived in Peru on the pretense of dealing with a rival in the region, saying he had been instructed by Hernandez to stay with Cabrera for a couple of days. During that time, Diaz never asked Cabrera about his drug use. Instead, he waited for an opportune moment and sneaked into the *celeno's* private bathroom, where he collected a few hair samples. He returned to Colombia and had hair follicle tests performed on them, then presented the results to Hernandez.

The boss had been pleased with the manner in which Diaz had confirmed Cabrera's guilt. It showed guile, ingenuity. Others might have tried to catch Cabrera in the act, but not Diaz. He'd used his head. As a reward, he was given Cabrera's position.

All he had to do was make it vacant.

He did that three days later. Accompanied by Diaz, Hernandez arrived in Peru unannounced. They were shown into Cabrera's study, where Hernandez levelled his accusation. Cabrera vehemently denied everything, but when presented with the evidence, his demeanor changed from indignation to rage. He reached for his gun, but Diaz was quicker. By the time Cabrera's men stormed the room, their old boss was dead and Jose Diaz was sitting in his place.

From that day, Diaz had run the Peruvian operation. He would have preferred to live closer to Lima, where he could indulge his passion for fast cars, but it wasn't to be. The coca was grown close to Tingo Maria, and Hernandez liked his men to be on top of production. Not close enough that the authorities could link a *celeno* to the cocaine, but not so far away that they couldn't readily keep tabs on the staff. Diaz dreamed of bringing his three supercars to the villa one day, but first he had to complete the road to town. He wasn't about to trash a car worth half a million dollars by driving it on a dirt road. For now, his collection would remain in Colombia.

His position afforded him wealth and power, but Diaz's ambitions were not yet fulfilled. Felix Hernandez was not a young man, and one day he would have to choose his successor. Diaz was the forerunner to take over the running of the cartel, and he was prepared to wait for that moment.

In the meantime, he had this woman to keep him entertained.

And what a beautiful specimen she was. Her shoulder-length hair was black as night, and he could tell that beneath the red silk dress she had a well maintained body. She might hold his interest for a few nights, maybe longer. Time would tell.

"Remove her dress," Diaz told Costa.

The giant took the knife from its scabbard on his belt and walked toward the bed, just as gunfire erupted from the floor below.

Chapter 5

Sonny drove with the lights off, guided by his green-tinted night vision glasses. Though he and Eva played the carefree couple out to enjoy life, they knew that trouble could hit them at any moment, and equipped their car for all eventualities. A secret compartment under the rear seat contained their stash: cash, passports in various names and nationalities, and a change of clothes in go bags so they could grab them and go at a moment's notice. They also had a variety of arms, including pistols, assault rifles and grenades, as well as the NVGs Sonny was wearing.

As the bartender had promised, the road transitioned from concrete to dirt without notice. Sonny was half-way there, just over two miles to go. He had to slow to a frustratingly sluggish twenty miles per hour for the next mile or destroy the car's suspension. That was as close as he dared go on wheels. If there were guards at the gate, a car driving without lights would alert them to danger.

He pulled off the road and killed the engine, then marked the position on his phone. He then geared up. He put on his webbing harness and took the two assault rifles, plus two pistols, one fitted with a suppressor. He filled the webbing pouches with spare magazines and settled on three grenades. Two were the fragmentation variety, the other a flashbang designed for disorientation.

Keeping the NVGs in place, he ran along the dirt road. He'd changed into black jeans and T-shirt at the hotel, and the dark beanie on his head rendered him all but invisible in the moonless night.

After seven minutes he stopped to rest, figuring he'd covered another mile on foot. He rested up for a couple of minutes, and once he'd caught his breath he set off again, this time at a slower pace. If the bartender had told the truth, Sonny would see the target soon.

Sonny suspected he'd reached his destination when the trees suddenly ended and he found himself at the corner of a ten-foot white wall. Just to be sure, he crossed the road and melted into the jungle, staying fifteen yards in as he crab-walked parallel to the dirt track. When he saw the gates, he knew he had the right place. Backtracking, he crossed over the road again and slid down the side of the compound, between the wall and the trees. Halfway down, he stopped. This was a good a place as any to make his entry.

He wished he had back-up. Len would have been his first choice, but his best friend was dead. Tom Gray would have been a close second, but he was hiding from the ESO with his daughter. The only person Sonny had left in the world was Eva, and he was confident she was somewhere inside the building.

If he had known the layout, he'd have a better chance of rescuing her, but he would have to wing it. The best option was a stealthy approach until things went noisy, and then, maximum aggression.

36

The thought brought a smile to his face, but it was fleeting. Eva was in there, and there was no telling what they had done to her. He had to get her out as soon as possible.

Sonny took a running jump and leaped to grab the top of the wall, then pulled himself up and peered over. It looked clear. There was a fountain atop a circular pool opposite the entrance to the house, and a gravel drive leading to the gate. The rest of the garden was grass cut smooth as a pool table. A few garden ornaments dotted the place, but nothing that would give him adequate cover if things went to shit.

He was just about to pull himself up and over the top of the wall when he saw a figure walk around the side of the house. The man held an automatic rifle casually as he strolled along a path underneath an overhanging balcony, and he looked bored.

That was just what Sonny wanted to see. It would take the man a second or two to wake to any danger and that was all the advantage Sonny needed. He waited for the guard to disappear around the side of the house, then slid over the wall and dropped quietly to the ground. Sonny waited a moment to see if the noise had alerted anyone, but when no shouts went up, he ran in a crouch to the back of the house, figuring he'd have more success entering there than through the front door.

The back door was closed, but Sonny could see a light through its frosted glass. As he got closer, he saw two silhouettes facing each other. One of them raised something to his lips. That told him the alarm hadn't been raised.

So far, so good.

Sonny knew he had to act fast. There was no telling what Eva was going through. Assuming she was still alive…

Sonny cast the thought aside. He *knew* she was in there.

37

He took a deep breath, then opened the door and rushed in, his silenced pistol up and ready to fire. One of the two figures he'd seen was a woman with short hair, dressed in chef's whites. The other was a man who was trying to unsling his automatic rifle. Sonny gave him a double-tap to the head, then turned back to the cook. She was frozen with shock. Sonny didn't want to kill her, but he couldn't just leave her here to raise the alarm.

"Turn around," he said, using hand gestures to reinforce his instructions.

She hesitated, her eyes wide and fearful, then slowly turned away from Sonny.

He grabbed an iron skillet and brought it down on the back of her head. The cook slumped to the floor. He kicked her shin, but there was no reaction, though he could see her breathing. She'd live, with hopefully nothing worse than a concussion.

Sonny put the skillet back on the stove and cracked open the kitchen door. He decided to clear the ground floor first—that was where guard quarters were most likely to be found—then check for a basement. If he hadn't found Eva by then, he would go upstairs.

He saw a hallway with four doors. He reckoned the staff quarters would be one of the side rooms, so he started toward a door to the left of the main entrance. He'd only gone a couple of paces when he heard a familiar sound: a safety being released. Sonny broke into a sprint and turned his head in the direction of the sound in time to see a guard swing a rifle up to his shoulder. Sonny fired as he ran, but his shots went high and wide. The guard missed, too, as Sonny rolled into a crouch and fired again, hitting his target in the shoulder. As the man's rifle dropped, Sonny steadied himself and put two shots in the man's head.

The noise from the guard's rifle would have alerted the rest of the house, so Sonny holstered the pistol and unclipped one of the assault rifles, an HK G36. No need for stealth now.

The door he'd been heading toward burst open, and two men piled out into the hallway. Ready, Sonny emptied half a magazine into them. They danced like marionettes before hitting the floor, and Sonny leaped over the bodies into the room they'd come from. It was empty, with no other entrances. As he retreated to the hallway, shots peppered the door frame millimeters from his head. He ducked back inside as more rounds smashed into the door where he'd been standing moments earlier.

If he didn't move, he'd be dead. It sounded like he was facing at least two weapons, but it could be more. The angle of attack gave him a vague idea where they were, so he unclipped the flashbang and pulled the pin. The fuse was set for a five-second delay, so he let the handle fly, counted to three and lobbed it into the hallway.

He was ready, but the guards were not. When seven million lumens flooded the hallway with a two-hundred decibel bang, Sonny was on the move. He had around five seconds before the effect of the flash-bang wore off, but that proved enough. He dispatched one guard on the ground floor, near the kitchen door, then turned his attention to a second at the top of the stairs. A three-round burst took him down.

Sonny deftly switched mags and brought his weapon up to his shoulder once more, scanning for threats as he made his way to another ground-floor door. He kicked it in, but there was no response from inside. He stuck his head around the frame for an instant, trying to draw fire, but still no shots came. He ran inside, checked every angle, then mentally marked it off as clear. The next room was also empty. As he emerged from it, a figure ran into the hallway and skidded to a stop when he saw Sonny. He raised his weapon, but far too slowly. A burst from Sonny's HK put him on his back.

There was only one more room on the ground floor to check. It turned out to be the living room, and there was no one inside.

That left the top floor.

Sonny climbed the stairs carefully, checking the landing as well as his six. When he reached the top unmolested, he faced a choice of closed doors. With no sounds to give him a clue, he went left.

* * *

When Eva heard shots from somewhere deep in the house, her heart leaped. She knew that Sonny had managed to escape his captors and had come to rescue her. Another burst of gunfire resonated, and she recognized it as the HK G36 that Sonny favored these days.

She had to help him somehow, but that wouldn't be easy with her hands cuffed behind her back. Thankfully, the muscle relaxant had almost completely worn off. Her only hope was that Costa and Diaz would forget about her, giving her a chance to free herself.

Costa snatched a radio from his pocket and screamed for someone to update him. Conflicting messages came back as several men tried to update him at once.

"What the hell's happening?" Diaz shouted.

Costa swore at the radio. "I don't know. They're all reporting shooters, I can't tell how many there are." He stuffed the radio under his arm and took out his pistol, ensuring there was a round in the chamber. More shots could be heard from downstairs.

"It's Alvarez," Diaz growled. "It has to be. If that bastard snake thinks he can take my turf, he can think again."

"Jun, talk to me," Costa said into the radio.

There was no reply.

"Diego, Raul, come in."

"We've got a shooter in the hallway," a voice came back. "Engaging now…"

There were more bursts of automatic fire, but when Costa asked for an update, there was no reply.

He turned to Diaz. "We have to go," he said. "We have no idea how many there are. We have to get out of here and regroup."

"I'm not running away from that scum," Diaz growled. "Get me a weapon."

"*Jefe*!" Costa shouted. "I've lost contact with our men. We don't know how many are left, or how many we're facing. Better to retreat and call Hernandez for reinforcements. Once we are safe, we can plan a counterstrike. But we have to go *now*!"

Eva could tell that Costa was uneasy speaking to his boss like that, but it seemed to have the desired effect. Diaz slowly nodded, then the pair walked toward the door, Costa taking the lead. As an afterthought, he turned to Eva.

"What about her?"

"Bring her," Diaz said. "We can use her as a shield."

Costa grabbed Eva's upper arm, yanking her from the bed. She tried to resist, but because of her restraints and the fact that Costa was holding her elbows high, all she could do was kick out. She landed a blow on Costa's leg, but with bare feet, it barely registered.

When there was a lull in the shooting, Diaz opened the door. Eva saw a man run to the top of the stairs and fire a sustained burst. Seconds later, the guard fired again until an explosion rocked the house. The guard at the top of the stairs recoiled, then his body jerked as rounds slammed into him.

Diaz ducked back inside the room. "We can't go that way."

"The balcony," Costa replied, and dragged Eva toward the window. She struggled to free herself from his grip, but her efforts had no effect on the giant.

Diaz slid the French window open and scanned the night, then gestured for Costa to follow.

Costa pulled Eva out into the warm darkness. The balcony ran along the length of the house and disappeared around a corner, and she saw Diaz heading to her left at speed. Costa followed, and Eva had no choice but to tag along.

They'd just reached the corner when another set of French windows burst open behind her.

* * *

Sonny was in the process of clearing the second room on the top floor when he saw the silhouettes of three figures run past the window.

One of them looked to be female, and she was being pulled along as if against her will.

It had to be Eva.

Sonny kicked the window open and stepped out, his rifle ready to dispense death, but all he saw was a woman's bare ankle as it disappeared around the corner. Sonny gave chase, stopping at the corner and kneeling to look around it in case someone was waiting to blow his brains out. There were three fleeing figures running down a set of external stairs, and he recognized two of them. One was the giant from the bar. The other was Eva.

Sonny ran to the top of the stairs just as the trio reached the bottom. One of them, a shorter man wearing a dressing gown, was running ahead toward an SUV. Sonny ignored him and focused on the big man who was pulling Eva behind him. Sonny sighted his rifle on the tall figure, but he hesitated to shoot at a moving target so close to Eva. He had to do something, though. They were ten yards from the SUV, and if they managed to get Eva inside, he would lose her again.

She was looking at him, but instead of a pleading expression, she looked calm.

Like she had a plan.

"Linda Mainwaring!" she shouted.

Sonny wasn't expecting instructions, and certainly not one so obscure.

He didn't know what she had in mind, but did know he would soon find out. He sent a short burst into the grass a few feet behind and to the left of Eva, and she immediately grunted in pain and went limp.

Sonny's heart almost stopped. Had he hit her with a ricochet? Had his aim been off?

He saw the tall man falter, look at Eva, then drop her and run to the vehicle. He leaped into the passenger side before

Sonny had a chance to gather himself. Rage coursed through Sonny as he emptied the magazine into the rear of the fleeing SUV, but it sped away as the rounds bounced off what appeared to be an armor-plated chassis.

Sonny sprinted down the stairs and ran to Eva, who was lying still. He threw himself down beside her and cradled her in his arms.

"Eva!"

She opened her eyes slowly and smiled up at him. "Yep, you shoot like Linda Mainwaring."

Eva and Sonny had visited a shooting range in Bolivia a few weeks earlier, the kind of place where tourists got the chance to play soldier with an array of weapons. There was a choice of automatic rifles and pistols, shotguns and revolvers, and the rounds were dirt cheap. Sonny and Eva had spent a few days there, sharpening their skills after a couple of months of inaction. That was where they'd met Linda and John Mainwaring, a rotund, elderly couple from Alabama. John was ex-military—very-ex, he insisted repeatedly—and a keen shot. Linda, however, had evidently never fired a rifle in her life. On their first visit to the range, they took the booths to Eva's left, and Linda's first effort went high and wide. She was told to allow for the kick of the Armalite rifle, but she overcompensated from that moment on. Every round she fired hit a few feet below the target, and she always pulled left when she fired. From that moment on, whenever Sonny missed the bull by a fraction of an inch, Eva would taunt him by calling him Linda Mainwaring.

Sonny dumped Eva on the ground and stood up. "Not funny. I thought I'd killed you."

Eva pulled the handcuffs down over her backside and pulled her legs to her chest as she brought the restraints around in front of her. She got to her feet. "Aw, come on. Don't be grumpy."

"Seriously, I thought you were hit."

"That's what I wanted him to think, too. No way he was going to drag a corpse into the car." Eva gave him a peck on the cheek. "That's for caring. Now, let's find a key for these and get the hell out of here before they come back with reinforcements."

Sonny put a new mag in the pistol and handed it to her, and they jogged back to the house.

"It should be in the room they were holding me in," Eva said. "I'll go look, you check the bodies."

Sonny went through the pockets of the men he'd killed, but none had keys for the handcuffs. He also checked the chef he'd knocked unconscious. He was glad to see that she was still breathing. When he returned to the hallway, Eva was waiting. The cuffs were nowhere in sight, and she'd changed back into her own clothes. Sonny gave her the second assault rifle that was strapped to his back.

"The car's about a mile down the road," he told her.

"Then what are we waiting for?"

Chapter 6

Jose Diaz's eyes flicked continually from the road ahead to the rear-view mirror as he gunned the SUV. The vehicle juddered angrily as they hit a pothole, bouncing Diaz and Costa violently in their seats.

"*Jefe*, slow down. The car wasn't built for this."

Diaz ignored him, keeping his foot hard down. Another jolt threw them both from their seats, but the speed never dropped.

"I want Alvarez dead," Diaz growled. "I want him dead, I want his family dead, I want his fucking dog dead!"

Costa rubbed his head where he'd banged it on the roof of the car. "If I'm honest, I don't think it was Alvarez," he said. "He would have sent more men, but I only heard one shooter."

"Then he sent an assassin," Diaz insisted.

Costa hesitated before answering. "I don't think so. When we were running for the car, he fired and hit the woman. Why didn't he finish us off? We were out in the open, an easy shot for a trained killer. It's almost as if we weren't the targets."

Diaz, fueled by adrenaline, was struggling to make sense of Costa's words. He slowed the car so that he had one less thing to concentrate on. Eventually, the answer came to him. "He was after the woman?"

"I think so."

"Then why shoot her?" Diaz asked.

Costa looked over at his boss. "Maybe he didn't. She shouted something, I don't know what it was. A name, a place, I don't know. Then he fired, and I heard her grunt and she collapsed, so I assumed she was hit. I wasn't about to hang around and check her vital signs."

Diaz slammed on the brakes. "You mean she could have been faking?" He was beyond angry. "You let her trick you?"

"*Jefe*, what was I to do? It sounded like she was hit. She collapsed. I had no way of knowing…"

Diaz spun the wheel and performed a three-point turn.

"We're going back?" Costa asked.

"Yes, dammit! You're going to go through the video tapes and identify the attacker."

There were several cameras dotted about the house, and the recordings were accessible from a secret room hidden behind a wardrobe in Diaz's suite, and only Diaz and Costa knew about it.

"But what if he is still there?" Costa asked.

Diaz looked determined. "Then we kill him."

Costa took out his phone.

"Who are you calling?" Diaz asked.

"Xavier. I told him and Hector to deal with the boyfriend." Costa listened for a few moments, then cursed. He tried another number, with the same result. "They're not answering."

It was all too coincidental for Diaz. "Who exactly was that girl?"

Costa shrugged. "Just some *puta* I found in a bar. She was sitting alone when I saw her, but then some gringo came along claiming to be her boyfriend. I told him to leave, and he just went crazy. He hit Hector with a bottle before I laid him out. The girl was a fighter, too. She went for Xavier like a wildcat, but he managed to knock her out. I brought her back here and told the others to deal with the boyfriend. They said they would take him into the jungle and bury him."

"Obviously they didn't, and now he's back for revenge."

"Maybe not," Costa said. "Maybe he just wanted the woman back."

Diaz looked over at Costa. "You think that makes a difference?" Diaz slapped the wheel. "He attacked my house!" he bellowed. "He killed my men and tried to kill me!"

Costa nodded solemnly, his responsibility clear. "I will find him. Both of them."

"How?" Diaz asked. "You think they're going to hang around for you to find them, eh? You think they'll rent a room in town and wait for you to knock on their door?"

Costa lowered his head slightly, a penitent act. "I have her wallet," he said. "I haven't been through it in detail, but I know there's a driver's license."

"There is? Show me."

"I haven't got it with me. It's in my truck."

"Then when we get back, give me her ID. I'll instruct the local police to set up roadblocks in a fifty-mile radius."

"We're going to need more men, too," Costa pointed out.

48

Diaz had already thought of that, but it meant calling Felix Hernandez and explaining the situation. He knew the boss wouldn't be happy to learn that six of his men were dead just because Costa had taken a fancy to a woman. Hernandez would be even more pissed to learn that she and her boyfriend were still alive. Hernandez would see an attack on one of his *celenos* as an attack on himself, and that was something he wouldn't tolerate. The call had to be made, though. Trying to bury the incident would only make Hernandez angrier.

"I'll arrange that," Diaz said reluctantly.

* * *

When they reached the gates to the house, Costa told Diaz to stop the car.

"I'll go ahead and make sure it's safe."

"No, give me a weapon," Diaz responded. "Better if we go in together."

Costa was glad that Diaz was a fighter. His previous boss had been hands-off, letting others do the messy work, but Diaz was happy to get his hands dirty. It was how he'd earned his reputation and his position.

"Okay." Costa got out, his pistol up in a two-handed grip, ready to fire at the first movement. He moved quickly, zigzagging across the grass until he reached the front door. It was open, and he stuck his head inside. He saw no movement, just five bodies. Costa waited by the door for a moment, listening, but there was no sound coming from inside the house. He crept inside to the nearest body. He didn't bother checking for vital signs, but took the man's rifle and spare magazines. As an afterthought, he went to the next corpse and took that man's weapon, too. One for Diaz, the other for himself.

Costa ran back to the car and Diaz climbed out, taking the rifle from Costa.

"No sign of anyone, but they could be hiding, waiting for us."

Diaz didn't seem to care about the danger. With a gun in his hand, he looked ready to take on the world.

Costa followed as Diaz strode confidently toward the house, kicked the door wide and walked in, as if daring anyone to take him on.

Not wanting to appear cowardly, Costa followed, marching into the house with all the swagger he could muster. He stood looking around, waiting for something to happen, and with each passing second he grew more relaxed.

"Check upstairs," Diaz said as he walked into the living room.

Costa stopped at the top of the stairs, listening for sounds of movement. All he could hear were Diaz's footsteps below him. Costa tried each bedroom in turn, and when he reached the room where the girls changed before being presented to Diaz, he saw that the woman's clothes were missing.

Costa left the room and found Diaz on the landing.

"All clear."

"Good," Diaz said. "Let's check the CCTV and see who it was."

They went to Diaz's room and the boss hit the hidden button to open his secret room. Inside was a chair facing a large monitor flanked by two smaller screens. Diaz tapped on the keyboard to display the view from the camera mounted at the top of the stairs, facing the front door. He rewound to the time of the attack, then let it play. It wasn't long before a lone figure came into view.

"That's him," Costa said. "That's the boyfriend."

They played the video for the next half-hour, and the final action was the couple leaving the house together.

"Looks like it's just the two of them," Diaz said.

"Then we should be able to stop them before they get too far. Come."

Diaz led Costa downstairs and into Diaz's study. The *celeno* poured a drink of straight whisky and stared at the secure cell phone on his desk. It was a direct line to Hernandez, the only way they communicated.

Costa could tell his boss's mind was in turmoil. He was probably dreading the call to the cartel boss, and Costa wasn't looking forward to it, either. His part in this would come out, and it was a coin toss whether Hernandez would let him live or die.

"Bring me her ID, then check on the cook," Diaz said. "She's in the kitchen."

Costa ran to his truck and took the wallet from the glove box. He had a quick look at the name on the driver's license, Harriet Danes. He returned to the house and gave it to Diaz, who took out his cell phone and called the police chief. He read off the details on the ID and gave the cop descriptions, telling him he wanted the woman and her male partner contained, or heads would roll. Diaz hung up, put his phone back in his pocket, then returned to staring at the phone on his desk.

Costa waited, hoping to hear the conversation between Diaz and Hernandez, but Diaz gestured toward the door with his head.

Costa reluctantly left.

Alan McDermott

He found Anastasia, the cook, sitting up against an island in the kitchen, massaging the back of her head. She looked woozy, confused.

"You okay?" he asked.

Anastasia looked at him as if he was a complete stranger speaking a different language.

Costa didn't want to waste time on her. He helped her to her feet, and when it was clear she wasn't going to collapse, he told her to go and lie down, then returned to Diaz's study. His boss was just ending the call when he entered the room.

"What did he say?" Costa asked, his hands resting on his hips, inches from his pistol. If Diaz had been ordered to kill him, he wasn't going without a fight.

"We're to wait by the phone," Diaz said. "He'll look into the woman and get back to us."

"That's it? He wasn't pissed?"

"Oh, he was pissed, trust me."

Costa believed him. Diaz had a ferocious temper, but compared to Felix Hernandez, he was a teddy bear. Hernandez had no tolerance for fuck-ups. He had once had a chef killed for over-seasoning a dish and then having the temerity to say it was cooked to perfection. Costa didn't dare think about what Hernandez would do in this situation.

"Maybe the local cops will find them soon," he offered, though he wasn't sure that would be enough to calm Hernandez.

"Even if they do, the damage has been done. Felix won't forget this."

* * *

Felix Hernandez put the phone down and took a couple of deep breaths, then slammed his fist into the mahogany table. "*Jorge!*"

One of his men ran into the room. "*Jefe.*"

"*Get me Jimenez!*"

The lieutenant ran to comply with the order, leaving Hernandez alone to fume.

"How *dare* they attack my operation!"

Hernandez stood and stuffed his hands in his pockets, looking out the window over his expansive estate.

"*Jefe.*"

Hernandez spun to see Romeo Jimenez striding in. The man reminded him of death. Tall, skinny, gaunt, bald, he had the look of a cadaver.

"Someone just hit the Peru operation," Hernandez said. "A man and a woman. Diaz said his idiot lieutenant picked the woman up at a bar and told his men to kill the boyfriend, but instead he showed up and went on the rampage. I want to know who they are." He went back to the table and gave Jimenez the piece of paper with the woman's details on it.

"Give me a few moments, *Jefe.*"

Jimenez walked away and took his phone out. He tapped the screen and began talking almost immediately.

Hernandez went to his bar and poured himself a drink, then lit a cigar and puffed angrily.

In all his years, he'd never seen anything so insulting. Sending just two people—one of them a *woman*—to kill one of his *celenos* was arrogance in the extreme. It was almost an affront to Hernandez himself. In fact, it *was*. It was a slap in the face, and he would destroy those responsible. He hadn't spent thirty years building his empire to have his reputation sullied this way.

And he would kill them himself. It wouldn't be the first time, and it wouldn't be the last. Over the course of his life, Hernandez had personally taken dozens of lives and ordered the deaths of hundreds more. Maybe thousands. He'd lost count a long time ago. Each death had helped cement his reputation as the most feared cartel boss in all Colombia, probably the world.

He'd even killed to get control of the organization. When the previous boss had died, three men had been in contention to take over, but Hernandez had judged none of them suitable. They certainly didn't have his vision or ruthless streak. They would have made weak leaders, leaving the cartel open to takeover by a rival, and Hernandez wasn't about to let that happen. Two of the candidates had taken a bodyguard each to a meeting in a restaurant to discuss becoming joint leaders. Hernandez had killed all four men. The one remaining hopeful had sent six of his best men to take Hernandez out, but they'd failed miserably. Their heads were delivered by Hernandez personally, and a seventh was added to the pile.

With all opposition quashed, Hernandez took over and immediately made changes. Those he knew to be loyal were promoted, while those who had wronged him in the past were dealt with swiftly until there was no one left who would dare to question his leadership. Not within his own organization, nor his rivals.

Until now.

After twenty minutes, Jimenez returned to the room. "I just spoke to my contact in the States. There's no record of the woman with that name and date of birth. No social security number, criminal record, IRS filings, nothing."

Hernandez was confused. "The license was a forgery?"

"I would think so."

"Then they were not simply tourists, as the woman claimed."

"It appears not. If I had to guess, I would say DEA. I can't think of any other reason why they would be in a shit hole like Tingo Maria except to target Diaz."

That made sense to Hernandez. The Drug Enforcement Agency was always looking for ways to infiltrate his organization.

"Can you be sure?" Hernandez asked. Jimenez was the best in the business, but even he had his limitations.

"If I can get DNA and hair samples, I should be able to identify them. Once I do, it will be a case of tying them to the Americans. I have people who can help me with that."

"Then I want you on a flight to Peru as soon as possible," Hernandez said.

"You want me to go there?"

"Of course. Jose screwed up, so I can't trust him on this. Get what you need and report back to me."

"I will, *Jefe*. It is imperative, though, that Jose doesn't touch anything in the house. I need to see it as it is now. He might try to clean up and destroy any evidence that is lying around."

"I'll let him know," Hernandez said. "Go and tell Julio to make the travel arrangements."

Jimenez nodded and left, and Hernandez picked up his hotline to Peru.

* * *

Diaz and Costa had plenty of time to think about the consequences before the phone rang again. They'd agreed that Diaz would put it on speaker.

Diaz cleared his throat. "*Jefe.*"

"I want you to tell me the truth," Hernandez said. "What really happened tonight?"

Diaz looked at Costa, confused. "It was just like I told you," Diaz said to Hernandez. "Costa found a woman at a bar and got involved in a fight with her boyfriend. Two men took the gringo away to bury him in the jungle and Costa brought the woman back to my home. An hour later, the place erupted. We checked the CCTV afterwards and it was the boyfriend. He killed six of my men and tried to kill me."

The phone went silent, adding to Costa's discomfort. It was unnerving that Hernandez thought they were being economical with the truth. Eventually, though, the cartel boss spoke again.

"We checked her details," Hernandez said. "She doesn't exist."

"Then the license must be a forgery," Diaz said. "I'll have it couriered to you immediately and—"

"No need," Hernandez interrupted. "I'm sending someone to you."

Costa could see that Diaz was getting flustered.

"There's no need, *Jefe*," Diaz said. "We have mobilized the local police. We'll have them within hours."

"Really?" Hernandez replied, his voice dripping with sarcasm. "You still think they were just tourists? You told me earlier that he had an assault rifle and grenades. You think he picked them up at the local supermarket. Eh?"

Diaz had no answer, so Hernandez filled in the blanks for him. "They are DEA!" the boss screamed down the phone. Diaz recoiled, and Costa almost jumped.

"Are you sure?" Diaz asked once he'd composed himself, then immediately flinched. It wasn't wise to question Felix Hernandez, especially when he was in such a foul mood.

Costa was surprised when Hernandez didn't explode.

"Not yet, but I have people working on it," Hernandez said. "In the meantime, do not touch anything in your house. Leave the bodies where they are, don't touch any shell casings, nothing. I'm sending Romeo Jimenez to track them down. If they can kill six of your men and escape unhurt, a few local cops are not going to stop them."

The call abruptly ended, and Costa slumped into a chair.

"That went better than I expected."

Diaz shot him a look. "You think? You invited the DEA into my house and you think things are going well?"

Costa squirmed. Time to change the subject. "Who is Romeo Jimenez?"

Diaz drained his glass of whiskey. "An ex-Fed from Bogotá. You remember Juan Perez, the enforcer from Chapinero?"

Costa nodded. "Of course." Perez had been caught in the act of dismembering one of his victims and sentenced to life in prison. Instead, he offered to turn state's evidence on Hernandez in return for witness protection.

"And you remember what happened to Perez?" Diaz asked.

The picture was still clear in Costa's mind. Juan Perez, stripped naked, his innards dangling from his body as he hung from an overpass. "I remember."

"Jimenez was the one who tracked him down. It took two months, but he eventually found him in Puerto Escondido. New name, new look, it didn't matter. If anyone can find this pair, it's Jimenez."

Chapter 7

"Satisfied now?" Eva asked as they got into the car.

They'd run from Diaz's house, staying inside the tree line in case any vehicles passed by. It had been a good call. Five minutes after they left, they heard the roar of an engine as it passed them on the way to the villa. They didn't see the occupants, just the flash of white as the headlights cut through the night, but it could signal police or reinforcements. They had to get out of the area, and fast.

"What do you mean?" Sonny asked as he put on his NVGs.

"This afternoon, you said you craved excitement. I just hope you got it out of your system."

Sonny started the car and backed out of the trees. He pointed it in the direction of town, keeping the lights off.

"I didn't want this," he said. "I never wanted to put you in danger."

Eva looked across at him. He seemed genuinely remorseful. She put her hand on his knee.

"Thanks for coming back for me," she said.

"Of course. You think I'd leave you there?"

"I thought I'd lost you," she said. "The big guy, Costa, said you were dead."

Sonny smiled and glanced at her. "You think I'd let something as trivial as death keep me from you?"

Eva squeezed his leg. "Did you get that from a Hallmark card?"

"No, that's one hundred percent original Sonny Baines."

"Speaking of which," Eva said, suddenly getting serious, "we need new IDs. Costa took mine, and I have a feeling they won't take your little incursion lightly."

"You think they'll come after us?"

"I do," Eva said. "Diaz came across as powerful, influential. You don't rise that high selling sunglasses to tourists."

"What do you think?" Sonny asked. "Local mafia?"

"Could be. A lot of coca is grown in this region. Could be a drug lord." It wasn't as if they could ask around town, and for now, it didn't really matter. The only thing she cared about was getting as far from Tingo Maria as possible.

"Where do you want to head?" Sonny asked, as if reading her mind.

Eva took out her phone and opened the map. After a few moments, she made a decision. "North."

"Ecuador?"

Eva shook her head. "Colombia. There's nothing east of us other than jungle, and I don't know anyone in Bolivia who can get us new papers. Once we get new IDs in Colombia, we can find a way off this continent."

"Then north it is."

Eva sat quiet as Sonny drove. It wasn't long before he noticed her silence.

"Something wrong?" Sonny asked.

"Yeah," Eva said. "I fucked up."

"How?"

Eva sighed. "I used your real name when I was with Diaz. Well, not Simon Baines. I called you Sonny."

"Ouch," Sonny said. He tapped his fingers on the steering wheel, a sure sign that he was deep in thought. Eventually he said, "Let's just hope Diaz wasn't ESO. If he is, we're proper fucked."

"Even if he isn't, all it takes is one call to the authorities and they'll flag us up immediately. A man and woman matching our description, the male called Sonny, involved in ninja shit…"

Sonny shook his head slowly and sighed. "It had to happen sooner or later," he said. "Don't blame yourself. It depends on Diaz's reach. If he's just a local gangster, we should be okay. If he's got major connections, it makes it harder to cross borders." He turned and smiled at Eva. "But we'll find a way. We always do."

They didn't come across any other vehicles on the track into town, but given the late hour, that wasn't unexpected. What did surprise them was the police presence when they drove into Tingo Maria. Sonny had taken off his NVGs and turned on the car's lights as he neared the town, and it was just as well. Riding slowly without lights was a sure way to attract attention, and the occupants of the two cop cars, parked next to each other in the middle of the main street, would surely have noticed.

"They must be looking for us." Sonny said.

"They're not here to control all the unruly revelers," Eva said, looking down the deserted street. "Take a right."

Sonny did as she said, then fixed his gaze on his side mirror. Eva did the same on her side, and cursed when she saw one of the police cars light up and follow them.

"Speed up a little," she said.

Sonny increased his speed to sixty, but the cop was soon on his tail. "How do you want to handle this?"

As much as Eva hated to do it, they had little choice but to kill the cop. If they didn't stop soon, he'd call in back up, and things could get messy. She checked the map on her phone. "Go another half mile, then pull over. When he gets out, I'll take him down, put him in the squad car and drive it to the roundabout. Take the first exit and drive a hundred yards, then stop. I'll put the cop in the driver's seat and join you."

"Got it," Sonny said.

He checked the odometer, then slowed and pulled to the side of the road. Eva had her fingers crossed that the cop was alone, but it was impossible to tell. When she looked back, there were no streetlights, just two headlights surrounded by darkness.

The police car stopped ten yards behind them and the driver got out. That made Eva feel better. If there had been two cops, the passenger would be the one to approach the vehicle while the driver remained alert in case they tried to drive off. At least, that was how it usually played out in other countries. Here, the passenger might be sighting an automatic rifle on them at this very moment.

There was only one way to find out.

Eva gently eased her door open a crack. She had the silenced pistol in her right hand, and she waited until the officer was five yards from the car before jumping out and putting two rounds in his chest. She continued moving, running to the passenger side of the cop car, but it was empty. She opened it, then went back and dragged the dead cop to his vehicle. Sonny came to give her a hand getting the corpse in, then he ran back to his own car and took off. Eva got in the cop car and followed.

Six miles later, they came to the roundabout. Sonny took the first exit and stopped fifty yards past a house. Eva drew up behind him and cut the engine, then got out and pulled the dead officer into the driver's seat. She arranged his body so that he looked to be sleeping, then closed the door quietly and went to join Sonny in their own car.

"Double back and take the next right," she said. With any luck, the cop's buddies would find him and think they were heading east, which should give them a clear run north.

Her heart went out to the cop she'd killed. *Murdered*, she corrected herself. He could have had a wife, kids, parents, a whole host of people waiting for him to return home safely from another shift. And she'd gunned him down, her only concern her own preservation.

"It had to be done," Sonny said.

"Huh?"

"You're thinking about the cop."

"I am," Eva admitted. "Why can't people just leave us alone? Why does death follow us everywhere?"

"To be fair," Sonny said, "tonight was the first time in a year, and most of them deserved it."

"Even the cop?"

"Maybe," Sonny shrugged. "To get mobilized so quickly, he might have been on Diaz's payroll. That makes him fair game."

"Or," Eva countered, "the police chief was in Diaz's pocket, and the one I killed was just a family man following orders."

Eva had killed many men in her time, but none had affected her like this one.

"You can't beat yourself up about it," Sonny said, caressing her cheek. "If you didn't kill him, we'd be dead by now. He'd have handed us over to Diaz and that's that. Game over."

Eva knew he was right, but it didn't make her feel any better.

"So," Sonny said. "What's the plan?"

Eva knew he was just trying to take her mind off the kill, and she silently thanked him for it. Sonny always knew when something was troubling her, and he was adept at changing the subject.

"We take a boat ride," she said.

"A boat?"

"It's the only way."

Sonny looked confused. "Then shouldn't we be heading west, to the coast?"

"No, we're taking the river."

Chapter 8

"Is that him?" Costa asked, his rifle trained on the Range Rover that had just pulled through the gates to the house.

Diaz waited until the vehicle stopped and a tall, rake-thin figure stepped out. He was bald, with a nose that looked two sizes too big for his gaunt face.

"That's Jimenez."

Costa lowered his weapon as Diaz went to meet the man Hernandez had sent.

"Romeo," Diaz smiled, extending his hand. "It's been a long time."

Jimenez took his hand and offered a brief shake, but there was no warmth or geniality. "Jose."

"Are you hungry? I can get the chef to whip up—"

"This isn't a social visit," Jimenez said, walking past Diaz to the house. He took in Costa with a brief glance, then walked past him. "Did you touch anything?"

Diaz ran to catch up. "No, we left it as it was."

Costa found it strange that a man of Diaz's standing should fawn over anyone, but he clearly held Jimenez in high regard. Few people could treat Diaz with such distain and live to see the end of the day, but Jimenez appeared to be one of them. After the phone call the previous day, Diaz hadn't said much more about Jimenez, other than the fact that he and Hernandez were close, and that the woman and her boyfriend, Sonny, would be captured sooner rather than later.

Costa watched Jimenez put on latex gloves and cover his mouth with a handkerchief before squatting down next to one of the victims. Jimenez used his index finger to carefully open the corpse's jacket and he looked at the bullet wounds to the chest. He then glanced around and his eyes settled on nearby blood spatters. Jimenez stood, looked from the blood stains to the corpse, then walked a path to where the shooter would have stood. He aimed an imaginary rifle, then looked down to his right, to see shell casings on the ground. Jimenez took a clear plastic bag from his pocket and used a pen to pick up the first casing. He examined it closely before putting it back on the ground. He tried a second, then tossed it away, cursing under his breath.

"Where did the woman spend her time?" Jimenez asked Costa.

"Upstairs, mostly. She showered and changed in one room, then I moved her to another room."

"Show me."

Costa walked ahead, up the stairs and to the changing room. He stood by the door and let Jimenez walk in first.

The ex-cop looked around before his eyes settled on the red dress lying on the floor. "Did she wear this?"

Costa nodded, and Jimenez took another bag from his pocket along with a pair of tweezers. He knelt down, his head a couple of inches from the dress, moving slowly until he spotted what he was looking for. He plucked a black hair from the material and placed it in the plastic bag.

Jimenez stood. "Show me the CCTV."

Costa was getting annoyed at the man's brusque manner, but he didn't let it show. If Diaz accepted it, he would, too. "This way."

He led Jimenez to Diaz's bedroom and pointed to the viewing room. Diaz had lied when he said he hadn't touched anything. He had transferred the recordings of the girls Diaz had slept with—and in some cases, killed—to a different hard drive.

"Play it," Jimenez said in his monotone voice.

Costa sat down and found the sequence showing the man called Sonny entering the house. He looked young, perhaps mid-thirties at the most, with short blond hair. Jimenez watched as the slight figure moved with a practiced step and then took down his first kill. Jimenez nodded appreciatively, and once the action had ended, he left the room and walked downstairs, Costa following.

Diaz puffed on a cigar as he stood among his dead bodyguards.

"You're lucky to be alive," Jimenez said to the *celeno*. "This man knows what he's doing. There were no fingerprints on the shell casings, which tells me he didn't want to be identified. I'd say special forces, perhaps DEA or CIA."

"He didn't sound like an American," Costa said, earning a glare from Jimenez.

"You didn't think to mention that earlier? I have my contacts searching the U.S. databases for this man!"

"I'm sorry...I didn't think—"

"No, you didn't!" Jimenez took out his phone. "Was he British? Australian?"

Costa shrugged. "I don't know, he just—"

"Didn't sound American." Jimenez hit a number and walked out into the sunshine.

It was clear he wanted to be alone, so Costa and Diaz remained inside the house.

A few minutes later, Jimenez returned. "What have you been doing to find them?"

Costa looked at Diaz. He was the *celeno*, it was his house that was attacked, so he should answer.

"The local police have set up roadblocks around the town," Diaz said. "If they try to escape, we'll catch them."

Jimenez looked at him with disgust. "Then they've already gone."

"Perhaps not," Diaz said, and Costa could see that he wasn't happy with the way he was being treated. "I mobilized the police minutes after the attack, and this road leads only into town. If anything, they are now on foot. They won't—" Diaz's phone rang. He took it from his pocket and checked the caller ID. "Speaking of which, this is the chief of police." He answered, then listened for a moment.

Costa noticed Diaz's face grow steadily paler. When the boss ended the call, he was almost white.

"What's wrong?"

"An officer spotted a suspicious car last night and set off in pursuit. They lost contact a few minutes later. They searched for his vehicle all night and they just found it near the Pumahuasi roundabout. The cop was shot twice."

"Take me there," Jimenez said, walking out of the house to his vehicle.

Costa followed Diaz to his own four-by-four and drove to the gate, waiting for Jimenez to follow.

"Of all the people," Diaz said, "why did Felix have to send this man?"

Costa knew it was a rhetorical question, so he let it hang.

"The man is an arrogant sonofabitch," Diaz added. "Did you see the way he disrespected me?"

Costa nodded. "You don't deserve such treatment, Jefe."

"He's already insufferable. Imagine what he'll be like if he completes his mission."

"It wouldn't look good," Costa agreed. "We let the gringos escape and he comes in to clean up our mess."

Diaz turned to Costa. "*Your* mess," he growled. "This is all your doing."

Costa had to accept the responsibility. He'd been the one to bring the woman to the house. He tried to convince himself that Diaz wasn't blameless, though. If the boss hadn't taken a fancy to her, she'd be dead by now. Costa would have had his way with her, then disposed of the body. But then, her boyfriend would still have come looking for her, and if Sonny had found her corpse, things might have turned out differently.

"I can fix this," he said.

"How?" Diaz fumed. "How could you possibly make this right?"

Costa didn't know, but he had to do something. Diaz was right. If Jimenez succeeded, it would reflect badly on Diaz, and ultimately on himself. His only option was to ensure he was the one who found the gringos, but he lacked the skills to do so.

One thing he didn't lack was guile.

"I will go with Jimenez," he said. "I will offer my help, and when he finds them, I will kill them all. Jimenez, Sonny, the woman, all of them. I'll say the boyfriend killed Jimenez, then bring them back here so that you can present their bodies to Hernandez. Your reputation will be restored, and that arrogant prick Jimenez will never disrespect you again."

Costa waited for Diaz's response, and was eventually rewarded with a smile.

"That could work," Diaz said, but his expression changed to concern. "But what if he doesn't accept your offer to help?"

Costa thought quickly. "Then I shall track him while he tracks them. Once he finds them, I will kill them all."

A horn interrupted their conversation, and Costa looked in his mirror to see Jimenez in the Range Rover. Costa put the car into gear and set off.

"Whatever it takes," Diaz said. "Whatever it takes."

* * *

They had no trouble finding the dead cop's car. When they reached the roundabout at Pumahuasi, they found several police vehicles and a crowd of onlookers.

Jimenez watched Diaz and Costa leave their car, then he climbed out and joined them. Diaz headed straight for a Peru National Police officer with thick black hair and a spreading waistline. The cop shooed away the man he was talking to and strode toward Diaz.

"*Capitan*," Diaz said. "What have you got?"

"We found him an hour ago," the officer said. "He's down here."

He led the trio past a cordon of police and to the squad car.

Jimenez looked through the window, then put a handkerchief over his mouth and opened the door. Despite his face covering, the stench was overpowering. He stepped back for a moment to let some air into the car, then stuck his head in to give the body a quick examination. He batted away a few flies, then looked at the two bullet wounds in the corpse's chest. They were close together.

"Nice grouping," he said to himself.

He pulled the body forward and checked the dead man's back, then stepped away from the vehicle and took a couple of deep breaths.

"They went that way," the cop said, indicating in the direction the squad car was pointing. "I've called all available resources into action and we've set up roadblocks on all turnoffs between here and Aguaytia. We'll find them."

Jimenez was dismayed that such an imbecile could rise to such a lofty position within the police. When he was in law enforcement, the people he worked with were bright, sharp. They would have spotted the inconsistencies in the crime scene and seen it as a ruse, but not this man.

"Tell me what you think happened," Jimenez said to him.

The cop looked at Diaz, a question in his expression. "I'm with Interpol," Jimenez said, producing his badge.

"Well," the officer said, after glancing at the ID, "We think—"

"We?" Jimenez interrupted.

The cop swallowed. "I...believe officer Rojas stopped their vehicle here, but before he could get out of his car, they shot him and drove off in that direction."

"You think they went south." It was a statement, not a question. "And they shot Rojas in his car?"

"That's right."

"They surprised him by walking to his car, opening the door and shooting him before closing the door again and driving away?"

71

The captain looked uncomfortable.

As well he should, Jimenez thought.

"As I said, we only just found him, and that was our...my...initial assessment of the situation."

"You were wrong," Jimenez said. "If he was shot in the car, there would have been more blood. I checked the entry and exit wounds, too. He was shot from the front, not by someone standing next to his door. Also, there are no impact marks on the seat. Rojas was killed elsewhere, and his body placed here to make it appear the gringos are heading east. They are not. You can stand your men down. The people we are looking for are long gone."

"Are you sure?" the captain asked.

"What time did Rojas pursue them?"

"Just after one this morning."

"Then I'm sure," Jimenez said. "That was over eight hours ago. They could be two hundred miles from here." He took out his phone and opened a map. The roads in this country were poor, which would thankfully hamper the gringos' progress. They might have made that distance, but they would have to stop for fuel and food. They might even have changed cars. "At least tell me you got a license plate."

"We did," the captain said. He reached into his breast pocket and took out a notepad, then read out the plate number.

At least they had that to work on. "Alert the PNP in Tarapoto, Cajamarca and any other major town within that area." Jimenez said. "I want to know the moment they see that car or anyone matching their descriptions. Get them to send alerts to small hotels, hostels, and car rentals."

The captain wrote the instructions down.

"And check the road leading from town to here. If it didn't rain last night, you should see a blood trail where he was dragged to his car."

The captain called over an officer and relayed those instructions.

"These people are dangerous," Jimenez added. "They are not to be approached, do you understand?"

"I understand."

"Good. From now on, Captain…"

"…Suarez," the cop said.

"Suarez. From now on you will communicate directly with me. I want to know about every lead, no matter how trivial it appears."

The captain looked at Diaz, who returned a resigned nod.

"Okay," Suarez said. "But tell me, who exactly are—"

Jimenez put a hand up to stop him, then took a plastic bag from his pocket. "Take that to the nearest police lab and perform a DNA profile. Send the results here." Jimenez handed him a card, then turned and walked back to his car before the officer could say anything else. He'd had enough of the moron, and he wasn't willing to stand around and listen to him anymore.

Jimenez was playing catch-up, a game he hated. Hopefully his friends in the intelligence services would get real names for the couple and he'd be able to look for known associates in the area, people they might turn to in a crisis. If the man called Sonny wasn't American, there was a good chance he wasn't DEA. Luckily, his contact at Interpol would be able to query the British and Australian police databases to see if there were any matches.

As he reached his car, Diaz joined him.

"I'll prepare a room at the house."

"No need," Jimenez said. "I'm driving north."

"Okay," Diaz said. He hesitated. "What are you going to do when you find them?" he asked.

Jimenez thought it a dumb question. "Kill them."

"You personally?"

"No. I'll call Felix and have him arrange for someone to do it."

Diaz looked like it wasn't the best idea he'd ever heard. "Why don't you take Costa with you?"

Jimenez looked over at the big bodyguard. "The man who created this mess? Why should I do that?"

"As you said, this man, Sonny, knows what he's doing. What happens if you corner him and he decides to fight? Could you handle that?"

"You think your man could take him down?" Jimenez asked. "If that was the case, Sonny would already be dead, no?"

"Costa's job was to protect me," Diaz countered, "and he did that. He put himself between me and the shooter so that I could escape. I owe him my life."

Jimenez thought it a shame that Costa had been so diligent. Jose Diaz was a gutter rat, born and raised in filth. Not much had changed over the years. Jimenez had always found him a vile, loathsome creature. There were rumors that Diaz favored underage girls, though no one had ever offered proof. Those close to him were unlikely to betray him, and he wasn't foolish enough to flaunt his vice.

It didn't matter now, anyway. His episode with the gringos had soured his standing with Felix Hernandez. The head of the cartel believed the incident had been a DEA sting, and though Jimenez now suspected otherwise, he wasn't going to share his opinion. It was better to let Hernandez think

Diaz had jeopardized the organization by inviting the American drug enforcement agency into his home. It would hopefully accelerate Diaz's demise.

In the meantime, he would have to suffer the man's existence.

That didn't mean he had to like it.

Or trust him.

"I'll manage without him," Jimenez told Diaz. "He would only get in the way."

"No, he won't. He obeys orders to the letter, and he'll be useful for any dirty work. He can be intimidating when he wants to be."

Jimenez glanced over at Costa, who was peering through the window of the police car at the dead body. When the man stood upright, he was a good foot taller than everyone around him. Not exactly the type who would blend in.

"Also," Diaz added, "you'll need someone to drive when you get tired. There are two of them, and they can take turns sleeping while the other drives. If you go alone, you'll lose ground every time you stop to rest."

Jimenez hadn't expected Diaz to come up with such a cogent argument, and it just added to the distrust. Did he have an ulterior motive for offering the giant's services, or was he just trying to be helpful, to minimize the punishment inevitably coming his way? Jimenez suspected it was the former, though with Diaz's only concern being self-preservation, he wasn't so sure.

Diaz did have a point, though. If he was to catch up with the couple, Jimenez would need a driving partner. He would have preferred to choose his own man and have him flown from Colombia to Peru, but there wasn't time. He'd been awake for over thirty hours already, and would need sleep sooner rather than later.

"Okay, I'll take him."

Diaz called Costa over and explained his new role.

"Okay," Costa said. "I'll go back to the house and grab a few belongings."

"There's no time. Buy what you need when we stop for food. You drive the first stint." Jimenez tossed Costa the keys to the Range Rover and got in the back.

He saw Diaz give Costa last-minute instructions, then the big man got behind the wheel.

"Where exactly are we going?"

"Just head north," Jimenez told him. "Wake me in six hours."

Jimenez lay across the back seat and closed his eyes. He was asleep before Costa turned the car around.

Chapter 9

Eva dumped the bags in the trunk and climbed in the car beside Sonny, who was sipping a fruit drink through a straw.

"That's the clothes, insect repellent, food and water," she said.

"Sounds like almost everything," Sonny replied. "We just need a couple of backpacks and we're ready to go."

The backpacks were essential for their journey. After a couple of days on a boat, they'd have to trek on foot around thirty miles to the Rio Putumayo, which marked the Colombian border. For that part of the journey, they would be able to follow a dirt road all the way, but once across the river, they would have to walk another sixty miles through the jungle before they reached the first sign of civilization. Barring mishaps, they hoped to complete that leg in a week, aiming for a minimum of ten miles a day. The shorter leg from Puerto Arica to the Rio Putumayo would take a couple of days at most, and the boat journey—all four hundred-plus miles of it—would take around three days. They'd decided on two weeks' worth of supplies, just in case they got held up along the way.

Unfortunately, they were limited in what they could take, so most of the food was dry produce: protein bars, dried fish and meat, and lots of sugary sweets for energy. They already had a rudimentary first aid kit, water purification tablets and vitamin pills from an earlier stop, which meant they were just about set.

"We can get backpacks in Yurimaguas," Eva said. "I don't want to spend too much time in one place."

The port town was just under three hours away, and would mark the end of their travels by road in Peru. There, they would either rent, buy or charter a boat for the next leg of their journey out of the country.

"We should get some kind of tarp, too," Sonny suggested. "When it rains in the jungle, it really comes down."

"Get one when you buy the backpacks," Eva said. "And some Ziplock bags. I don't want the money getting wet."

That was one of the few things that they would be taking with them. The money, along with two pistols and ammunition. In truth, they didn't have many material possessions. They were constantly on the road, so apart from their weapons and a couple of suitcases of clothes and toiletries, they didn't have much to shed.

"Will do. I also think we should ditch the car rather than sell it," Sonny said as they set off.

"Yeah. And as they'll probably be watching the borders and airports, I thought it would be safe enough to spend one last night in a hotel before we set off." She reached over and kissed Sonny on the cheek, then bit her lower lip seductively. "That way, I can thank you properly for saving my life."

* * *

Three hours later, Eva and Sonny arrived in Yurimaguas. For a town in the middle of nowhere, it was much larger than either had anticipated, though there really wasn't that much to see. Most of the shops seemed to cater to the mototaxis—motorcycles attached to two- or three-seater sedans—that dominated the roads. There were a few food stores, and after half an hour of driving around, Sonny spotted a place where they might be likely to purchase some backpacks for the trip into the jungle. He noted the address, then went in search of a hotel.

He found one near the bank of the river, a three-story hostel that looked to have a maximum of two rooms on each floor. Eva's Spanish was better, so she asked about availability, and then beckoned him in. Sonny carried a handful of bags to their room. It wasn't the biggest place he'd stayed in, but it was far from the dirtiest.

"It beats what we're gonna be facing for the next two weeks," Eva said, flopping down on the bed.

Sonny had to agree. He'd spent many nights in jungles, from Belize to Malaya and Africa. None of them held pleasant memories.

"What do you want to do?" he asked. "Shop, or arrange the boat?"

"Boat. I never thought I'd say it, but I'm sick of shopping."

"Okay. I'll get the stuff we need and I'll see you back here…" he checked his watch, "…at six."

Sonny quickly changed into shorts, then left the hostel. After a ten-minute walk, he found the shop he'd noticed on the way into town, where he got what he needed. When he got back to the hostel there was no sign of Eva, so he dumped the shopping and left the room once more. He decided to drive the car to the outskirts of the town, find somewhere quiet and ditch it, perhaps in a river, or just drive it deep into the jungle and cover it with foliage.

When he stepped out of the hostel, Sonny's heart almost stopped.

A police officer was standing on the other side of the road, and he was talking into a radio while looking at Sonny's Toyota sedan. When he saw Sonny, the cop's face flashed recognition before he turned and walked away slowly. Sonny watched as the man glanced back once while talking into the mic dangling from his epaulette.

Shit!

Sonny ducked back inside the reception and ran back to the room. He stuffed as many of their belongings as he could into the two new backpacks, but there was no room for all the food and water. He took enough for two days, which would see them to Iquitos, where they could stock up again. He and Eva could have managed to carry everything between them, but for now, Sonny was on his own.

Sonny threw one pack on his back and carried the other by the strap out of the room, taking the fire escape out the back of the building and sneaking around the side. He poked his head around the corner and saw that the cop was a hundred yards from the hostel, walking away. With no time to waste, Sonny took out his car keys and crouched at the rear of the Toyota. He scratched a large letter X on the lid of the trunk, and underneath he drew two arrows pointing in the direction the car was facing. With a quick glance to check that the cop wasn't looking, Sonny sprinted down a side street.

The mark was a signal that they had been compromised. If Sonny didn't find Eva at the bank of the river, she would come back and see the warning. The arrows were a red herring, telling her to travel in the opposite direction. Two arrows signified two miles. Sonny would meet her there at their last agreed meeting time, six in the evening.

He didn't want to wait that long. If the police were onto them, he wanted to skip town immediately.

He ran to the next corner and took a right toward the river. The town stretched for about a mile along the riverbank, and Sonny was slap bang in the middle. He had to choose left or right. He settled on left, for no other reason than it took him farther away from the cop.

After a few hundred yards, Sonny began to think he'd made the wrong call. All he discovered were shops and restaurants. Once or twice a break in the buildings gave him a view of the river, but he saw no sign of Eva. He was about to give up and turn back when he jogged down a slope and came across what looked like a ferry terminal. Three vessels were moored at the bank, each large enough to hold at least a hundred people, and walking toward him was Eva.

"What are you doing here?" she asked, then saw the concerned look on his face. "What is it?"

"We have to go," Sonny said. "Now." He told her about the cop and the interest he'd taken in the car.

"Damn!"

He handed her the pack he was carrying. "I got everything apart from the food. There's enough for two days, that's it."

"It'll have to do." Eva turned back toward the river. "I found just one boat for sale, but it looked like it would sink the moment we got it. We can either take a ferry or try to hire a faster boat."

It wasn't the ideal option. If the police worked out that they were making their way on water, it would be easy to intercept them.

"Okay, but only as far as the next port. We'll find a car there."

"No can do," Eva said. "I already checked the map. The only place we can get off is Nauta, but the road out of there only leads to Iquitos. The rest of the stops are nothing more than fishing villages, with no roads in or out. We might as well stay on the boat all the way. The fewer people we come across, the better."

Sonny wasn't happy, but there was little else they could do. They might buy or steal a car, but there were no roads that took them where they wanted to be.

"Fast boat it is," Sonny said.

Eva walked over to one of the shore hands, a young man wearing a T-shirt bearing the ferry's insignia. She enquired about chartering a boat and was directed to a place a few hundred yards down the street.

They soon found the man they were looking for. His name was Papi. Sonny guessed it was a nickname, but grandpapi would have been more appropriate. He looked to be in his eighties, a stick-thin man with skin the color and texture of old leather. A pipe hung from his mouth like an octogenarian Popeye's.

Sonny tried to keep up as Eva conversed with Papi in free-flowing Spanish. From what Sonny could gather, Papi seemed reluctant to make the journey. He kept shaking his head and mumbling through nicotine-stained lips. Just when Sonny thought the negotiation had failed, Papi stood and nodded, then walked to the riverbank.

"What was the problem?" Sonny asked Eva as they followed the old man.

"He saw a couple of gringos and assumed we were rich. I offered him three hundred bucks to take us to Iquitos, but he wanted three grand."

"Greedy old bastard," Sonny smiled. "For that money I'd expect him to take us all the way to Puerto Arica and then carry us to Bogotá. What did you agree on in the end?"

Eva gave him a wry grin. "Three grand."

Papi ducked into a building and spoke to someone for a few moments, then reappeared and gestured for them to follow.

The boat they'd hired was better than Sonny had expected. There was no cabin, but at least there was an overhead canopy that would keep any rain off, with canvas flaps that could be folded down for extra protection from the elements. The boat was only about eight feet wide, but a large outboard motor hung off the stern, suggesting they wouldn't be spending too long on it. It was just as well, as the only places to rest were the wooden benches that ran along either side of the boat.

"How long will it take to get there?" Sonny asked Eva.

"He says two days at the most."

The outboard motor clearly wasn't as powerful as it first appeared to Sonny, but it was what it was. "Ask him when we can set off."

Eva did, and got an elaborate response, with Papi pointing to various places on the boat.

"Now," she said.

"He doesn't want to stock up on food or fuel?"

"He's all set, apparently. Says an old sailor knows to have his vessel ready to go at all times."

It was the first bit of luck they'd had all day. Sonny helped Eva aboard, then climbed in himself. Papi nimbly jumped from the dock to the stern and started the motor, then untied the vessel and waved for them to sit. He hit the throttle seconds later and aimed the nose out into the middle of the river.

Chapter 10

Romeo Jimenez was approaching Tarapoto when his cell phone rang. He'd been awake for an hour, and it was Fernando Costa's turn to get his head down on the back seat.

"Yes," he said. Jimenez never answered with his name if he didn't know who was calling.

"It's Captain Suarez. We got a hit on the car."

Jimenez slammed on the brakes and pulled to the side of the road. He snatched the phone from its stand on the dash and opened a map app. "Where?"

"Yurimaguas. It's about seventy kilom—"

"Got it. Where are the man and woman?"

"In a hostel," Suarez said. "Our officer saw the man only, but at least we know where they are staying."

"Have your men surround the building, but keep out of sight. They are not to show themselves or approach the suspects. If they blow this, it rests on you. Understood?"

"I understand," Suarez said, his voice cracking, "but I am hundreds of miles away. I cannot guarantee that the men in Yurimaguas will obey my instructions."

"Then I suggest you be very persuasive," Jimenez warned him. "As if your life depended on it." He paused to let the threat sink in, then added, "What's the name and address of the hostel?"

Suarez rattled off the details and Jimenez entered them into the search bar on the map.

"Don't mess this up," Jimenez said, then ended the call.

He spun the wheel and put his foot down, throwing up dust as he rejoined the road.

"What's happening?" a groggy Costa asked from the back seat.

"We found them."

Costa shot upright. "Where?"

"Yurimaguas. We'll be there in less than two hours."

* * *

They made it to Yurimaguas in an hour and a half, despite stopping in Tarapoto for gas. They switched drivers, with Costa now behind the wheel and Jimenez on his phone preparing for the take down. He'd already called Suarez and got the name of the officer in charge of the surveillance operation, a man by the name of Gonzales. Jimenez had called Gonzales and arranged to meet him two blocks from the hostel.

"Wait here," Jimenez told Costa. "They know what you look like, but they haven't seen me." Darkness descended as he stepped out of the Range Rover. He found the police chief talking to two junior officers and flashed a badge. "Jimenez, Interpol."

Gonzales was young for such a high-ranking officer. Jimenez guessed his age at around forty, and he appeared to look after himself. There was none of the fat Jimenez associated with desk cops.

"The suspects are still in the hostel," Gonzales told him. "We've had people watching for the last eight hours and there has been no sign of them leaving."

Jimenez almost choked on his anger. "Eight hours!? Why didn't you report this sooner?"

Gonzales looked perplexed. "I did. The moment Officer Nunez radioed it in, I contacted regional command, as ordered. If there was a hold up, it was at their end."

Jimenez was fit to explode, but it would have achieved nothing. He couldn't blame Gonzales or the officer who had reported the sighting. Besides which, if he'd known about them eight hours earlier, he wouldn't have been able to get there any quicker. If the gringos were still holed up in their room, no harm had been done.

Jimenez had already decided how to perform the take-down. If they went in mobhanded with uniformed police, the gringos would bolt, or at least have time to mount some kind of defense. Jimenez didn't want that. A shootout would draw attention, while his aim was to grab the couple and disappear without fuss.

"Are your men ready?"

Gonzales nodded and got on the radio. Four men, dressed in T-shirts and shorts, stepped out of a nearby café. They looked like manual laborers, which was just what Jimenez wanted.

"Are you all armed?" Jimenez asked the group.

They all raised their T-shirts to show service weapons tucked into their waistbands.

"Good. And you know what you're supposed to do?"

"We pretend we've just finished a shift and we're on our way to have a drink before we go home," one of the men said. "We go into the hostel bar, and if the suspects are not there, we go up to their room."

Jimenez was glad that Gonzales had briefed his men well. "When you storm the room, move fast and make lots of noise. It will disorientate them. And remember, these people are dangerous. We go in hard and secure them quickly, before they have a chance to think."

The men nodded.

"What are they wanted for?" one of them asked.

"Murder," Jimenez replied. "I'll go ahead. Wait two minutes, then join me."

Jimenez strolled toward the hostel slowly, pretending to take an interest in the shops he passed. When he got to the front door, he looked through the glass first. Seeing no one apart from a bored-looking receptionist, he walked in. He could see that the small barroom, through an arch to his left, was almost empty. He went in anyway, to make sure they weren't sitting in a corner, but the only drinkers were a couple of middle-aged locals.

Jimenez went back to reception and stood at the desk. He flashed his badge at the ponytailed woman. "Interpol. You have two foreigners staying here. What room are they in?"

The woman looked at the ID, then up at Jimenez, whose fierce expression said, "Don't fuck with me."

"Room three," she said.

Jimenez reached over the counter and snatched up the register. Only two rooms appeared to be occupied, and room three was in the name of Clark.

The four plain-clothes police walked in. Jimenez told them which room to search, then asked the receptionist for the spare keys for room three and to follow him.

The receptionist's hands shook as she fumbled in a drawer, but eventually found what she was looking for. She handed it over and stood awaiting further instructions.

Jimenez drew his pistol and led the way, with the receptionist behind him and the four cops at the rear. When they reached the first floor, Jimenez explained what he wanted the receptionist to do, and she nodded nervously. He positioned her next to the door, and the cops stood ready to storm the room.

"Now," Jimenez whispered.

The receptionist swallowed, then announced, "Room service," in as cheery a voice as she could muster. At the same time, Jimenez put the key in the lock, turned it and threw the door open before jumping aside. The cops rushed in, shouting as they did so. It only took fifteen seconds to check the bathroom, closet and under the bed before the room was declared clear.

"No one here," one cop said as he left the room, disappointed.

Jimenez walked in to check, finding nothing but a pile of food on one of the beds. They'd obviously left in a hurry, probably soon after the cop had spotted the one called Sonny. Jimenez went back into the hallway and asked the shaking receptionist if there was another exit. She pointed to a door, and Jimenez walked through it to find himself on an external staircase. He cursed as he turned and slammed the door, marching back down to reception with the others following at a safe distance.

Outside, Jimenez found Gonzales waiting expectantly. His face dropped when Jimenez stormed toward him.

"They're gone!"

"But…I…my men were watching all day."

"They slipped out the moment your officer spotted him," Jimenez fumed.

They had an eight-hour head start, but Jimenez wasn't about to give up just yet.

* * *

Fernando Costa got out of the car and walked over to Jimenez, who had walked into the middle of the road and was looking at his surroundings. It was clear the raid had been a failure, otherwise the two gringos would be in handcuffs by now.

"What happened?" he asked Jimenez.

"They're gone," was the succinct reply. "We missed them."

Costa looked over at the hostel. "That's their car," he said. "They must have other transport."

"Of course they have," Jimenez said. "And I know what it is."

"What?"

"A boat. The only reason they would come here is if they wanted to take a boat. If they planned to keep on driving, they would have gone north-west at Tarapoto. They wouldn't have chosen this cesspit."

If the gringos planned to cross the border on foot, it meant they were desperate. A couple on vacation wouldn't go to that much trouble. They had to be wanted, and not just by Felix Hernandez. It meant they were unlikely to go to the police for help, and that gave Jimenez the advantage.

He returned to Gonzales, and Costa followed.

"Have your men question everyone at the dock. I want to know if they took a ferry, or purchased a boat. Do it now. I'll be…" Jimenez looked around and his eyes settled on a cantina. "…in there."

Costa tailed Jimenez to the eatery and sat down at a table opposite him. He could see that the tracker was pissed over missing his quarry, and so was Costa. He wanted to get this over with so that he could return to Tingo Maria. It wasn't so much that he liked the small town, but at least there he was closer to Lima. He liked to go there on his days off, and his next one was overdue. Lima had everything Costa loved. The city was vibrant, the food excellent, the women beautiful...

What he missed most, though, was being treated with respect. He got that in spades when he was in Tingo Maria, and to some extent, in Lima, too. Here, though, he was treated worse than a dog by that *puto* Jimenez. It would be a pleasure to put a bullet between the man's eyes. He might even stab him in the stomach and watch him slowly and painfully fade away.

The thought brought a smile to his face.

"What's so funny?" Jimenez asked.

"Nothing," Costa said, removing the grin. "Just remembering a boat ride I went on as a kid." He picked up the menu and perused it, keeping his head down.

Jimenez grunted and looked at his own menu.

Costa knew he would have to be careful around Jimenez. The man was far from stupid, and if he suspected Costa's reason for being there, the shit would really fly.

Jimenez chose a fish meal, while Costa settled for beef. They were halfway through their dishes when Gonzales appeared at their table.

"You were right," the police chief said. "We spoke to a deck hand from one of the ferries. The woman was asking about hiring a boat to go north, to Iquitos. It appears they chartered a *lancha* from a guy named Papi."

"When?" Jimenez asked.

"Just after eleven this morning," Gonzales told him.

Jimenez stood and dropped a few notes on the table. "Who has the fastest boat in this town?"

Gonzales swallowed. "There are none that can make up an eight-hour head start."

If they ever wanted to catch them, they would have to come up with another mode of transport. Costa took out his cell phone and opened a map of the area. He hoped to find some unmarked roads, but spotted something infinitely more promising.

"Why don't we fly to Iquitos and wait for them?" he asked Jimenez.

"Sure. Just conjure a plane out of your ass and we're all set."

"Actually," Gonzales said, "we have an airfield. It's about two hundred metres from here."

Jimenez perked up. "Great. Book us on the next flight."

Gonzales looked pained. "I'm afraid there are no commercial flights to Iquitos. The airport is only used by a couple of local companies, but you might be able to charter one of their planes."

"Do it," Jimenez told him.

"It could be expensive."

Jimenez strode up to Gonzales and stood nose to nose with him. "I don't care if I have to buy the goddamn plane. I want to be in the air within the hour."

Chapter 11

Vincent May sucked on his Cuban cigar and puffed a cloud of blue smoke toward the ceiling of the conference room, where a state-of-the-art air conditioning unit erased it like a bad memory. The unit had cost over a hundred grand to install. That was a pittance to the ESO, and its whisper-quiet mechanism was almost undetectable.

"Then it's just a matter of who we get to do the job," he said to the others around the ornate table.

The topic of conversation was the removal of Jacobi Evergood as President of Bulasi, a small central African state that had recently gained independence after a bitter civil war. Few in the international community knew what had sparked the conflict, or why anyone should want to waste tens of thousands of lives to secure such an arid piece of land. These matters were usually tribal, but that wasn't the case here. Fighting had erupted without warning, and after many months of conflict and close to seventy thousand dead, the ruler of Malundi had capitulated and let Evergood have his land.

It was only after the dust had settled that Evergood announced the discovery of the world's largest neodymium deposit. The rare earth metal, vital for the electric car industry, was in short supply, and with several developed countries vowing to ditch gasoline and diesel cars by the end of the decade, demand was high. So high, that the price of neodymium had tripled in the last year alone.

U.S. companies had been among the first to court Evergood in an attempt to secure mining rights, but the Chinese were favorites to stake a claim. They'd already offered to provide major infrastructure projects as "gifts" to the new Evergood regime, including roads, railways and power stations. Beijing already had the U.S. by the balls when it came to the components for batteries used in electric vehicles, smartphones and laptops. Gaining control of the Bulasi deposit could enable them to squeeze every last cent out of Western consumers and manufacturers.

Larry Carter, who ran the military industrial complex, was first to speak. "The administration won't sanction military intervention," he said, sipping his coffee. "When the president of Malundi asked us to help stop the bloodshed last year, POTUS refused to send in the troops. If he did so now, his motive would be obvious. People would start demanding that he take action against other one-party states, like North Korea. It's too messy."

May had expected as much. Even though the organization he headed—the Executive Security Office, or ESO—was the most powerful on the planet, they didn't always get what they wanted. They might control the White House, but the decision to launch military action would have to go through the Senate. The ESO had a number of senators in its pocket, but not enough to sway the vote.

"Then we'll have to do it some other way," May said.

He looked at the vacant seat belonging to Ben Scott, who ran foreign affairs. It was unusual for a meeting to take place without all the members present, but Scott had called ahead to say he was delayed. May hadn't pressed for a reason, knowing Scott wouldn't be late to one of the weekly meetings without good cause.

"It'll have to be a private security company," James Butler said. "Won't be cheap."

Butler was the finance man. Like the others, he was a multi-billionaire, yet he moaned about every penny spent.

"Too risky," May said. "If we can't launch a full military campaign under the guise of ensuring democracy for the oppressed people of Bulasi, we'll have to go to the other extreme. If we send in a team of contractors, chances are one of them will be captured or killed, and that leads back to us. It has to be one person, someone we can disavow if things go wrong. An independent. A specialist."

"Ben can draw up a list," Carter said. "How about a sniper? One bullet, job done."

"Nice," Butler said, "but it still leaves the matter of who steps in to fill the void. We need to court Evergood's entourage, find someone who will be more receptive to our advances."

"I've got the CIA working on that." May said. "We should have some profiles in the next few days."

Ben Scott entered the room. He was a rotund man in his late sixties, the oldest of the group, and the only one to be losing his hair. Vincent May had a full head of black hair, while Carter and Butler were well into the grey stage.

"You'll never guess who just came back from the dead," Scott said, placing a manila file on the desk. He took a seat and poured himself a glass of water from a crystal decanter.

"Lazarus?" Butler sniggered.

Scott shot him a look. "Very droll. No, it's Eva Driscoll."

It wasn't often that Vincent May was shocked, but now he had every right to be. "That's impossible. They saw her get on the plane. They saw it take off…"

"…and as planned, it exploded over the Pacific," Scott added, "but somehow she survived. Not just her, but Simon Baines, too."

May sat with his mouth hanging open, unable to comprehend the news. No one, not even Eva Driscoll, could survive an explosion on a plane thirty thousand feet in the air. Even if she did, there was no way they could last more than a few hours in the middle of the ocean.

"Where did you get this information?"

"Interpol," Scott said. He took a pack of antacids from his pocket and stuck one in his mouth. "I had a flag running and forgot to cancel it when her plane went down. It seems she's caused a ruckus in Peru." He opened the file and read from the top sheet. "The Peruvian National Police put out a BOLO on a woman and a white male. They had a DNA sample from her hair that matched the profile held by Interpol. It says they're wanted for multiple murders, but no details as to the victims. There was a block on her record, so her real identity wasn't passed to the Peruvians."

"Good," said Butler. "Hopefully they'll catch her and stick her in prison for the rest of her life."

"I think that would be the least of her worries," Scott said. "I was curious to know who she'd killed, so I had someone run some checks. The cop who asked for the DNA match, a Captain Suarez, said it was at the request of someone called Jimenez from Interpol. They don't have anyone working for them by that name."

"Maybe the cop got it wrong," May suggested.

"Maybe, but Suarez works out of a small town called Tingo Maria, and there was only one murder reported in the last week, a local cop. A little further digging revealed that Jose Diaz lives on the outskirts of Tingo Maria, and before you ask, he's one of the top men in a Colombian cartel which just happens to employ an ex-cop named Romeo Jimenez. I had someone query Suarez for a description and they match."

"Which cartel boss has she pissed off?" May asked.

Scott scowled. "Our old friend, Felix Hernandez."

"Hernandez," May muttered. The Colombian was a major pain in the ass, and as far from a friend as anyone could be. The ESO had influence in government policy in just about every country in the world, but Hernandez was making life difficult for them in Colombia. Money was usually enough to sway politicians and the judiciary so that the ESO got its way, but that wasn't the case here. While the ESO dangled carrots in order to achieve their goals, Hernandez preferred the stick. A big, electrified stick, with nails in the end for good measure. No one with any relevant political standing was stupid enough to refuse Felix Hernandez, unless they wanted to end up in pieces after watching their entire family being slaughtered. The ESO had tried—and failed—to take Hernandez out. The six-man team sent to complete the mission was found in a Bogotá park the following day, their heads and limbs cut off and their innards removed.

"So Driscoll has got the Soldado cartel on her tail?" Carter smirked. "Ain't life a bitch."

Vincent May wasn't so sure. Hernandez might be the epitome of violence, but Eva Driscoll was no pushover.

"We should send someone to help them," Butler added. "Just to make absolutely sure she dies this time."

"Do we even know where they are?" Carter asked.

"I know where Jimenez is," Scott said. "I put a trace on his phone. That should be good enough."

May thought about it, and a smile crept onto his face. "Yes," he said. "Send a team."

Chapter 12

Graham Masters thumbed through the news headlines on his cell phone as he waited for the mechanic to give him the bad news. Thirty years ago, he'd have stripped the car down himself to investigate the knocking sound, but his life had changed dramatically in that time. For one thing, cars had evolved. He'd opened the hood a few weeks ago to inspect his car's carburetor, only to discover that his modern vehicle had a fuel injection system, instead.

You're getting old, he told himself, as he thought back to the days when he'd taken Land Rovers apart and put them back together in the blazing heat of the Afghan desert. It seemed a lifetime ago.

The man sitting next to him looked at his watch and sighed. Joel Grant was Masters' driver, an ex-soldier in his late twenties.

"I'm sorry about this, sir. I thought they'd be done by now."

"Don't worry about it," Masters said. "It's not like I've got anything better to do."

Which was true. There was no job to go to, no friends to visit, just shopping and a couple of runs to drop off and pick up his daughter from school. They'd actually been on the way to the mall when the knocking had started again. Joel had felt it through the steering wheel, and Masters had heard it from his seat in the back of the Ford Expedition. Masters had been heading to the mall out of boredom rather than necessity, so there was no rush to get back to it.

"I'll go see how they're doing," Joel said, getting up. "If it's not gonna be done in the next thirty minutes, I'll arrange a loaner so we can pick Melissa up."

Masters checked his watch. He had to collect his daughter from Poundmaker Elementary at three-thirty, and it was just after one now.

"Sure, but don't let them fob you off with a compact."

Joel looked puzzled at the British colloquialism.

"It means don't be pressured," Masters explained.

"Ah. Gotcha."

Masters returned his attention to his phone. Not much was happening in Okotoks, according to the local online newspaper. With a population of just under thirty thousand, it wasn't exactly a bustling metropolis. A man had been arrested for speeding and DUI after hitting a tree, and a fight had broken out at a bar, but that just about covered the crime section. Other headlines told of a charity bake sale and an upcoming band competition for a local high school, the kind of news that stirred the crowds in this small Alberta town.

That was why Masters had chosen it. Okotoks was small enough that there wasn't much in the way of crime, but big enough that not everybody knew everyone else. He was able to keep himself to himself, and that was his main goal. There were times when he'd been politely interrogated by the locals, usually at the store checkout or school activities, and especially when they heard his British accent. When forced to interact with anyone from Okotoks, he simply told them that he'd retired after selling his company in London, and had come to Canada for the quiet life. If pressed on the question of a Mrs. Masters, he simply told them that he was a widower, that it happened when Melissa was small, and that he didn't like to talk about it.

It was much easier than explaining that both of his former wives were dead, one from a suicide, the other murdered.

It was also preferable to telling them that Graham Masters wasn't his real name, and that he'd picked their little town to escape the attention of the most powerful group of people on the planet.

In order to do that, he had to stay under the radar and out of trouble. If arrested, his fingerprints would enter the law enforcement system and he'd be identified in no time. That was why he'd hired Joel as a driver. If there was an accident or traffic stop, the police would take an interest in Joel, not his passenger. The passport Masters held was British, and the real Graham Masters had died as a young child. A criminal gang had managed to get a birth certificate and national insurance number, and the whole package had cost Masters over fifty grand. Thankfully, he'd easily been able to afford it.

"Ten more minutes," Joel said as he returned to his seat. "They found the issue. A damaged bearing in the drive shaft."

Masters liked Joel. The kid was a year out of the army on a medical discharge. A land mine had gone off near him in Iraq, and though it killed his friend, Joel had escaped with a mangled knee. He'd taken the discharge and was currently studying for a business degree. The arrangement suited both people. Joel drove Masters and his daughter to the school and back each day, plus the occasional trip to the mall midweek and day trips out at the weekend. Apart from that, Joel's time was his own. In return, he had free lodging in the self-contained apartment over Masters' garage, plus three grand a month in cash. Joel didn't drink or smoke, and Masters had seen no sign of drug use. Just a level-headed young man trying to make his way in the world.

Masters' phone rang, and he checked the Caller ID. It was a call he'd been expecting for the last few days.

"Graham Masters," he said when he answered.

"Mr. Masters, this is Jenny Holgate from Poundmaker Elementary. There's been an incident involving your daughter."

"Is she okay?"

"Yes, she's fine, but she was involved in a fight and the other girl was hurt quite badly. I need you to come to the school right away."

"No problem," Masters said. "I can be there in half an hour."

He ended the call.

"Change of plan," he told Joel. "When the car's fixed, I need to go see Melissa's principal."

* * *

"I shouldn't be too long," Masters said as Joel stopped in front of the school.

"Take your time," Joel said, holding up a textbook. He always kept two in the car so that he could continue his studies while waiting for Masters to do his shopping.

Masters found Melissa sitting outside the principal's office. She didn't look upset, but he could see a red welt on the side of her face.

"You okay, sweetheart?" Masters asked, gently rubbing her cheek.

"I'm fine," she said, but a tear crept from the corner of her eye.

"What's wrong? Did she hurt you?"

"No," Melissa said. "I just…do we have to move schools again?"

Masters really felt for his daughter. In the last two-and-a-bit years, she'd been to three different schools, and it always seemed to happen just when she was getting settled and making new friends.

"I'm sure we won't," Masters said, and hoped it was true.

He'd seen this day coming and had prepared as best he could, but now it was in the hands of the principal.

The door to the principal's office opened, and a secretary asked Masters and Melissa to come in.

Masters ushered his daughter in first, and was surprised to see so many people inside. A man in an expensive-looking suit sat opposite the principal, Jenny Holgate, and three girls were standing against one wall.

But the one that troubled Masters the most was the sergeant from the Royal Canadian Mounted Police.

"Take a seat please," Holgate said, gesturing to a chair next to the suit.

"I'll stand, thanks," Masters said, his arm around his daughter. "So, what's this all about?"

"Melissa launched an unprovoked attack on my daughter and broke her nose," the suit said.

Masters looked at him. He was in his forties, with a hundred-dollar haircut and manicured hands. "You must be Madison Fraser's father."

Fraser looked surprised to hear his own name. "I am."

"I thought so," Masters said. "Madison has been bullying Melissa for the last few weeks." He turned his glare to Principal Holgate. "Isn't that right?"

Holgate had her hands clasped on the desk. "There have been allegations," she said, "but nothing has been substantiated."

"Which means nothing was done," Masters told her. "You had the opportunity, but you chose to ignore the situation. I had no choice but to allow Melissa to defend herself."

"Self-defense doesn't come into this," Fraser said from his chair. "Your daughter approached Madison, who was studying in her lunch break, and started beating on her for no reason."

Masters had met Fraser's kind before. Arrogant, unwilling to accept anything but their own truth, a stubborn refusal to admit when they were in the wrong. Masters couldn't help but smile. "Your daughter told you that, and you believed it?"

Fraser seemed irked that Masters found the situation humorous. "Yes, I believed her. I also believe my other daughter—" Fraser pointed to the three girls standing against the wall "—and her two friends. They were all there. They saw the whole thing."

"This is a serious allegation," the sergeant added. "The victim suffered severe trauma."

"Then let's get to the truth, shall we?" Masters turned and took a knee next to Melissa. "What really happened?"

Fraser scoffed, but reverted to silence when Masters glared at him.

"I was eating in the school yard when Madison and those three came up to me. Madison said, 'Where's your mom?' and I said, 'She's dead. You know she's dead.' Then Madison said, 'I bet she killed herself rather than be your mom.' And I said, 'Stop talking about my mom like that.'"

"Then what happened?" Masters asked gently.

"Then Madison said, 'Are you gonna make me?' And I said, 'I will if I have to.' And Madison got up in my face and grabbed my hair and pulled it. She said, 'Let me see you try.' Then she pushed me over and I fell backwards. When I got up, Madison slapped me across the face."

Masters looked at the sergeant. "That sounds like assault to me."

"Yeah," Fraser laughed. "If it really happened. But it didn't. We have four witnesses against one."

"Did you record it?" Masters asked Melissa.

She nodded. "When they started walking toward me."

"Let's see," Masters said. He held out his hand, and Melissa removed the pendant from around her neck. It was a black stone in the shape of a heart. Masters took out his cell phone, held the stone next to it, then opened Bluetooth and looked at Holgate. "I've sent you three emails detailing the bullying against Melissa. Each time, you replied that there was no evidence to suggest it was true. I still have your replies on my phone if you'd like to see them."

Holgate said nothing, and Masters stood and looked at his phone for over a minute. He eventually nodded and held up the pendant.

"This is a camera, and it recorded the incident. Would you like to see it, Sergeant?"

Fraser was on his feet. "Now you wait a minute. There's a law about recording images on school premises."

The sergeant ignored the outburst and took the phone from Masters, then watched.

"I'm going to sue you and your daughter over this," Fraser said to Masters. "My law firm is going to take you for every penny you have." He started counting on his fingers. "Assault, slander, illicit recordings—"

"Then let me quickly deal with these one by one." Masters looked at Principal Holgate. "Ask his daughter to hand over her phone and check her Gallery. I think you'll find a recording of Madison striking my daughter first."

"Don't you dare do that," Fraser glared at Holgate. "You have no right."

"Actually, I have every right." She snapped her fingers at the Fraser sister, and the girl stepped forward, looking at her father.

"Do as the principal says," the sergeant told her.

The girl reluctantly dug into her blazer pocket and handed over her cell phone. Holgate took it, and moments later she had the video playing. She turned up the volume, and the sergeant leaned over to watch. When it finished, they both looked at Fraser.

"Your daughter approached Melissa," Holgate said to Fraser. "She said exactly what Melissa told us, to the letter, then she grabbed Melissa's hair, pushed her over, and when Melissa got up, Madison slapped her."

"And your other daughter recorded the assault," Masters added. "Which is illegal, I believe."

Fraser was almost purple with rage. "This doesn't change the fact that my daughter is in the hospital right now with a broken nose."

"It does, actually," the sergeant said. "Madison started it. If you want me to press ahead with the assault charge, it'll be against your daughter. Melissa here was just defending herself."

"I could understand if she slapped Madison back, but I've seen Madison's face. Melissa must have stamped on her or something."

"It was one punch," the sergeant said. "I've just watched it."

Fraser took hold of his daughter's hand and dragged her toward the door. "You haven't heard the last of this," he said to Holgate.

"Before you go," she replied, "you should know that I'm suspending Madison for two weeks while we investigate this incident. Sarah, too. I should warn you that this could lead to expulsion in both instances."

"What? Expulsion! If you even consider expelling my daughters, I'll…I'll…"

"Sue me?" Holgate said. "I'm well aware that you're a prominent lawyer, Mr. Fraser, but that doesn't give you or your family free rein in this town."

"She's right," the sergeant chimed in. "From what I've seen, both of your daughters behaved atrociously." He looked at Masters. "Do you wish to press charges?"

Masters shook his head. "Hopefully, Madison has learned her lesson. Let's leave it at that."

Fraser stormed out, and Masters decided to give him a minute to get out of the building before making his own exit.

"You went through a lot of trouble just to prove a point," the sergeant said to Masters.

"In situations where it's someone's word against someone else's, the winner is usually the one with the loudest voice. Melissa told me there were always four of them, so I knew she had to be prepared. It's just as well, I think. Without that recording, Melissa would almost certainly be facing criminal charges."

"You could have just told her to walk away," Holgate suggested.

"Melissa did that on many occasions," Masters said, "and it didn't stop the bullying. I also sent you those three emails, and they didn't stop the bullying." He looked down at his daughter and smiled. "I think we just stopped the bullying."

"One thing I have to ask," the sergeant added. "Where did Melissa learn to punch like that? That shot would have taken me down."

"Daddy taught me," Melissa beamed. "He said if you have to hit someone, punch them so hard that they either go down or do some stupid things standing up."

"She's paraphrasing," Masters said guiltily, as a grin slid onto the cop's face. "I just showed her a few things I saw on some self-defense videos online." He looked at Holgate. "So, we good?"

She nodded. "I'm sorry this had to happen. You can rest assured that I'll be overhauling our bullying policy."

Bit late, Masters thought. "Okay. I'll let Melissa get back to class. Miss Holgate. Sergeant."

Masters kissed Melissa on the head and led her out of the room, closing the door behind him, then knelt down next to her.

"That was our little secret," he said. "Don't tell anyone else that."

Melissa pouted. "Why not? It's funny. The policeman thought so."

"I know, but that's something soldiers say, and I don't want anyone to know I was in the army. I told you, we have to be very careful."

"Okay," Melissa said, her head bowed. "I won't say it again."

Masters couldn't help but feel sorry for her. She'd been through so much in her nine years, and life wasn't about to get any easier. She was limited in what she could tell her friends, and it must have been confusing for her to be told to tell him the truth yet lie to others.

"Hopefully, it won't be for much longer," he told her. "In the meantime, to show you how proud you made me, how about we go to Wendy's after school?"

Melissa's face lit up. "Promise?"

"Promise. Now go, learn lots."

Chapter 13

Luke Fraser put Sarah in the back seat and slammed the door, then climbed in behind the wheel.

"Seat belt!"

Luke watched as Sarah scrambled. When she was fastened in, he turned to the front and jabbed his key in the lock.

Who the hell does he think he is, embarrassing me like that?

He started the engine and reversed out of his parking space, and when he checked his mirror, he saw Masters walking out of the school building, a smug look on his face.

Yeah, I'll bet you're loving this moment, aren't you?

Even though Masters couldn't see him, Fraser flipped him the bird and gunned the Porsche's three-liter flat six.

In all his years, Fraser had never had anyone blindside him like Masters had done. As a lawyer, he was used to surprises in the courtroom, but Masters had pulled the video from nowhere and made him look like a fool. Not only that, his children faced expulsion from school. That news would ripple through the town, doing his reputation no good at all.

You wanna mess with me? Fine.

"Daddy, you're going too fast."

Fraser gripped the wheel until his knuckles went white. "*Shut. Up!*" he screamed.

He looked in his mirror and saw Sarah shrink into her seat like she always did when he shouted at her. *Weak*, he thought. All of them. His wife, the kids, all weak. Whenever he raised his voice, they always cowered. When they didn't, when they looked at him defiantly, that was when the belt came off.

It's time to take the belt to Masters, too.

Masters had something about him, an air of menace. Taking him on in a straight fight wasn't in the cards, but Luke Fraser knew more than one way to hurt a man. In fact, he knew the best way: to cripple them financially.

He'd done it to others. Like Masters, they all had deserved it. DeShaun Bailey, high on drugs when he drove his uninsured four-by-four into a bus stop late one night. The girl he'd hit spent three months in the hospital and the prognosis was that she'd be in a wheelchair for the rest of her life. Fraser had taken Bailey for every cent. Theo Papadopoulos had skimped on maintenance for his rental apartment complex. Despite three warning letters from the local authorities, he'd failed to fix his heating system, and when two of his tenants died from the resulting carbon monoxide leak, Fraser took everything.

Then there was Michael Tornielli. Good old Michael. Handsome, witty Michael. Family friend, racquetball partner, business associate, and the man Fraser suspected of sleeping with his wife. Though he'd never caught them in the act, Fraser had a plethora of evidence. It didn't bother him that most was circumstantial: calls between Michael and his wife; Michael being at the family home when Fraser had arrived early from work one day; his wife's sudden loss of sexual appetite. It all added up, and Fraser had made him pay.

Earlier that year, Fraser and Michael had attended a conference in Winnipeg. In the weeks leading up to the event, Fraser arranged for a local prostitute to get friendly with Michael. He also slipped a small package into Michael's locker at the gym.

On the first night of the conference, Fraser met Michael in the bar and pointed the woman out, commenting on how it was such a shame a beautiful woman was all alone. Michael, ever confident around the ladies, had approached the hooker. She was dressed as an attendee, and they hit it off immediately. Within minutes, they rose from their seats and Michael threw Fraser a wink. The hooker stumbled as they left the bar, and Fraser commented to the barman that she seemed to have had a skinful. He said she'd only had two drinks, and Fraser and the barman watched as Michael held on to his catch as they walked to the elevators. When they got to the room, they had sex, and afterwards the hooker took GHB, the date rape drug. The next morning, Michael had trouble waking her, and she seemed dazed as he ushered her out of the hotel room.

Michael's world fell apart the next day. The hooker went to the police, claiming she'd been drugged and raped. A toxicology test was performed and the GHB was detected. She was able to give the police a description and a room number, and Michael was brought in for questioning. His hotel room was searched, but nothing sinister was found, so the police got a warrant to search his home in Okotoks. When that drew a blank, they took a look at his locker at the gym and found more GHB. With the date rape drug, the hooker's statement and the barman as a witness that the woman seemed out of it despite just two drinks, Michael was charged with rape.

It never went to court, but the damage had been done. Michael lost his job and his wife divorced him, taking Michael to the cleaners in the process. When the case came up in court, the hooker refused to testify, claiming it was too much of an ordeal. She withdrew her complaint and disappeared with the fifty grand Fraser had given her. Michael, now a broken man with his reputation in tatters, had relocated to Quebec to start afresh.

Now it's your turn, Masters.

Fraser took the cell phone from his pocket and placed it in the holder on the dash, then hit the number for Nathaniel Kane. Nat was a private investigator from Calgary, and he'd done several jobs for Fraser in the past. Nat's specialty was finding dirt on defendants, and he'd been the one to discover the warning letters that had been sent to Theo Papadopoulos. If anyone could discover a chink in Masters' armor, it was Nat.

"I've got a job for you," Fraser said as soon as Nat answered.

Fraser heard the rustling of paper. "Fire away," Nat said.

"Not over the phone," Fraser said, aware that Sarah could hear him. "Meet me at the Crab Pit tonight at seven."

"Seven…Crab Pit… got it. See you then."

The call ended, and Fraser finally managed to relax a little. Nat Kane was the best in the business. Not because of his experience, but because he wasn't afraid to venture outside the law if the situation called for it.

Fraser lifted his foot off the gas, his anger replaced by joy at the prospect of revenge.

Chapter 14

"So Japhet Nkosi is our only option?" Vincent May asked Ben Scott.

"I'm afraid so. We courted the other members of Evergood's high command, but they're loyal to their president. Nkosi is the only one who was willing to see him fall."

"In exchange for the chance to lead the country himself," Larry Carter added. "We'll just be swapping one power-mad dictator for another, with no guarantee that he'll give us what we want."

"He will," Scott said. "Once he sees how easy it is for us to get to the President, he won't think of crossing us."

"Unless he asks the Chinese to provide him with security in exchange for the mineral rights," James Butler mused. "They could send a few thousand troops as part of their infrastructure aid program and Nkosi would be untouchable."

"Trust me," Scott said, "Nkosi isn't that smart. All he's interested in is money and power, and we guarantee both. Also, as defense minister, Nkosi is well placed to prevent anyone else snatching the reins. The moment the kill is confirmed, he can have the rest of Evergood's cabinet arrested for treason before they have a chance to regroup and choose their own successor."

May considered the proposal for a moment. "There simply isn't time to consider any other options," he eventually said. "The Chinese delegation is due to arrive in Bulasi to ink the deal in the next two weeks. We have to act before that happens."

"I have just the man for the job," Carter said. "Travis Burke. Former SEAL sniper, two silver stars, three tours in Afghanistan with nine confirmed kills. And he's African American, so he won't stick out over there."

"Has he done anything like this in the past?" May asked.

"No. When he quit the navy, he formed his own trucking company, but it's been leaking money from the start. He's over six hundred grand in the red and the bank is ready to foreclose. If we offer to clear his debt, provide some working capital and throw a few lucrative contracts his way, I think he'll do it. He's got no connections to any government agencies, so total deniability. Plus, he's expendable."

"What if he fails?" Butler asked. "We should have a fallback."

Carter shook his head. "We only get one shot at this. If Burke isn't successful, Evergood will beef up security and our chance is gone. Forever."

The three men looked at May for the final decision.

"We go with Burke," he said. "James, leak a press release regarding the Chinese mineral rights deal. That'll drive down the share prices of the main EV companies and we can buy just before Nkosi takes over."

"Already drafted," James Butler smiled.

Chapter 15

Five years ago, a man in a suit knocking on his office door meant a new customer for his fledgling trucking business. These days, it meant trouble.

Financial trouble.

Travis Burke had spent most of the morning staring at the screen on his desk, but the figures stubbornly refused to change. As if they weren't enough, the foreclosure notice that had arrived a few days earlier was all the proof he needed that his business was sunk.

He should have listened. His friends and financial advisors had told him his prices were too cheap and unsustainable, but he'd refused to believe them.

If I get enough customers, it'll work out.

That lie had cost him dearly.

If he'd stuck to his original plan—lease a rig and be a one-man show—things would have been different, but he'd gone all in. The numbers worked in his head, but reality had kicked his ass. It didn't help that he'd been in the hole from the get-go. He'd borrowed to lease the second truck, then the haulage yard, then the next four trucks, and before he knew it, his home was also on the line, mortgaged to the hilt.

And now his creditors had come to collect.

Travis opened the door. The man on the landing was forty, maybe forty-five, with neat black hair cut short, and a strong face. His suit looked expensive, so they hadn't just sent a messenger. This was someone important.

Travis let the man in. No point being confrontational. He gestured to a seat on a leather sofa that took up one side of the office and asked if the man would like any refreshments.

"No, thank you."

Travis leaned his butt on the corner of the desk. How can I help you, mister…?"

"Johnson," the man said. He reached into a document case and pulled out a few sheets of paper. "Nice hole you've dug yourself," he said, flicking through the pages.

It wasn't the professional approach Travis had been expecting. "Times are hard, but we'll pull through."

"I very much doubt it. You've exhausted every line of credit, you're behind on your repayments to the bank, the truck company, even the IRS." Johnson put the papers on the couch next to him and smiled up at Travis. "Thankfully, I can make all your problems go away."

Travis narrowed his eyes. If something sounded too good to be true, it usually was. "How?"

Johnson picked up the first sheet of paper. "You owe the IRS twenty-two thousand." He chose another sheet. "Obetron Leasing LLC, ninety-eight thousand." Another, "First Medway Bank, three hundred and ninety-seven thousand. The list goes on, Travis. In total, you owe close to six hundred grand, and that pile is growing day by day."

"I know what I owe," Travis said, folding his arms across his well-built chest. "I asked how you can make it go away."

Johnson picked up the first sheet. "IRS. Consider it paid." He placed it back in his document case. "The leasing company. Paid. Medway, paid. We'll also give you a capital injection of four hundred grand, plus contracts with three national supermarket chains and two distilleries in the Tennessee area, all at the going rate. How does that sound?"

Travis just stared at Johnson. It couldn't be real, no way. "Is this some kind of joke? Did someone put you up to this? Who was it? Mike Berry? Chuck Sawyer?"

"No trick, Travis, and no joke. I'm serious."

"Bullshit. Who are you, anyway? You come in here with this crazy-ass story and expect me to believe you? Get the hell out of my office!"

Johnson didn't get up. Instead, he took out his phone and made a call. "He needs proof," he said, then hung up.

"So what's that supposed to prove?" Travis asked, still angry at the joke being played on him. He was sure it was Chuck Sawyer, his old army buddy. They'd bumped into each other a few weeks earlier, and Chuck was the original joker. He'd told Chuck about his money problems over a few beers, and Chuck had said something would turn up. Travis knew this was what he was talking about.

"Check your bank account," Johnson said.

"I just did," Travis said. "I've been looking at it all day."

"Look again."

Travis sighed, then turned the screen on his computer and hit refresh. His jaw dropped. The negative balance had been replaced by a healthy four hundred-thousand-dollar surplus. He looked back at Johnson. "How? I mean…how?"

"It doesn't matter how, just know that we can."

"Yeah, you said that before," Travis said. "Who's 'we'?"

"Need to know, and you *really* don't *want* to know."

119

Travis folded his arms again. "And what's to stop me keeping that money and throwing your crazy ass out of here?"

"Look again," Johnson said. "It'll be gone by now."

Travis refreshed the screen, and the red figures were back. He stood up straight. "What the hell kind of game are you playing?"

"No game, Travis. We just want to show you what we're capable of. Now, do you like our offer?"

Travis was too confused to think straight. Of course he liked the offer, but no one was going to give him so much without asking a lot in return. And Travis had nothing to give. "What do you want in return?"

"Your skills with the TAC-338," Johnson said, crossing his legs and leaning back on the couch.

It all made sense now. No one was going to offer him a million dollars unless there was something illegal at the other end.

Travis tried to think of alternatives, but there were none. He was going to lose everything, and all he could do after that was private contract work, where there was a strong chance he'd have to kill someone anyway. He had no other discernable skills, and his bad credit would follow him around for the rest of his life.

He sighed. "Who's the mark?" He closed his eyes, hoping it wasn't the President of the United States of America. *Not the President. Not the President.*

"A high ranking official," Johnson said, "of a small foreign nation."

Travis exhaled audibly.

"What?" Johnson asked. "Did you think we'd ask you to kill someone on home soil? No, that would be murder."

"And this isn't?"

"No," Johnson said. "This is statecraft. There's a big difference. This man threatens the national security of our nation, and he has to be stopped."

"So send in the SEALs," Travis said, instantly regretting it. He was talking himself out of a million bucks.

"It can't be traced back to the government," Johnson said.

Travis had more questions, but hesitated to ask them in case Johnson changed his mind about the offer. One had to be cleared up, though. "What's to stop you reneging on the deal once I've killed him? What guarantees do I have that you'll keep your end of the bargain? I've already seen you take money from my bank."

Johnson raised one eyebrow. "Are you expecting me to produce a contract that says we'll pay you the agreed amount in return for killing a man? For one, do you think that would hold up in court? No, you're just going to have to trust us."

It was a fair point. It was also decision time.

"How long do I have to think about it?" Travis asked.

Johnson looked at his watch. "I'll give you ten seconds."

"What? You can't expect me to make a decision in that time!"

"Seven."

Travis had never been one to panic, but he saw his lifeline slipping away.

"Four…three…"

He wasn't a hundred percent sold on the idea, but he also didn't want to see his company go under. He had no choice.

"One."

"I'll do it," Travis blurted out breathlessly.

"I thought you might."

Travis ran his hand over his shaved head, only now having time to reflect on what he'd just agreed to. *A high-ranking official of a small foreign nation.* That could be anyone. The British prime minister, the guy that runs the European Union, anyone.

What have I got myself into?

It was too late to back out now, even if he wanted to. He'd only known Johnson—and that probably wasn't his real name—for a matter of minutes, but he could tell he wasn't the kind of person who shrugged off disappointment readily.

"I can see you're struggling to come to terms with this," Johnson said. "Take a few minutes if you need to, but know this: you're committed now. There's no going back."

Travis could only nod his understanding.

"And if you're worried about who the target might be, don't. We wouldn't ask you to whack an ally. No, this guy is an enemy of the state, and you'll be doing your country a service, just like you did all those years ago."

Travis' head bobbed once more as the surreal situation sank in. At least he wasn't being asked to put a bullet in a good guy, and it wasn't as if he hadn't killed America's enemies in the past.

One final question begged to be asked. "Why me? I know plenty of other SOCOM snipers who would do it for a lot less."

"Because you're the only African-American on record with five kill shots at over fourteen hundred yards," Johnson said.

"Then maybe I should have asked for two million," Travis managed to smile.

Johnson did likewise. "We would have paid three." He stood and removed a bottle from his pouch and sprayed a clear liquid onto the couch, then wiped it with a paper towel. He became serious. "Wipe the security footage on that hard drive," he said, nodding at the CCTV rig in the corner of the room. "I don't want my visit recorded, for obvious reasons."

Travis did as he was told, erasing the last hour from the disk.

Johnson took a cap from his jacket pocket and put it on, pulling the peak down low over his face. "You'll get an email with a meeting place within the next few hours. Go there alone."

He stood by the door, and Travis wondered why he wasn't leaving. Then it occurred to him: Johnson didn't want to touch it. He was making sure there was no evidence of his visit. Travis rushed to open it for him.

"Good luck," Johnson said, and walked out of the office, his head down.

Chapter 16

As Johnson had promised, an email arrived an hour after he had left. It contained a name and the address of a park in Franklin, Tennessee. When Travis arrived, he saw the man wearing the white Fedora sitting on the bench by the fountain. When Travis approached him, the man stood.

"Let's walk."

Travis got in step. "You got a name?"

The man looked at him as they strolled toward a pond. "You can call me Smith."

Smith was in his sixties, with grey hair and mustache. He was a little shorter than Travis' six-one, and his jacket betrayed the middle-age spread around his waist.

"So, who's the target?"

"Jacobi Evergood," Smith said. "He's the president of a new state called Bulasi. It's in central Africa."

"And what's he done to deserve a bullet?"

"I could tell you, but—"

"—but then you'd have to kill me, I get it."

"Actually, I was going to say, I could tell you, but you're going to do the job regardless, so there's no point. Let's just say he's no friend of ours."

Travis didn't push it. He hadn't expected an answer, in truth. "When do I go in?"

"Three days. A diversion will be in place, which will make things easier for you. You'll get all the details when you arrive. One of our men will meet you at the airport. He'll give you all the necessary intel and provide you with logistics."

"Do I need to take anything with me?"

"No. Everything you need will be provided." Smith took an envelope from his jacket pocket. "Plane tickets and passport."

"I already have a passport."

"Use this one. It's in the name of Tyrone Glenn. We need total deniability if things go south."

"Does that mean if things get hairy, I'm on my own?"

"Yes," Smith said, "but if you stick to the plan, nothing should go wrong."

Travis wasn't so sure. He knew from experience that any one of a million random incidents could trash a mission: a guard where he wasn't supposed to be; a flat tire that causes a convoy to be late for an RV; a last-minute change of route; a jammed weapon.

None of that mattered now, though. It was too late to back out.

Smith walked away, leaving Travis to his thoughts.

* * *

Three days later, Travis stood in the line for the immigration desks at Malundi's Derrek Okanza International Airport. His only baggage was the knapsack on his back, which contained toiletries and three changes of clothes. They were purely for show. The plan was for him to execute his mission and be back on the plane within the next twenty-four hours.

Travis got through the border controls without incident. At the arrivals lounge, he looked for someone holding a board with "Tyrone Glenn" on it.

There were a dozen men waiting, all holding up pieces of card, but none were for him.

"Mr. Glenn?"

Travis wheeled and saw a man a foot shorter than himself. "I'm Danny. Welcome to Malundi." It sounded like English was definitely his second language.

Danny was skinny to the extreme, with prominent teeth and skin the color of night. He was smiling like he'd just won the lottery.

Travis held out a hand and Danny shook it, his hand like that of a child.

"Come. This way."

Travis followed Danny out of the airport terminal and into the fierce heat of a Malundi lunchtime. Sweat was pouring from him by the time they reached a beaten-up Toyota with a two-tone color scheme: blue and rust. Danny beamed with pride as he opened the door for Travis, who threw his bag in the back seat and climbed into the front. The seat moaned as he sat, and Travis could feel the springs threatening to give him an impromptu colonoscopy.

"First time in Malundi?" Danny asked as he coaxed life into the engine.

"Yeah."

First and last.

The spattering of buildings they passed on the highway were all single-story, made of wood with corrugated tin roofs, and in need of repair. It looked like a dire place.

Travis had done his research on Malundi. It was one of the poorest African nations, and the recent civil war hadn't done much for the country's economy. At sixty miles wide by a hundred long, it was also the smallest. It had been larger, but the secession of Bulasi had cut the overall size by more than a third. The most important things he'd learned were how to get into Bulasi, and how to get out again.

Travis' first stop was a small village a couple of miles from the border. It was so small, it wasn't even named on any maps. When they reached it, Travis could see why. It consisted of five huts built of wood and mud, and a pen shared by chickens and goats.

Danny led Travis into the largest hut. It was dark and empty, with a dirt floor and a few sticks of apparently home-made furniture. The large circular clock on the wall stood out. On a table in the center of the room was a black leather rifle case next to a battered Browning Hi-Power pistol.

Travis sat down and opened the case, and his fingers caressed the weapon inside. It was a McMillan TAC-338, the same model of sniper rifle he'd fired so many times during his SEAL days. It had been stripped down and oiled, and Travis wasted no time putting it back together.

"Where can I test it?" he asked Danny.

"This way."

The small guide took him outside and around the back of the hut, past a small diesel generator. There was open ground for a couple of hundred yards before a thin line of trees broke up the horizon. Travis stuck a magazine into the rifle and fired off all five rounds at the nearest trunk, making small adjustments to the Vortex scope after each shot. By the time he'd emptied five mags, he was satisfied with the set up. He emptied the mag on the handgun, too, just to be sure it was in working order.

They went back inside, where Travis dismantled the rifle once more. He took his time cleaning it, then wrapped the pieces in oil cloth and put them in his backpack, along with four full magazines and two spares for the pistol.

When Travis was done, Danny shouted something in the local language and a woman appeared with a tray of food. There were strips of roast meat and a vegetable medley, and although Travis was famished, he wasn't about to risk anything prepared in such unsanitary conditions. The last thing he needed was food poisoning right before the mission kicked off. At the same time, he didn't want to upset the locals, especially as they were the ones responsible for his exfiltration—getting him safely out of the country. He picked at some root vegetables and explained to Danny that he was vegan, and to thank the woman for her efforts.

"Vegan?" Danny asked.

"I don't eat meat," Travis explained.

Danny relayed the message, and the woman adopted an impressive facial reaction that portrayed both confusion and shock. She picked up the bowl of meat and walked away, muttering to herself.

When she was gone, Travis asked to see the intel. Danny retrieved a laptop and a satellite phone from the car. After powering up the computer, he opened a password-protected folder.

"We are here," Danny said, indicating a point on a satellite photo, "and you will cross the border here."

"It is guarded?" Travis asked.

"Usually, yes, but tonight, General Nkosi is hosting a military parade in honor of President Evergood. Most of the country's troops will be there, so the border will be thinly patrolled."

"Where does Evergood live?" Travis asked.

"Here," Danny said, holding out a photograph, "in his palace, but it is better if you take him on his way to the parade. His palace is heavily guarded."

It wasn't much of a palace. Most houses in the Flagstaff suburbs were bigger and better maintained.

"I've marked three potential sites along his route," Danny continued. "Any of them should give you a decent shot at him."

Travis checked each of the locations in turn, immediately ruling out the second. It would mean hitting a moving target side on from twelve hundred yards. The first was promising, but he opted for the third. It was closest to the border—and therefore his exfil—and provided a degree of elevation and a near head-on shot from just under a thousand yards.

"What vehicle will Evergood be traveling in?"

Danny produced another photograph, this time of a Cadillac Escalade.

"Is it armor-plated?" Travis asked.

"No."

Travis hoped he was right. If not, the TAC-338's Lapua Magnum rounds would bounce off from that distance.

He fired off a few more questions: what time would Evergood leave his palace? What time was sunset in Bulasi? What was the weather forecast? All of the answers worked in Travis' favor.

Travis was starting to feel like he was back in his team, only this time there would be no back-up if the mission turned ugly. No chopper to call on, no teammate to watch his six as he retreated. If he got this wrong, he wasn't going home.

Travis checked his watch. He had an hour before he had to set off, so he strolled out of the hut and walked around aimlessly, visualizing every step ahead through the mission. Once he was satisfied that things were as nailed down as they could be, he took out his phone and brought up a picture of Jacobi Evergood. He'd stared at the face many times before leaving Tennessee, looking into the eyes of the man he was going to kill. Evergood didn't look like a monster. There was nothing evil in his appearance, and his bio didn't paint him as a mass murderer. All he'd really learned in his research was that the president of Bulasi was about to sign a trade deal with the Chinese. Was that what this was all about? Travis neither knew nor cared. Not anymore. His government wanted the man dead, and for a million dollars, Travis Burke would pull the trigger.

* * *

Travis left the hut at three in the afternoon, heading north. He'd changed into local clothing so that he wouldn't stand out, and swapped the backpack for one Danny provided. It was at least twenty years old and non-brand so as not to display any kind of wealth. Malundi was a poor country, and Bulasi even more so.

As promised, the border was clear. It had been marked out with fence posts every five yards, but the actual construction of a fence hadn't yet begun. The dirt on the Bulasi side was well worn, suggesting heavy foot traffic, and Travis was glad of the distraction of the military parade.

From the border it was another three-and-a-bit miles to the place he would wait for Evergood. By the time he arrived, he had drunk two of the four large water bottles he had brought and was soaked in sweat.

The location was as good as he'd hoped. He was on a rise, with the road about fifty yards below. The bushes all around gave him a clear view while obscuring him from the road. Evergood would come from Travis' left, and the angle was better than he'd envisaged from the overheads. The car would approach at an angle of about forty degrees, so he would be able to see into the vehicle but wouldn't have to lead it so much. He had to fire in front of a moving target so that the bullet and subject intersected at the right moment.

He checked his watch again. Evergood was due to leave his home at six, which was half an hour away. It would take him just ten minutes to reach this point.

Travis assembled his rifle, thoroughly checking each component for dirt. He placed a round in the chamber and slapped a five-round magazine home. That would give him six shots before he had to swap out.

Next, he cut off some branches from a nearby bush to further obscure his hiding place.

At exactly six in the evening, Travis made himself comfortable behind the blind.

If there was one thing that could be said for Jacobi Evergood, he was punctual. Travis saw a plume of dust from a couple of miles away at eight minutes past.

He pulled the stock of the rifle into his shoulder and forced himself to calm his breathing. Having been out of the game so long, it wasn't easy.

A mile and a half.

In…out…in…

Travis' pulse quickened as he identified five vehicles, which wasn't what he had been hoping for. Two, maybe three tops, would have been something he could handle. He'd asked Danny how many there would be, but the small guide had only shrugged.

He checked his breathing again as the lead vehicle got to the mile marker, a gnarled tree ten yards from the road.

Shit's about to get real…

The road bent to the driver's left, which changed the angle and allowed Travis to see inside all the vehicles. Jacobi Evergood was in the third, sitting next to the window.

Travis took a deep breath and held it as the center of the scope settled on Evergood's forehead. He let his breath out and squeezed the trigger at the bottom of the exhale. The scope jumped momentarily, and when it settled back on Evergood, his head was hanging to one side and there was a large red patch on the cream leather seat.

But Travis' job wasn't done yet. The five vehicles were capable of traveling off road, so he couldn't run until they were out of commission. He started with the nearest one, putting a round through the driver's chest and then switching his attention to the wheels. He popped the nearside front tire, then moved on to the second vehicle. The rest of the convoy had had to stop behind the first two vehicles, so Travis concentrated on disabling the cars. He destroyed three more tires, then switched out the mag and set his sights on the last of the vehicles.

He didn't get the shot off. Gunfire erupted from below, and rounds chewed up the ground in front of him. Travis backed away until he was out of the line of sight, then threw the pack on his back and ran two hundred yards at a lung-bursting pace until he found a good spot to throw himself to the ground. As he brought the rifle up to his shoulder, the remaining usable vehicle bounced into view. Men were firing automatic rifles from both rear windows, but Travis ignored them and focused on the driver. He hit the man in the throat, then chambered another round ready to put it through the grille.

He didn't have to bother. The dead driver fell against the steering wheel and the vehicle slewed to the left, hit a termite mound and cartwheeled half a dozen times. The gunmen flew through the air like rag dolls. Silence descended.

Travis knew it wouldn't last long.

He got up and ran, calculating as he went. Four cars left, say four men in each, was sixteen. Take away the driver he'd killed, plus Evergood, and that meant at least fourteen on his tail.

And fourteen rounds left for the TAC.

He would have to make every shot count, or let them in close enough for the pistol to be effective.

Bullets whizzed past his head a split second before the sound of gunfire reached him. He threw himself behind a tree and brought his rifle up. There were three of them, all dressed in army green and firing from the hip as they ran toward him. Travis took two down in quick succession, but the third dived behind cover and fired blindly. Travis waited for him to run dry, then sprinted away again. He got another three hundred yards before his lungs cried enough, and he fell behind a tree to catch his breath. After a few seconds he peeked around the trunk and saw four soldiers heading his way. They moved warily, having seen their mates fall.

Travis gave them more to think about. He got the lead soldier in his sights and squeezed the trigger. As soon as the bullet left the rifle, Travis cycled the bolt and chambered another, switching to a new target and letting fly. This shot missed, and he had to endure more incoming fire from the three hostiles.

He would have given anything for some grenades. Smoke, frag, it didn't matter. Anything to give him a few seconds of respite.

As the assault on his position continued, Travis shuffled his backside away from the tree until he was lying on his back, then switched onto his stomach and stuck his rifle around the base of the trunk. The three men were still advancing, and he took another out of the equation. The other two sprayed bullets his way, and Travis waited until the first ran dry, then focused and registered another kill.

Nine men left, and only eight rounds.

Two more men had appeared, and they were shouting at their fellow soldier as he cowered behind a tree trunk. Travis took advantage of the situation and took one of them out, and the other newcomer realized why his friend was hiding. He ducked into cover, too, and Travis took it as his cue to leave.

He was already two hundred yards from them, and he soon doubled that distance. He allowed himself the luxury of slowing. His enemies were carrying AKs, which had an effective range of about four hundred yards, which was how far he was from them now. They could still get lucky with a stray round at up to double that distance, but when he checked his six, they didn't seem to be pursuing him.

Travis wasn't about to let up. He'd kept up his fitness regimen after leaving the navy, and it was paying off now.

He took a couple of seconds to check the compass on his wristwatch, then adjusted his heading a few degrees and ran out into the open. There was no more cover for another half a mile, and halfway across the open ground was the makeshift border.

Four hundred and forty yards, he told himself as he pushed on once more, his legs and arms pumping. He could do that in under a minute and a half on the track, but today he would try to cover it in two.

He was halfway across when he felt a sting in his buttock. His step faltered and Travis tumbled to the ground, rolling twice. More bullets flew toward him, the earth near his head erupting in fountains of dirt. He saw a lone gunman running from the border. He looked young, maybe mid-teens, and his uniform appeared two sizes too big.

That didn't make the rifle he was carrying any less deadly.

Much as he hated to, Travis stuck the stock into his shoulder and got the advancing child in the center of his scope. His heart skipped a beat at the thought of what he was going to do, but his survival instincts kicked in and he squeezed the trigger.

Travis' head dropped as he saw the boy go down like a marionette that had its strings cut.

This wasn't part of the deal. One shot, one kill, that's all he signed up for. If he'd known he had to kill kids, he would have turned the offer down flat.

Move!

Years of training ingrained into his brain spurred him into action. If there was one border guard, there would no doubt be more, and the shooting would draw them in.

Travis got to his feet, his ass stinging from the bullet he'd taken. He limped as fast as he could to the line of fence posts and didn't stop once he'd passed them. He wanted to get as deep into Malundi as he could before he let up the pace.

After another mile, Travis allowed himself a rest. He fell against a tree and checked all around, but there was no sign of Evergood's men. Darkness had fallen, and hopefully that meant they'd lost both his scent, and their courage.

He felt for the wound in his buttock. His hand came away bloody, and he used his knife to cut a swathe of cloth from his T-shirt. He balled it up and pressed it into the wound, then staggered onwards, keeping pressure on the painful area. Each step brought a fresh wave of discomfort, but he'd gone through worse during his SEAL training.

Twenty minutes later he saw the outline of the small village in the distance. Putting on a final spurt, he got to the largest structure and pushed the door inwards.

Danny rose from his seat as Travis staggered inside and collapsed on the dirt floor.

"You're hit," Danny said.

"No shit." Travis pulled his pants off. "Get me a mirror."

When Danny fetched one, Travis inspected the damage. Thankfully, the bullet had only grazed the flesh, leaving a furrow a couple of inches long and maybe a quarter of an inch deep.

"I'll take you to the doctor," Danny said, putting on a jacket.

"No, get me a first aid kit."

Danny looked at him with a blank face, and Travis realized he was going to have to improvise. "Just fetch me a couple of clean towels, hot water, some salt and a roll of Scotch tape."

An hour later, with a makeshift dressing on his butt and a soft blanket to sit on, Travis was heading back to the airport in Danny's car. It was a mercifully short journey, and Travis did his best to mask his discomfort as he walked through the airport terminal.

The next hour was the most nerve-wracking of his life. At any moment he expected the police or army to arrest him for murder, but soon enough, he handed over his boarding pass at the gate and took his seat on the flight.

Only when the wheels left the ground was Travis able to relax a little. There was still a chance that the authorities would demand that the pilot return to Malundi, but it wasn't enough to keep Travis from enjoying a couple of inflight beers.

At Amsterdam's Schiphol Airport, he purchased a bandage and some antiseptic cream from a pharmacy and dressed his wound properly in the washroom, then headed to a bar for some liquid pain relief before the connecting flight to London Heathrow. From there it was another hop to Memphis and he was all but home.

As he sipped a Jim Beam, Travis wondered if it had been worth it. He'd been offered private security work by a couple of former SEALs after leaving the navy, but he'd turned them down. He was done with killing, he'd told them, and it was time to begin a new life.

Look how that turned out.

When he got home, he was going to use some of his payoff to hire a real manager to run the business, someone with actual haulage experience. It was something he should have done from the start, but he'd been determined to make it on his own. The last five years had proven that he didn't have the right skills for that. He was big enough to admit that he'd been wrong, but as far as he was concerned, the past was the past.

It was time to look forward to the future, one where there would be no more killing.

He downed his bourbon and ordered another, holding it up before him in a silent toast.

The future.

Chapter 17

If it weren't for the incessant chugging of the outboard motor, the river cruise would have been idyllic.

Idyllic, but boring as hell.

Eva stood and stretched her legs for the umpteenth time. Other than staring at the passing jungle, there was nothing for her to do. She envied Sonny, who'd brought his Kindle along. He took it with him everywhere, a gift from his dead friend, Len Smart.

"More war stories?" she asked.

"No, I've gone for a legal thriller this time. *The Professor*, by Robert Bailey. It's great so far."

"I didn't know that was your thing," Eva said, taking a seat next to him.

"It isn't, normally, but after we watched The Rainmaker a few weeks ago, I developed a craving for courtroom dramas. The characters in this one are vivid and the storyline is riveting."

"Please tell me you didn't download it recently," Eva said, suddenly concerned.

"No, it was one of Len's books. It was already on the Kindle when he left it to me."

Her relief was instant. "Phew. The last thing we need is to leave more tracks."

Sonny turned off his Kindle and put it in his cargo pants pocket. "You think we'll ever stop running?" he asked.

"From the ESO? I don't think so."

He looked out over the water for a moment. Eva followed his gaze and saw a river dolphin breach the surface before disappearing once more beneath the brown water. Sonny didn't seem to have noticed it.

"We could take the fight to them," he said, then looked at her for her reaction.

Eva sighed. She wanted to agree with him, but it was one fight they couldn't win. "We got lucky when we discovered Henry Langton was the head of the ESO, but that's all changed now. I wouldn't know where to begin looking for them."

"We could bring them to us," Sonny suggested. "Leave a trail, wait for them to strike, then capture one of them and work our way to the top."

Eva cradled his hand in hers. "You've been reading too many war stories," she said. "It's not how it works, and you know it. If they send a team after us, we won't know about it until we're dead."

Sonny's head drooped. "I just…"

Eva kissed his cheek. "Yeah, I know. Me too."

She looked at her watch for the fifth time that hour. It was almost six in the evening, and the sun was on its way down. According to Papi, they were making ten knots, so by her earlier calculations they would reach Iquitos by ten the following night.

Just twenty-nine hours to go.

Eva absently dropped her hand over the side, then immediately pulled it back. Papi had warned her about the piranhas that swam in the river.

"Where do you want to go after this?" she asked. "Stick to South America, or move on?"

Sonny shrugged. "I'm easy, but one thing's for sure: once we get to Colombia, we're gonna be in serious need of some down time."

* * *

Romeo Jimenez cursed as he lay in bed. He hated working to the schedule of others. It was one of the reasons he'd quit the police, though not the driving factor. That had been money. More money than he could ever have hoped to dream of.

For Jimenez, policing hadn't been a calling. He'd fallen into the role at a time when jobs were hard to come by. After answering an advertisement in a local newspaper, he'd been accepted with the minimum of fuss and immediately sent for training. That hadn't been the most rigorous process, and before he knew it, he was ready to pound the streets, protecting the great city of Bogotá.

He was surprised to discover that he actually enjoyed the job. He thought it would have been monotonous, directing traffic or issuing parking tickets. However, as soon as his training ended, he'd been chosen for detective training. His aptitude test score had been off the charts, his talent recognized.

Jimenez rose through the ranks swiftly, but after seventeen years his passion for the job was gone. The hours seemed to increase year after year, while the money was

141

barely enough to maintain a decent bachelor lifestyle. He knew that most cops took backhanders to help with living costs, but he'd seen too many get greedy and fall into departmental stings to try it himself. Instead, he had a more profitable idea. Having cultivated a sizable list of contacts— both in the police and intelligence community and the criminal fraternity—Jimenez quit the force and set up his own investigative agency.

The early months were barren times, with few clients and little in the way of income. Then he got his big break, a missing persons case.

The moment the woman had walked into his office, Jimenez knew something wasn't right. She'd claimed her husband had gone missing, but something about her story didn't ring true. Jimenez had promised to do all he could, but his initial investigation had been into the woman herself. It didn't take long to establish a link between the woman and the Soldado cartel.

Jimenez had seen this as a life-changing opportunity. He'd promptly found the missing husband, but rather than contact the woman, he'd gone straight to Felix Hernandez with the man's location. It was a calculated gamble, but one that paid off handsomely. Jimenez had offered his services to Hernandez, explaining how easy it was to link the woman to the cartel. By using his deep knowledge of law enforcement, he could ensure such ties were obfuscated in future. That, and the fact that he'd found a man Hernandez had spent two years looking for, sealed the deal.

Jimenez had been working for Hernandez ever since, and in those eight years he'd tracked down over a dozen men and women who had incurred the wrath of his boss. For each success, Jimenez had received substantial bonuses on top of his already generous salary. He now had over five million dollars saved in various banks on the continent, though they were all in safe deposit boxes, not standard bank accounts.

Now in his mid-forties, he reckoned on another five years with Hernandez, then he would disappear and enjoy his retirement. His time would be his own, and he wouldn't have to worry about deadlines.

As it was, he was stuck in a hotel in Yurimaguas until morning because the only person willing to charter his private plane wasn't willing to fly at night. A storm was coming, the pilot had explained, and no matter how much money Jimenez offered him to take off immediately, the man had dug his heels in.

It made no difference in the end. The locals said Papi, the man who had taken the couple down river, had never completed the 440-mile journey to Iquitos in less than thirty-six hours. Even if Jimenez flew late the following morning, he'd be in Iquitos at least nine hours before the gringos.

A roll of thunder boomed overhead, and rain fell like rocks, bouncing off the windows of the hotel room. Jimenez stood and opened the drapes, but all he could see was a river of water running down the pane. Perhaps the pilot had been right after all. Flying in this weather wouldn't have been a pleasant experience.

He returned to the bed. All that remained was to come up with a plan to capture the gringos. He thought the best way would be to wait until they docked, then surprise them as they left the boat. They would be weary from the journey and unlikely to put up much resistance. He would get Costa to hide upstream and send a signal when he saw the boat approach Iquitos, giving himself plenty of time to get into position. The dock would hopefully be quiet so late in the evening, so there would be no crowd for them to disappear into.

It sounded perfect.

Another boom of thunder shook the room, almost jolting Jimenez from his bed, and a fierce wind rattled the window. He knew that he wouldn't be able to sleep through such a racket, so he dressed and went downstairs to the bar. It was tiny, with two stools up against the bar and one small circular table with two chairs. All of the seats were occupied, so Jimenez ordered four bottles of beer and took them back to his room.

He knew he wouldn't get much sleep that night, but at least he wasn't stuck on a tiny boat floating in the middle of nowhere.

Chapter 18

Eva had never seen a storm like it. One minute they were sleeping soundly, lulled by the sound of the motor, and the next they were being lashed with raindrops the size of marbles. Each one stung as she tried to help the others to pull down the flaps and secure them to the side of the boat, but a ferocious wind whipped the tarpaulin from her numb fingers time and again. Sonny fared no better. Even Papi, accustomed to such hostile conditions, seemed ill at ease.

The worst part was the wind. It seemed to come at them from all sides and caught the roof of the boat like a sail, lifting the vessel out of the water and slamming it back down, jarring them violently.

Eva finally managed to get one panel secured, but as she moved on to the next, disaster struck.

Papi had steered the boat closer to the bank, where the water was a little calmer, but it was still a rollercoaster ride. Lightning pierced the darkness and slashed into the forest by the side of the river. A giant tree took the brunt of the strike and exploded. The top half of it came crashing down toward them. As it landed astern, one of the thick branches slapped into the outboard motor, flipping it off the boat like a tiddlywink.

The impact threw Sonny backwards. His head cracked against one of the poles that supported the roof, leaving a long gash in his scalp, and he stumbled and lost his footing. Eva reached out to grab him, but he slipped over the side and crashed into the water below. She peered into the dark, angry river, but there was no sign of him.

"*Sonny!*"

The boat bobbed like a cork in a maelstrom, powerless and rudderless. Eva looked to Papi for help, but he lay motionless on the deck, waves soaking him as they washed over the side.

Eva turned her attention back to the water. It was almost impossible to make out shapes as the rain continued to attack her from all angles. It was only when another lightning bolt crashed overhead that she saw Sonny floating in the water. He was about ten yards from the boat, face down and helpless.

Eva dove in and powered through the water, fueled by adrenaline, until one flailing arm touched what she prayed was a leg. She pulled herself next to Sonny and flipped him over on his back. Putting her arm over his chest, she grabbed him near the armpit, then pulled him backwards to keep his head out of the water as she tried to swim one-handed to the shore. Progress was painfully slow. Wave after wave washed over her face, foul water flooding into her mouth with each breath she took. Debris whipped up by the storm assaulted her with every stroke as the rain continued to sting her face. The raging river threatened to drag them out into deeper water, away from safety. Eva's muscles screamed for mercy, but she fought through the pain. With gritted teeth, she made one last huge effort, kicking wildly and clawing at the surface of the water. It was working. Ever so slowly, she could see the bank getting closer, and she eventually managed to grab onto a tree root and drag herself, and then Sonny, clear of the river. She placed him on his back and checked his breathing, but with the wind howling through the trees, it was impossible to hear anything. She cleared his airway and pumped his chest, then held his nose and blew into his mouth.

There was no response.

"Don't you dare die on me, you sonofabitch!"

Eva pounded his chest once more, and was rewarded with a face full or river water as Sonny coughed out the contents of his lungs. He took gulping breaths, and Eva fell on top of him, cradling his head to her neck.

"I thought I'd lost you," she whispered, but her words were carried away by the storm.

"What…happened?"

"You fell in, you clumsy British asshole!"

Sonny tried to sit up, then winced and touched the back of his head.

"Lie still," Eva said.

She looked out over the river. The boat was drifting out to deeper water, aimlessly following the storm's commands. It was already too far out for them to swim to it, and even if they managed to get on board, there was no way they could steer it.

"Why are we on land?" Sonny asked. "What happened to the boat?"

"It's gone," she said. Not only that, all of their possessions were on board. All they had to survive were the clothes on their backs. No food, no weapons, no money, and no shelter.

"Our bags…?" Sonny asked.

Eva just shook her head.

Sonny grimaced and closed his eyes, ignoring the rain streaming down on him.

"You know I said I wanted a little action in my life?" he said.

Eva nodded. "I remember."

"Well, I've had enough now."

Eva couldn't help but chuckle. Despite their dire situation, he was still able to make jokes.

"Come on," she said, pulling him to his feet. "Let's get inland and find some shelter."

* * *

"How are you feeling?" Eva asked when Sonny opened his eyes.

She'd been staring at him as he slept, reflecting on how lucky she was to have him. When she'd first met him, she hadn't been impressed at all. He'd come across as immature, irritating, probably the most unprofessional soldier she'd ever encountered. That had only lasted a few hours, though. The moment he was pressed into action, he showed his true colors.

The incident that had killed his best friend, Len Smart, had also claimed the life of her lover, Carl Huff. Soon after, Eva and Sonny had gone their separate ways, and Eva hadn't expected to see him again. The ESO had changed all that. Forced to do a job for them in North Korea, she'd recruited Sonny to help, and in their time apart he'd changed beyond recognition. The happy-go-lucky playboy had become a self-taught chef and restaurant owner.

Eva knew she could have her choice of men, but what she needed was a kindred spirit. Sonny was that man.

"My head's pounding," Sonny said, rubbing the back of his neck.

"I'm not surprised. You took a real bang. I cleaned it as best I could, but you should really get it checked out."

"That's not gonna be easy," Sonny said, sitting up. "Not many hospitals around, I'm guessing."

"There's not much of anything," Eva agreed, though their surroundings teemed with life. A cacophony boomed out of the jungle, birds and insects competing to make the most noise. As long as that was all they had to contend with, they should be okay. If they came across any of the predators, like panthers, things could get real ugly, real quick. There were also myriad spiders, bullet ants and giant centipedes to avoid on their travels. Eva was almost sorry she'd done her research before getting on the boat.

"Any idea where we are?" Sonny asked.

"None. Also, our phones got waterlogged during the swim. Even your Kindle, I'm afraid."

"Then we're in the shit," Sonny moaned. "I vaguely remember you saying we lost all our gear. Please tell me I was dreaming."

"Afraid not. It's all gone. And unless you can use that jungle training of yours to fashion some sort of teleporter out of twigs and moss, yes, we're in the shit."

"I was absent the day they taught that," Sonny said, getting to his feet. "Where are my socks?"

"Hanging on that branch," Eva said. "I dried them while we were sleeping." She reached into her pocket and took out some notes. "That's the last of the money. I had to dry it out, too. You take half, just in case."

"Good thinking." He checked his socks, turned them inside out to make sure they hadn't been used as a sleeping bag by the local insects, then put them on. "Have you got a needle?"

Eva shook her head.

"Didn't think so. I could have made a compass. I was there for that lesson."

"East is that way," Eva said, pointing. "I was awake when the sun came up. The river is back that way."

Sonny stood, concentrating. Eventually, he said, "We slept at about ten, and it would have taken at least an hour for that storm to brew, so let's say we were on the boat for twelve hours. At ten knots, that's…"

"…Two hundred and twenty klicks," Eva said. "I already did the math. The question is, where do we go from here?"

"We follow the river," Sonny told her. "There has to be a small fishing village or something like that. From there, we can get a lift to the nearest big town and regroup."

"Sounds like a plan," Eva said, putting her socks on. She checked her sneakers for spiders and ants, then stuck them on her feet. "Lead the way."

Chapter 19

Graham Masters looked down at Melissa as she slept. The book she'd been reading was open on her bed sheet, and he put her bookmark in before placing it on the nightstand and turning off her light.

She deserves a real life, he told himself, but it wasn't something he could promise to deliver. He'd done things in his life that he regretted but couldn't change. Over a decade earlier, he'd chosen a course of action that led him to this point. He often wondered what his life would be like if he hadn't kidnapped those five boys and threatened to kill them live on the internet.

You would still be Tom Gray, not living a lie as Graham Masters.

If he'd let the death of his wife and son go, life would have been much different. He wouldn't have met Andrew Harvey from MI5, and subsequently his friends Sonny and Len wouldn't have been hired to help the Driscoll woman. That was when any hopes of a semi-normal life disappeared. Until that point, he'd been content with his life in Italy, but that all changed when the ESO used Melissa to get to Driscoll. Since then, he'd been running from them, and he would do so for the rest of his life.

The flip side was, if he hadn't been spirited away to the Philippines by the UK government, he would never have met Vick, his second wife, and therefore Melissa wouldn't have been born. Maybe that would have been a blessing. Melissa wouldn't have to watch every word she said for the rest of her life, and constantly move around to evade their enemies.

My enemies, he corrected himself.

None of this was Melissa's fault, yet he'd dragged her into it. Would she have been better off with her grandparents, Ken and Mina Hatcher? Perhaps. But that ship had sailed. Once he'd become a person of interest to the ESO, there was no option but to run. It was too late to place Melissa with relatives; that was the first place the ESO would look, and the moment he contacted them, their lives would be over.

"I'm sorry," Gray whispered as he gently brushed a strand of hair from his daughter's cheek.

He left her room and pulled the door, leaving it open a crack so that the light from the hallway could penetrate the small gap. She'd had nightmares in the past, which was understandable, given what she'd been through, and she could no longer sleep with the lights off. He'd tried turning the hallway light off a couple of times, but her screams had soon woken him.

Downstairs, Gray took a beer from the refrigerator and sat down in front of the TV. It was the same routine every night. Two light beers, a film, then bed. He'd lost count of the number of times he wanted two beers to become six, or eight, but he had to keep a clear head. If the ESO found him, they weren't going to give him advance notice, so he had to be alert and ready to fight at all times.

Almost as big a problem as the threat of imminent capture was the boredom. He couldn't afford to make friends in case they became too nosey, and he couldn't go out at night because of Melissa. He'd left her with a babysitter once, and that hadn't ended well. He'd considered sharing a brewski or two with Joel, but that would have invited awkward questions about Gray's past. As he took another mouthful of beer, Gray thought about the times he'd shared with his friends of old, and how he'd give anything for one more night with them. Len, Sonny, Carl, Jeff, Tris…but it would never be. Len was dead, and Sonny was in the wind, like himself. If he tried to contact the others, the ESO would be on to him immediately.

No, solitude was his only companion during the dark hours, and Melissa was there before and after school. That was the way it was always going to be.

Gray took a swig of beer, and a smile played on his lips as he thought back to the video the girl had taken on her cell phone. As the sergeant had said, it was one hell of a punch.

You taught her well, Gray.

But the more he thought about it, that was all he'd taught her. He wasn't the most studious father on the planet, and when she got to trigonometry at school, there was no way he was going to be able to help her with her homework. Advanced math might not be his forte, but he did know one thing, and that was how to fight. Even if the ESO wasn't looking for them, self-defense lessons would still have been part of her daily routine. It was a mad world, where the stranger walking toward you could have love or violence in their heart. Gray wanted her to be prepared for the latter, especially in the years to come. She'd soon be old enough to make her own way in the world, without Daddy there to look after her. When that time came, Gray wanted to be confident that she could look after herself.

Judging by today's performance, she was well on her way to achieving that.

Gray sank the last mouthful of beer and went back to the kitchen for the second bottle. When he resumed his seat, he wondered how much longer they could stay in Okotoks. He didn't much care where they lived, as he'd be spending most of his life in the house, but Melissa liked the town, especially her school. Madison Fraser and her entourage apart, Melissa had made some good friends and was always cheery when Gray picked her up. It would be a real shame to have to up sticks and find a new home.

It would have to happen eventually, though. Something always came up that caused them to move on. In the last town, it had been a neighbor who simply refused to give Gray and Melissa any privacy. If he ventured into the back yard, she was there, standing by the fence, waiting to ask questions. Whenever he went to the mall, she was there, just itching to spark up a conversation. Eventually, Gray had hired a U-Haul and parked it down the street. That night, he'd loaded it up with their meagre possessions and they'd skipped town.

There had been no such issues in Okotoks, but the incident at the school could become a problem. He'd made a wise choice investing in the pendant. Without that video evidence, Melissa would have no doubt been expelled. Worse, she could have faced criminal charges.

Could I have handled it differently?

He didn't think so. Maybe instruct Melissa to walk away from Madison Fraser, but what life lesson would that have been? You should always let the bully win? No, that wasn't the way. He'd handled it correctly, making sure they had proof that Melissa was in the right.

At least he wouldn't have to worry about Fraser. His kid might be a bully, but the father was weak. Gray had seen it when he'd silenced the man with just a glare. Better men would have stood up to him, but not that worm. There'd be no comeback from that quarter.

Gray looked at the half-empty bottle in his hand, then went to the kitchen and poured the contents down the sink. He drank to relax, but most nights—tonight included—he found himself reminiscing, pining for a life long gone.

Forget the past. It's time to make new memories with Melissa.

Gray decided to check for amusement parks on the internet in the morning. Melissa's school term would be over in a couple of weeks, and she deserved a treat.

He tossed the empty bottle in the recycling box and went up to bed.

Chapter 20

When Luke Fraser thought of private investigators, he pictured Magnum, with his flashy cars and chest hair, or Columbo, with his rumpled trench coat. Men with distinguishing appearances or affectations. Nat Kane wasn't like that. He was five-ten, with neat but slightly long hair combed over to the side, and a face that was instantly forgettable. The kind of man you could meet at a party and not recognize ten minutes later. Nat claimed his looks were what made him so good. He was able to blend into a crowd and go unnoticed. Fraser didn't care what worked for him, as long as he got the job done.

Nat arrived at the Crab Pit a couple of minutes early and took a seat opposite Fraser. He signaled a passing waitress and ordered the special plate and a diet soda. They'd done business in this seafood joint enough times that Nat knew his order before he even stepped in.

"I'm intrigued," Nat said. "What kind of job can't you discuss over the phone?"

Fraser recognized the opening gambit. Nat was looking for extra. He always did when the lines between legal and illicit were blurred.

"Nothing special. I just couldn't talk with my kid in the back seat," Fraser said.

Nat's face dropped a little. He took a piece of bread from a basket on the table and took a bite. "So who am I looking at?"

"His name is Graham Masters. My daughter says he lives on Phillips Drive in Okotoks."

Nat took out his phone and opened a memo app, adding the details.

"What's he done?"

Fraser hesitated, looking around for anyone within earshot, then leaned in. "It's personal."

Nat perked up again and gave Fraser a knowing grin. "Need another hooker?"

It was Nat who had engaged the services of the prostitute used to frame Michael Tornielli. He'd hired her, coached her on her role and handled the payment. He'd even provided the GHB. Nothing could be traced back to Fraser.

"Maybe," Fraser said. "All I know is that he's British and his kid's mom is dead. I found that out today."

"Do you know where he works, how long he's been in Canada…?"

Fraser took a sip of his vodka tonic. "No. I just came across him this afternoon."

"Must have been one hell of a first impression if you're ready to destroy him already. What did the guy do to you?"

"He humiliated me and got my kids kicked out of school," Fraser said. He picked up a fork and squeezed the handle until his knuckles were white. "Ten grand a semester I pay that place, and the first time my kids step over the line, they kick them out."

"Tell me about it," Nat said, as his food arrived.

Fraser did. He recounted the entire episode, telling Nat how Masters had used sneaky, underhand tactics to set his girls up. Young Masters had goaded Madison into hitting her just so that she could try out her Jiu Jitsu shit on her and film the entire thing so that they could go home and have a good laugh about it.

Nat popped a sauteed prawn into his mouth. "The Masters girl, what's her name?"

"Melissa."

"You say Melissa recorded the fight?"

"Yeah. She was wearing some kind of camera in a necklace. Real spy shit if you ask me."

Nat looked surprised. "Sounds like he'd planned the whole thing." He made a note of it on his cell phone.

"He did," Fraser said. "I'm sure of it. He must have known I was Madison's father, and he orchestrated the entire episode just to set me up."

"Or, he's been in this situation before," Nat suggested, as he typed that thought into his memo.

"Whatever," Fraser said with a dismissive wave. "I just want everything you've got on him."

Nat put his phone back in his pocket and cracked open a crab leg. "How are things with you and Holly now that Michael is out of the picture?"

"The same." Fraser took another gulp of his vodka tonic and eyed Nat's plate. He'd opted for a liquid supper, but the calamari sitting on the side of Nat's plate looked tempting. As a waitress passed by, Fraser got her attention and ordered a basket of squid.

"Then maybe they weren't having an affair after all," Nat said. "Maybe you ruined your best friend's life for nothing."

Fraser thought he detected a hint of mirth. "Bullshit," he spat. "They were going at it like rabbits, believe me. The only reason she's no longer interested in sex is because her lover is gone. The bitch has probably found someone else already."

Nat wiped his hands on a napkin and threw it on top of his empty plate. "Well, I'll leave you to sort that one out. If you haven't got his exact address, I'm gonna need pictures of this guy so that I can tail him."

"I haven't got that, but I do have one of his daughter. Drop by my office in the morning."

"Will do," Nat said. "When do you need the info on Masters?"

"As soon as you can," Fraser said.

"Okay. I'm going to need an advance. I've got people to pay off."

Fraser took an envelope from his inside jacket pocket and put it on the table.

Nat slipped it into his pants pocket. "I'll see you tomorrow." He stood and left, leaving Fraser to pick up the check.

* * *

Nat whistled as he walked to his car, patting the stuffed envelope in his pocket. Luke Fraser might be a pain in the ass to work with, but he sure paid well.

The job should be easy enough. Usually with a task like this, he'd tail the guy for a while, find out who his friends are, then get cozy with them, pretending to be an old school friend. With Masters being British, that approach would raise red flags. He'd instead pretend to be an old work colleague. Nat would also check public records and social media to see what kind of footprint Masters had left. It was amazing how many people were open with their personal information. They used their real name, date of birth, sometimes even their phone number on Facebook. That kind of carelessness was just inviting trouble.

It certainly made Nat Kane's job much easier.

Would Graham Masters be so accommodating? Time would tell. First, Nat would have to stake out the street until he determined which house the girl lived in. Then he would photograph the father. From there, it would just be a matter of tailing him for a few days before taking the next step.

He felt the bulge in his pants pocket once more and smiled.

Easy money.

Chapter 21

It had been a tense few hours, but it was almost over.

Romeo Jimenez sat outside a café near the ferry dock and sipped his coffee as he waited for news from Costa. He'd sent the giant five miles upstream to keep an eye out for the boat the gringos were traveling in, and hopefully he'd have news soon.

It wasn't going to be as straightforward as he'd imagined, though. Iquitos sat on the left bank of the Amazon river, where an inlet ran down the eastern edge of the town. That meant his targets could land anywhere along a two-mile stretch. To counter this, Jimenez had enlisted the help of the local police. Ten men were currently out on the water, in two boats of five. Once the vessel was identified, they would tail it until it made land, feeding instructions to the team of ten on the shore. They would surround the couple and take them into custody, and Jimenez had arranged for them to be taken to the airfield. He'd already spoken to Hernandez, updating him on the progress he'd made, and the boss had promised to send a plane and four men to escort the gringos back to Colombia.

As for Costa, he could make his own way home.

Jimenez didn't trust the giant. He had a constant look in his eye that said he couldn't wait to put a bullet in Jimenez's head. The same went for Jose Diaz. Jimenez knew his offer to have Costa tag along wasn't altruism. Whatever they had planned, though, it would fail. By the time Costa returned to town, Jimenez would be on the plane to Bogotá. It would then be up to Felix Hernandez to decide their fate.

From experience, Jimenez knew it wouldn't be pleasant.

A smile crept onto his face, but only briefly. He still had work to do, and he wasn't happy having to rely on the vigilance of others.

Jimenez checked his watch again. Almost half past ten, and no word from Costa. He wondered—not for the first time—if the couple could have been delayed by the storm that had struck the region the night before. Chief Gonzales had assured Jimenez that Papi had sailed in rougher weather many times before, so there was no reason to suspect it would affect this particular journey.

So why are they late?

Jimenez cursed himself for not going with his gut instinct to send a couple of plain-clothes cops upriver to search for their boat. At least that way, he would know they were on their way. Now, he would just have to sit and wait, not something he was comfortable doing. Hernandez, for one, would want an explanation for the delay, and at the moment all Jimenez could offer was, "I don't know."

The radio on the table next to Jimenez cackled into life, and he snatched it up. "This is Jimenez."

"No sign of them," Costa said.

Jimenez swore under his breath, at both the giant and the gringos.

"I told you not to contact me unless you spot them," Jimenez growled.

"I know, but they're late. You said they'd be here by ten o'clock. It's already half-past."

A dozen rebukes sprang to mind, but Jimenez wasn't going to waste them on the big oaf. "Just keep looking," he said. "And stay off the radio until you have something to report."

"But what if they know we're waiting for them?" Costa persisted, fueling Jimenez's anger. "What if they decided to stop somewhere else?"

Jimenez pictured himself with a pistol, Costa standing in front of him. He raises the weapon, pulls the trigger…

But Jimenez knew that would never happen. That was his only weakness. He wasn't a killer. All those years spent in the police, and he'd never fired his weapon, other than in training. In fact, he'd only ever had to draw his sidearm on three occasions. He hadn't let Hernandez know that, though. If you wanted to work for an organization with a reputation built around violent murder, you didn't admit that you had qualms about taking human life.

Thankfully, Hernandez had never asked him to kill anyone. So far, his remit had been to locate the subject and let the enforcers do their job. He'd expected it to be the same this time, but the gringos weren't playing ball.

Could Costa be right? Could they somehow know he was on their tail? Jimenez doubted it. They probably guessed that the cop they killed had called in their license plate, and when the local police took an interest, they ran.

That had to be it.

"No," he told Costa, "they couldn't possibly know we're looking for them."

Jimenez also didn't think they would stop anywhere, because he was convinced they were trying to reach the Colombian border. To do that, they need to follow the river for at least another two hundred miles past Iquitos. Maybe they would want to stock up on food to make up for the supplies they left at the hostel, but they would have a better chance of finding what they needed in a big town than a fishing port. No, there had to be a rational explanation for the delay, and he suspected it was the storm the previous evening.

"I'm going to look into it," Jimenez told Costa. "Remain where you are."

The group of ten officers—nine uniforms and their chief—were gathered nearby. Jimenez targeted the senior officer. "I want you to send a fast boat up river and see what the hold-up is."

Papi had been sailing the Amazon for over sixty years and was well-known, so they knew what the boat looked like. They also had detailed descriptions of the man and woman. If they were still on the water, they would be found.

If not…

"I also need you to put me in touch with a tracker," Jimenez added. "If they got off along the way, I want someone familiar with the area to track them down."

The cop scratched his chin. "If that's the case, you will need a local man. Not someone local to Iquitos, but to the area where they landed. There are tribes all along the Amazon, and each knows its territory better than you know your own home. First you have to find where they got off the boat, then recruit someone from the nearest tribe. That won't be easy, as few—if any—speak Spanish."

"Then get me someone who can communicate with these people," Jimenez said, exasperated.

The chief turned and barked orders, and two of the uniformed officers peeled off and disappeared toward the center of town.

"They will bring someone," the cop said.

"Good. And send that boat, now."

* * *

Jimenez woke with a start to see the police chief standing over him.

"We found the boat."

Jimenez shot upright. When the search had yielded no results by three in the morning, he'd found a hotel room. It felt like he'd only been asleep for minutes.

"What time is it?" Jimenez asked.

"Just after seven."

Jimenez stood and shook away sleep's cobwebs. "Where are they?"

"As I said, we found the boat."

Jimenez glared at him. "What's that supposed to mean?"

"Papi was found by a ferry late yesterday. They towed his boat back to Yurimaguas. He said they were caught in the storm and he was knocked unconscious. When he woke, the weather had cleared, but the couple were gone and so was his engine. It appears the people you are looking for left everything they owned on the boat, including weapons and money. Lots of money."

Why would they do that? Jimenez wondered. *Why abandon all of their belongings?*

"They must have been forced to flee the boat," he mused out loud.

"Or they were thrown overboard," the police chief suggested. "Papi said it was the most violent storm he'd seen in years."

If that was the case, it would make Jimenez's job much easier. They would be in an unfamiliar jungle with nothing but their wits. They could even be dead. Drowned, or eaten by river creatures. It was possible. In fact, it was more than probable, but he wasn't going to offer that scenario to Hernandez without checking it out first.

"Arrange for a boat to take me to the place they found Papi," Jimenez said. "And where is the guide you promised me?"

"The guide is already on his way to the location. It is over 250 miles from here, so he should be able to locate a local tracker by the time you get there. As for a boat…I found something better."

"What?"

"I've arranged for you to use the local air ambulance." The cop beamed proudly. "For a fee, naturally."

It was the first bit of good news he'd had in a long time. Jimenez opened his phone and brought up a map. "Show me where they are."

The view on the screen moved dizzyingly until the cop zoomed in on a stretch of the river. "Papi said that the last thing he remembered, they were here."

The area looked deserted, apart from a small fishing village about fifteen miles north of their last known location. If they stuck to the river—and anyone with half a brain would do so—they would have reached it within a day or so. Thankfully, there appeared to be no roads out of the area.

That meant they would either have to walk or take another boat. Jimenez knew they would do the latter.

"I want you to contact every police station between that village and Iquitos and tell them who we're looking for. When you've done that, get every available man in a boat. If the gringos are not already back on the river, they soon will be. Find them."

Chapter 22

Nat Kane sat in his three-year-old Toyota Camry, rubbing his chin as he reviewed the notes he'd made on Graham Masters. There was the name, and that was it. No social media presence whatsoever, not even for the kid. Masters wasn't listed as a homeowner in Okotoks, either, so he must be renting his property. It was highly unusual to gain so little information from an internet search in this day and age, but he'd been unable to dig up anything in the last thirty-six hours, which had tickled Nat's curiosity.

He checked his watch again. It was almost eight-fifteen, and if Masters was going to drop his kid off at school, they would have to leave their house in the next few minutes. Nat picked up his camera with the telephoto lens and played it up and down the street, scanning each front door in turn.

There you are.

She had the same pigtails as her photo, and there were two men with her. One was young, maybe in his late twenties. The other was much older. Nat took several photos of each of them as the younger one got behind the wheel of an Expedition. The older man and the girl got in the back.

Nat waited until the Expedition pulled out of the drive, then followed at a distance. He knew they would be going to school, so there was no need to get too close at the moment.

Ten minutes later, the Expedition pulled up outside Poundmaker Elementary and Melissa got out. As soon as the door closed, the car was on the move.

"Time to see where you work," Nat said to himself as he eased into the same lane, a few cars back.

He was disappointed. The Expedition returned to the home on Phillips. Both men got out of the car and entered the house. Either Masters was taking a personal day, or he worked from home. Nat wasn't prepared to spend the next few weeks scoping out the place to discover the answer.

There were easier ways.

* * *

The moment he saw Masters and his young companion get into the Expedition for the afternoon school run, Nat got out of his car and walked down Phillips toward their home. Nat knew he had twenty minutes, tops, to get in and out.

The house had two stories and an apartment over the garage. The front lawn was neatly trimmed, and a sturdy wooden fence led around the back of the building. Nat checked the street, then walked up the drive, put on a pair of skin-colored latex gloves and tried the gate. Its lock was only a minor inconvenience. Nat grabbed the top of the gate and easily pulled himself up and over. As he landed, he braced himself for the sound of a guard dog.

Nothing.

Nat checked his watch. Thirteen minutes.

He walked around and peered through the glass of the back door. There was no sign of life. The lock was one that he could easily pick. Within seconds he had it open, but the door wouldn't give. Nat knew it must have been bolted on the inside.

Damn!

He checked the ground floor for open windows, but Masters was obviously security conscious. Everything was firmly locked.

Nat was about to give up when he spotted a window on the second floor above the two-car garage. It was slightly ajar and easily big enough for him to squeeze through. He tested the drainpipe, but it was too flimsy. Fortunately, the brickwork had a feature that looked like narrow steps. Every fifth row, a brick stood out, which would allow him a toe hold. Nat climbed up and grabbed the window ledge before hauling himself inside.

The room was neat, with just a bed, a wardrobe and a desk which was piled high with textbooks next to an open laptop. Someone was clearly studying for college, and as the girl was too young, it had to belong to one of the men. A quick check in the wardrobe confirmed that this was a man's room.

Nat walked out into a hallway, looking for the master bedroom. He found it at the end of the hall, and like the loft, it was immaculate. The bed was made, the lone dresser dust-free, the wooden flooring polished to a shine. Masters was either a clean freak, or ex-military. Nat favored the latter. He opened the drawers one by one and found neatly folded socks and underwear in the top, T-shirts in the second and towels in the third. He switched his attention to the nightstand, but the drawers held nothing of note.

170

Nat knew from experience that most people kept their passports and other valuable documents in the bedroom, but clearly not this guy. Nat tried the wardrobe, but it only contained a few polo shirts and slacks. There were a couple of suitcases, but a quick inspection revealed them to be empty.

Nine minutes.

Nat walked downstairs and checked the drawers in the living room, kitchen and den, but there was no sign of any personal documents. Frustrated, he walked back upstairs and into the main bedroom once more.

Why are you hiding them?

More importantly, where?

If Masters was going to so much trouble, he had to be hiding a secret of some kind. Nat was determined to discover what it was.

He got down on his knees and checked under the bed, but it was clear. As he stood once more, the floorboard beneath his foot flexed. It was only a few millimeters, but enough to tell Nat that he'd found the hiding place. Taking out his penknife, Nat eased the floorboard out and put his hand inside the hole, feeling around. His fingers came across some kind of material, and he pulled it out to reveal a cloth bag. Pulse racing, Nat checked his watch—seven minutes— then eased open the drawstring. Inside was at least fifty grand in U.S. currency and the equivalent in Canadian money. There were also two passports. Nat opened them both and used his cell phone to take photos of the documents, then put them aside and dipped back into the bag. He came out with two birth certificates and a small notebook. He flicked through the pages, but only the first three had writing on them, and it was just a sequence of

171

numbers. They had to be bank accounts. He took photos of them, just to be thorough.

There was nothing else in the bag, so Nat put everything back inside and replaced it where he'd found it. He then put the floorboard back in place and swept the area with the palm of his hand to ensure he hadn't left any clues.

Three minutes.

Nat returned to the loft room and climbed back out of the window, then dropped to the ground and launched himself over the garden gate. The street was clear, so he walked back to his car and drove it a couple of streets away.

Just who the hell was Graham Masters, and why was he hiding his valuables like that?

There was one way to find out. Nat took out his cell phone and found the contact listed as Jane. He hit the Call button.

"It's me," he said. "I need something."

"The usual?"

"Yeah. I can be there in an hour."

"I'll be here," the voice said, and hung up.

Jane was a pseudonym for Nat's ex-brother-in-law, Peter Walton, who worked for CSIS, the Canadian Security Intelligence Service. The cell Nat had called was a burner purchased especially for the two of them to communicate, and Peter insisted that they only use it to discuss meeting up, nothing more.

Nat got in his car and drove back to Calgary. He parked outside an old factory building that had been converted to apartments as part of an urban regeneration scheme a few years earlier. The one he wanted was on the top floor. Nat knocked on the last door on the left. He saw the spy hole go dark, then locks turned and the door opened.

The man who answered was in his fifties, with receding hair and round glasses. He stood aside so that Nat could enter, then checked the corridor before closing and bolting the door. When he turned, Nat held out a handful of hundred-dollar bills. "Two grand."

Peter put the money in a cigar box on top of a racing form. He had a penchant for the horses, which had ultimately cost him his marriage. Nat, who rarely passed up an opportunity—even if it was a result of the misfortune of others—was only too happy to provide Peter with stake money in return for occasional access to the expansive government database.

"What do you need?"

Nat held out his cell phone. "Everything you've got on this guy. He's British."

Peter took the phone and sat down at a computer terminal, one of three in the room. His fingers danced across the keyboard. After a couple of minutes, he sat back in his chair.

"Hmm."

"Something wrong?" Nat asked.

Peter leaned forward and typed some more, then started shaking his head slowly. "He entered Canada a couple of years ago on a six-month tourist visa and he's renewed it three times since. He did that online using a pre-paid credit card. That's it. There's nothing on him."

"No driver's license? Bank accounts?"

"Nada."

"What about before he came here?" Nat asked. "Can you get access to the British database?"

"No," Peter told him. "I could ask the Brits, but I'd need a good reason. If he's a person of interest in a serious crime, that would do it."

Nat cursed. Masters' only crime had been to get on the wrong side of Luke Fraser. "What about an immigration check?" Nat suggested. "Would that cut it?"

"I suppose so," Peter admitted, "but there's an additional risk." He looked up at Nat. "To me. When people have such a shallow footprint, it usually means they're not who they say they are. This could come back to bite us."

Nat sighed. "How much?"

"Another two grand."

"One."

"One and a half," Peter countered.

"Done. When will you have something for me?"

"Depends on how quickly the Brits act on the request. Maybe tonight, could be a few days."

Nat headed for the door. "Call me. I'll have your money the next time we meet."

"Hang on," Peter said. "With these requests, they usually want more than just a name and passport photo. Can you get fingerprints and DNA?"

Nat was sure he could. "It'll take a couple of days."

"Okay. I'll hold off until you get them." Peter stood and unlocked his door, checking the hallway before letting Nat out. "And don't forget my money."

Chapter 23

When it came to getting DNA samples, Nat had a surefire strategy. All he had to do was wait for the right moment.

Nat followed the Expedition to the school the next morning. After dropping Melissa off, the young driver had gone to a local mall and stayed in the car while Masters went inside.

Nat followed him.

It was easy to spot Masters' brown leather jacket among the crowd, which enabled Nat to keep his distance. Nat wasn't interested in the shops Masters visited. He was hoping for him to stop off at a coffee shop or the food court.

He didn't have to wait long. Masters came out of a kid's outlet with a small bag and walked to a Starbucks. Nat gave him a five minutes start, then walked into the coffee shop. Masters was sitting at a table in the middle and had his back to Nat.

Perfect.

Nat ordered a drink, and while he waited for it to be prepared, he took out some hair grooming clay and put a pea-sized drop on the palm of his left hand, rubbing it in.

When his drink was ready, he took it and walked past Masters' table. When he was directly behind him, Nat ruffled Masters' hair vigorously.

"Mark! How you doing, buddy?"

Masters shrugged him off and turned around. He shot Nat a look of sheer menace.

"Hey, man, I'm really sorry," Nat said. "I thought you were someone else."

Masters ran a hand through his hair, putting it back in place. "That's okay," he said in a crude British accent. He turned back to his table and sipped his coffee.

Nat found a table at the back of the room and took a small plastic bag from his pocket. He checked his left hand and saw that three hairs had stuck to the styling clay. Using a pair of tweezers, he put them in the bag one by one. With one of his tasks complete, Nat took out his phone, making sure not to look in Masters' direction. For half an hour he scrolled through the news, always keeping Masters in his peripheral vision, until his target rose and walked out the door. Nat waited until he'd disappeared out of sight, then got up and went to the table Masters had been sitting at. He picked up the cup by the rim, poured the remnants of the coffee into the saucer, then stuck the cup inside his jacket and left.

Back at his car, Nat put the cup in a plastic bag and drove back to Calgary.

His first stop was to a lab he'd used many times before. It specialized in DNA profiling, and he handed over the hairs he'd collected from Masters. He was told he would have the results the next day.

Nat drove home. His house was a simple one-story bungalow in the suburbs, with a tiny yard that didn't require much maintenance. He lived alone and planned to do so forever. Even though he could afford a much bigger place, he didn't see the point. He had his den, his bedroom, and his office, and that was all he needed.

In his office, he took the cup from the bag and dusted it with powder, then snapped off a few photos of the resulting fingerprints before taking impressions using tape. He stuck these onto clear slides, then called Peter Walton.

"I'll be there tomorrow at seven.'

Chapter 24

"When I think back to my jungle training," Sonny said, "it was never this hard."

They were sitting on a fallen log, with Sonny doing his best to wipe the sweat from his face with his damp T-shirt.

"That's because it was forty years ago," Eva groaned, fanning herself with a large leaf. "We got old."

"Hey, less of the old. It was only twenty years ago, thank you very much."

It feels like forty, though.

He kept himself fit, and forty-two wasn't even close to what he considered old, yet here he was, sweating like a teenager on his first date.

"I reckon we've only covered about seventeen klicks," he said, looking into the trees to try to identify the sender of a particularly loud call. It could have been a monkey, or maybe a large bird. In the day-and-a-bit since they'd emerged from the river, they'd heard nothing that sounded like a big cat, which was Sonny's biggest worry. He'd fashioned a crude spear out of a branch using a splinter of rock, but that was all they had to defend themselves.

"We'll come across someone soon," Eva said. "There are tribes throughout this area, and most see the river as their main source of food."

"Just as long as they're not cannibals." Sonny stood, shook a kink out of his thigh muscle, then set off again.

It was hard going on uneven ground in inappropriate footwear, and Sonny was starving. They hadn't eaten since the gas stop on the way to Yurimaguas, and that had only been a snack. One thing he did remember from his training with the SAS all those years ago, was that not everything that grew in the jungle was edible. Some plants would kill, while others had strong hallucinogenic qualities. There was plenty of protein to be had, though. Grubs, insects, amphibians and rodents were plentiful. They'd spent a couple of hours fishing, but for all their efforts they only landed one small specimen. Rather than expend energy building a fire to cook such a puny morsel, they'd eaten it raw.

"If you see any taco plants, let me know," Sonny said. "My stomach thinks my throat's been cut."

Eva stopped suddenly. "No plants that grow tacos, but I do see a hut."

Sonny peered through the trees and spotted it, too. "Please let that be a McDonald's."

They picked up the pace and reached the rear of the wooden building minutes later. It appeared to be derelict, the walls rotting, but Sonny's disappointment was tempered by the view as he walked around the side of the shack.

They'd reached an inlet, and it was swarming with people. Boats were either preparing for a day on the river or unloading the day's catch, and the houses stretched for hundreds of yards along the far bank. Beyond them, Sonny could see taller buildings, suggesting the town was a decent size. The best part was, no one was dressed like they were part of an indigenous tribe. They could have all come from Yurimaguas for the day, which meant they would probably speak Spanish.

"Let's find some food, then we'll consider our next move," Sonny said, abandoning his homemade spear.

They headed left along the bank to a bridge that led across the bay. It was old, yet thankfully sturdy. Once across, they followed their noses.

Sonny and Eva got some strange looks from the locals, which was to be expected. They'd emerged from the trees on foot, with no possessions. They wouldn't have seen many foreigners do that.

There was a wide variety of street vendors offering cooked food, but Sonny wasn't about to take the time to browse. He stopped at the first stall and pointed at something that looked like beef. It could have been alligator for all he cared. Eva was more picky, taking her time to eye the selection before going for a fish dish that came loaded with vegetables. They paid with crinkled notes and ate as they walked down the street.

"We need to find some transport to get us to Iquitos," Sonny said with a mouthful of meat. "There's no way we'll be able to replace our gear in this place."

Quaint as the place was, it was no shopper's paradise. There was also something strange about the place, as if something was missing, but he couldn't put his finger on it.

Eva picked up on it, though. "It'll have to be another boat. There don't appear to be any cars here."

That was it. The street was teeming with people, but not a vehicle to be seen, not even a motorcycle.

The thought of another couple of days on the water was almost enough to ruin Sonny's appetite.

Almost.

He shoveled another spoonful of food into his mouth as his eyes searched for a suitable conveyance, but most of the boats looked to be simple kayaks. It would take weeks to get to Iquitos under their own steam. Going back to Yurimaguas wasn't an option, either. The cop there had taken an interest in their car, which meant there was surely a nationwide manhunt for them. They had, after all, killed a police officer.

"No matter where we go, the police are going to be looking for us," he told Eva.

"Which is why we have to get out of this country fast."

"Easier said than done," Sonny said, spitting out a chunk of gristle. *Maybe it's rat.*

Eva looked like she was about to say something, then she frowned and tilted her head. "Hear that?"

At first, all Sonny could hear was the hustle and bustle of people going about their business, but then the faint buzzing became louder. It was definitely the sound of a motor, and Sonny hoped it belonged to a powerful boat.

It wasn't.

It was something even better.

"That's a Huey!"

"It's our way out of here," Eva corrected him.

They watched as the helicopter circled slowly over the town. It was white, with a red cross on the fuselage. Sonny saw it settle into a hover and descend behind a tall building a few hundred yards away.

"Must be an air ambulance," Eva said. "Come on."

She dumped her food and set off at a jog, and Sonny hurried after her.

It only took them a couple of minutes of darting through narrow streets before they found the chopper. As they emerged from an alleyway, they saw it had landed on a green lawn outside a large grey building, and the rotors were winding down. A large crowd had gathered. Sonny and Eva stood at the back of it.

They wouldn't be able to do anything with so many people around, but they also couldn't afford to wait too long in case the helicopter took off again. Sonny craned his neck to see if it was dropping off or picking up a patient.

What he saw was enough to make him feel sick, himself.

He grabbed Eva's arm and crouched as he dragged her back toward the alley. She naturally copied his action, and once they were hidden from view, Sonny straightened.

"Did you see who got off?" he asked.

"No, I was looking around for a fuel truck. We'll need a full tank if we're gonna fly out of here. Why, who was it?"

"The giant from the bar," Sonny said.

"Costa?"

"Yeah. I never forget an ugly face."

"Shit."

Sonny was thinking the same thing. "He can only be here for us," he said. He looked at Eva for guidance, but she seemed as shocked as he was.

"He can't know for definite that we're here," Sonny said. "If someone spotted us and called him, he wouldn't have got here so quickly. He must have known we went in the water and figured this was the closest town, so we would show up here."

"That must be it," Eva agreed, "but that doesn't make it any better. You saw the looks people were giving us when we arrived. It won't be long before word gets back to Costa and he seals the place off. We have to get to that chopper before he figures out we're here."

"That won't be easy," Sonny said. "Costa and the guy he was with were met by a couple of cops. If one of them stays by the chopper to keep the crowd back, we're screwed. If we had weapons, we'd have no problem, but I haven't even got my pointy stick."

"Then let's go get some."

* * *

Jimenez wasn't happy that Costa was still with him, but he was forced to admit to himself that he needed the thug. The couple might have lost all of their possessions, including their weapons, but from what he'd seen on the CCTV at Diaz's home, the blond male appeared to be an experienced soldier. He surely wouldn't go down without a fight. According to Costa, the woman was handy with her fists, too. During his time in the police, Jimenez had dealt primarily with homicide investigation. His job was to identify the suspects, not take them down. He might have been able to handle someone accused of domestic violence or a street punk, but these two were a much different proposition.

The helicopter began to descend, and a crowd was already gathering to watch it land. When it settled with the slightest of bumps, Jimenez sat patiently until the rotors had slowed, then got out. He was met by two uniformed police officers.

"Welcome to Saramenas," one of them said. "If you'll follow me…"

Costa eased his large frame out of the helicopter and followed Jimenez to a nearby building.

"How many men do you have here?" Jimenez asked the cops.

"Three. Marcos and I, plus Juan. My name is Hector."

"Only three?"

Hector shrugged. "We're a small town, maybe five hundred people, and we get few visitors. Three is enough."

It might be enough for you, Jimenez thought, *but I want an army looking for these people.* "I was told there would be a guide waiting."

"He's inside," Hector said.

"Good. I want to get started straight away. We'll take a boat to where we believe the suspects left the river, then—"

A shout interrupted Jimenez, and he turned to see the third officer, presumably Juan, running toward them.

"They're here!"

"Where?" Hector asked.

"Somewhere nearby. I was telling shop owners to keep an eye out for them, and a dozen people had already spotted them. They came out of the jungle, crossed the bridge, bought some food, then ran down Alfonso Street toward the helicopter."

Jimenez was off like a shot, leaving the others trailing in his wake.

* * *

"Go buy a couple of knives and a lighter," Eva said as they ran back to the row of shops facing the inlet. "I'll meet you at that building at the far end of town, the one with the red roof."

She peeled off in the opposite direction, leaving Sonny to fulfil her shopping list.

The first item was easy to find. Every twenty yards, there was someone sitting beside a box, selling cigarettes. He dropped a note into a woman's hand and took a plastic lighter, testing it as he searched for the next item. Unfortunately, there didn't appear to be an ironmonger in the market, so he improvised. In a butcher shop, he picked up a seven-inch blade and offered the man behind the counter the equivalent of a hundred dollars. The man almost tore Sonny's hand off as he grabbed for the money, and Sonny scanned the stall to see if there was another knife he could purchase. The butcher saw him looking and produced another blade from under a counter. Sonny went to take it, but the man held out his hand for more money. Sonny reluctantly handed over another hundred, then ran down the road to the rendezvous point.

Eva turned up a few minutes later carrying two gas cannisters, the kind used for camp stoves. They entered the red-roofed building to find a few empty rice and flour bags littering the floor, but no people inside.

They got to work, gathering handfuls of kindling. Sonny created a small fire, and they piled more wood and other combustible material on top. Once it was burning fiercely, they each placed a cannister in the fire, then ran out of the shack and closed the door.

"How long do you reckon?" Sonny asked as they made their way through the trees, aiming to skirt the town and emerge near the helicopter.

"Could be a few minutes, might even be half an hour. Depends on how sturdy the tanks are and whether they were filled at high or low pressure."

To be safe, they ran as fast as they could. They wanted to be within sight of the helicopter when the gas bottles exploded. They hoped that everyone in town would run to douse the fire, and they could board the chopper and force the pilot to take off.

They got their wish. They reached the edge of the clearing six minutes before the bottles went up, and when the explosion came it was violent enough to shake the ground under their feet. A plume of fire, then dense black smoke rose into the sky half a mile away.

The dwindling crowd near the chopper turned as one, then like an army of ants, they ran in the direction of the burning building.

"Come on," Eva said, and she broke from cover.

They approached the chopper from the rear and split up when they reached the tail, with Sonny going around one side of the fuselage and Eva the other.

Eva snatched the pilot's door open and placed the point of her knife against the side of his neck, then checked him for a weapon. He was clean, probably the normal paramedic pilot.

"Do as I say and you'll live," she said in Spanish. "Understood?"

The pilot, eyes wide, gave a shaky nod, his hands already in the air.

Sonny opened the other door and got into the co-pilot's seat. He produced his own blade and held it against the pilot's stomach. "Phone."

The pilot slowly and nervously reached into his pants pocket and produced a cell phone. Eva climbed into the back of the chopper, and Sonny handed her the pilot's device.

"Go," Sonny said to the pilot. When he got no response, Sonny jabbed him in the ribs with the knife. Not enough to break the skin, but it got the man's attention. "Come on. Get us in the air."

The pilot didn't move. He stared at Sonny unblinking, his head shaking involuntarily.

"He's in shock," Eva said. She recognized the signs. When faced with life-or-death decisions, the human body produced a fight or flight response, only sometimes the person was simply unable to choose. Instead, they froze.

Eva jumped out, opened the pilot's door and dragged him out of the seat. She climbed in and strapped on her harness. "Looks like you're flying," she said to Sonny.

"But I've got no time in this model," Sonny said, taking in the dials and controls.

"Shouldn't be a problem. That's the collective, that's the cyclic, those are the pedals. What more do you need?"

"Another thirty hours of flying lessons would be nice," Sonny said, powering up the engines and watching as the rotors began to turn.

"You've had ten. That'll have to do."

Sonny didn't answer, his face now a mask of concentration. His eyes flitted from the controls to the rotors overhead, and once the chopping sound of the blades became a solid hum, he pulled up on the collective. The bird

Alan McDermott

wobbled into the air and began to spin to the right. Sonny pressed down on the left pedal to correct the movement, then tugged the collective higher. The helicopter shot upwards, catching Eva by surprise. She cursed as she gripped her harness.

"Sorry," Sonny said, pushing the cyclic forward.

The chopper followed his command, easing forwards and out over a sea of green.

* * *

As the three police officers ran toward the burning building, Jimenez hesitated. Costa stopped alongside him, looking at Jimenez for guidance.

Something's not right, Jimenez thought.

He'd been a cop long enough to trust his gut instinct, and right now it was telling him he was being played. A sudden unexplained explosion, just when he was closing in on his prey? Too much of a coincidence, it had to be a distraction, which meant whatever was happening was in the opposite direction. Jimenez turned, and saw the tall white building they'd landed next to.

They're going for the helicopter!

Jimenez sprinted back to the landing zone, knowing his huge shadow wouldn't be far behind. As he navigated the side streets, Jimenez heard the sound of the rotors winding up. When he ran onto the lawn, he saw the chopper pilot running away from the craft as it rose slowly, then shot upwards like a cork out of a champagne bottle. Jimenez drew his weapon and fired as it settled into a hover a hundred feet off the ground, and moments later he heard the *Boom* of Costa's weapon joining in. As the chopper

188

began to pitch forward, Jimenez swapped out his magazine for a new one and emptied it in seconds, but the chopper flew on, heading out over the jungle.

Bastards!

After being so close to catching them, he could only look on as the helicopter whisked his targets away.

A chill ran through him. He would have to report this to Felix Hernandez, and his boss hadn't been pleased to hear about the previous delay. This was more than a merc setback; they'd stolen a fucking helicopter!

In his rush to get to the village, Jimenez had asked the pilot how fast it could go: more than 160 miles an hour. If the chopper was carrying enough fuel, they could be in Ecuador, Colombia or Brazil within three hours. How was he going to explain that?

A sudden loud bang and a plume of smoke from the helicopter's gearbox meant he might not have to. He watched the aircraft shimmy from side to side, then veer to the left and lose height. One of his bullets must have found its mark.

"They're going down!" he shouted to Costa. "We've got them now!"

* * *

"What the hell—"

Eva looked out the side window and saw Costa and his companion firing up at them. Another couple of rounds pinged off the fuselage as the chopper inched slowly toward the jungle canopy in front of them. "It's Costa. Get us the hell out of here!"

Alan McDermott

Sonny pushed the cyclic forward as the aircraft took more hits, and just when Eva thought they were almost out of range and out of danger, there was a tremendous *bang!* and the chopper shuddered as metal shrieked above their heads.

"We're hit!" Sonny said, as oil began to run down the windshield. The copter started to pitch to the left, and Sonny pushed the cyclic in the opposite direction. "Come on…come on…!"

Eva braced herself. It looked like Sonny had arrested the turn, but they were dropping too close to the treetops for her liking. "Can't you take us up?"

"Throttle is at max," Sonny said through gritted teeth as he used every ounce of strength to keep the chopper flying straight. "I'm not sure how long I can keep us in the air. We need… somewhere to land."

Eva scanned the area, but all she could see were swathes of green on both sides of the brown river.

"Can you put us down in the water?"

"Maybe," Sonny grunted, "but I really don't think we wanna do that."

Eva didn't like it, either, but there were no other options apart from crashing into the jungle.

"We've got no choice," she said.

The stretch of water was over three hundred meters wide at this point. Easy enough to hit, if they could reach it. Sonny eased off on the cyclic and the helicopter responded by leaning over to the left again, toward the Maranon River, but it rapidly lost height at the same time. Sonny corrected and brought the bird level once more.

"No way. If I try to turn one more time, we go into the trees. I just can't get any lift out of it." They flew on in a straight line. "All I can do is keep it in the air until we either run out of fuel or the gearbox chews itself apart."

"Then get us as far from that village as you can. If we have to go down, at least we'll have a head start on them."

"There's no *if* about it," Sonny said, his arms straining at the controls.

The inevitability of the situation spurred Eva into action. If they were going down, they would need more than just their wits to survive, so she turned in her seat and looked in the back. Among the various pieces of medical equipment, she saw a first aid kit that they could use, as well as a flare gun. Everything else was stored in lockers, which she would have to search once they landed.

Or crashed, she reminded herself.

She turned to the front and looked for gaps in the trees. Given the state of the aircraft, it would have to be big, as Sonny would have a hard time squeezing into a tight space.

There were none.

To make matters worse, the vibrations were getting stronger by the second.

"It's no good," Sonny said, as the tops of the trees grew closer. Branches began to whip the undercarriage, the impacts growing steadily stronger until the inevitable happened.

The nose pitched down violently, and the spinning blades slashed into the trees. Severed branches pounded the glass in front of them before the rotors shattered and the fuselage plummeted to the ground. It dropped through the thinner outgrowths, but as it reached the larger branches below, their progress stalled, before eventually they came to rest forty feet above the jungle floor.

Eva and Sonny hung forward, secured in their seats by the harnesses.

"You okay?" Sonny asked as he flipped off the power to prevent a fire.

"I'm good," Eva replied. "What about you?"

"Spiffing."

Eva looked down at the ground, then up the trunk of the tree they were stranded in. The branches stopped about five feet below the front of the copter, and the tree was too large to wrap her arms around and shimmy down. They would either have to jump the last thirty-five feet, or find something to lower themselves to the ground.

"We need a way down," she said. She braced her feet against the dash and unclipped the harness, then crawled slowly over her seat into the rear compartment. Sonny followed her, his actions equally gentle.

The lockers had come open, but there was no rope. If they were going to lower themselves, they would have to use something else.

"Let's dump whatever could be useful out the door, then find something to climb down." Eva started with the flare gun and spare cartridges, then the first aid kit. She was about to drop it out of the chopper when Sonny stopped her.

"Wait. See if there are any bandages in there."

Eva opened the box and took out six rolls.

"I'll secure these," Sonny said, taking them from her, "you see what else you can find." He crawled out onto a branch and opened the first of the bandages, tutting as he studied the flimsy material. "I'm going to have to ply them."

As Sonny prepared to layer the bandages to make them more robust, Eva checked the rest of the compartments. Being an air ambulance, there was a lot of medical kit on

192

board, but little of it would be useful on a hike through the jungle. She discarded any machines, but found two bottles of medical alcohol that could come in useful. There was nothing else that could be used as a ready-made weapon, so she thought about how to make her own. A couple of ideas sprang to mind, and she looked around until she eventually found a suitable length of cord. She cut the electrical wire from a monitoring machine, emptied out a bag of face masks and filled it with her haul.

"How we doing?" she asked Sonny.

"Almost there."

Eva crawled out to see that he'd put the ends of all six bandages together and had let the rolls drop below him. He'd tied his end to the branch he was on and was in the process of twisting the bandages together. A few minutes later, he tugged at the makeshift rope.

"That should do it," he said. "Here goes nothing."

Sonny eased himself off the branch and slithered down, dropping the last few feet.

"It's fine," he said, holding out his hands.

Eva dropped the bag to him, then climbed down.

"How far do you think we've come?" she asked when she reached the ground.

"Dunno. Ten, maybe twelve klicks."

"That's not much of a head start," Eva said.

"I know, and the locals will know the jungle a lot better than us."

Eva lifted the bag onto her shoulder. "Then we'll just have to be smarter."

Chapter 25

Charles Squires was lifelong MI5. He'd joined the agency straight out of university and had spent the next twenty-six years in the same office on the first floor, handling inter-agency requests. The work was easy, sometimes mind-numbingly so, but that suited him fine. He never had to take his work home with him and was never called in on his day off.

This morning, he'd come into the office to another virtual pile of requests. Everything was done electronically, and Squires always dealt with them in chronological order, starting with the oldest.

First up was from the DGSE, the French equivalent of MI6. They wanted details on a British national who had been seen associating with a suspected far-right terrorist. Squires prepared the usual file, following internal security protocols to ensure that no classified information was included. Once he sent it off, he passed the original request to the analysis team.

His next request was from the Americans. They'd arrested a Scottish woman at a drug bust and wanted her background. Squires sent it, then went to get a coffee.

When he returned to his desk, he opened the next item. This one was an immigration enquiry from the Canadians. Normally they would just ask for someone's criminal history, but this one wanted the full work-up. Squires opened another window and did a search for Graham Masters, then sat back in his chair and stared at the screen.

There was almost nothing. A passport had been issued two years earlier, backed up by a birth certificate and national insurance number, but that was it. No tax history, no credit file. Squires had seen this before. Document forgers would apply for a passport in the name of someone who had died at an early age, and as death certificates had only been digitized back to 1957, this kind of fraud was hard to detect.

Protocol dictated that he create an alert for the subject. The address the document had been sent to would go on a watch list which would be sent to HM Passport Office and an investigation into the occupants would be initiated.

The second step was to find out who was currently using the passport. Using the number, he searched the database for the photograph and set it running through facial recognition software. While he waited for that to yield a result, he checked the rest of the request. There were fingerprints and even a DNA sample. These went into separate search programs, and Squires sat back and sipped his coffee as he waited for the first of them to throw up a name.

When the fingerprint program found a match, Squires saw something he'd never encountered in all his years with MI5. A warning screen appeared, informing him to cease all further activity and contact the director general, quoting Priority Sigma.

If there was one thing Charles Squires knew, it was that curiosity could be a dangerous thing in his line of work. He'd seen colleagues get dismissed, some for stupid reasons like doing background searches on neighbors or people they had grudges against, but a couple of them had poked their noses in where they weren't appreciated.

He wasn't about to throw his career down the toilet in the same way.

Squires picked up the phone and told the operator he wanted to speak to the boss. When she told him the DG was busy, Squires informed her that he had a Priority Sigma alert. Seconds later, Arthur Haines was on the line.

"Where are you?" Haines barked.

"First floor, room one-oh-seven."

"Stay there, touch nothing."

The phone went dead, and Squires stood and backed away from his terminal as if it was venomous.

Two minutes later, the DG entered the office. He was a barrel-chested man in his fifties, and he appeared to have run the entire way. He jumped into the chair in front of the screen, where the warning message was still flashing red.

"Did you look at the file?" Haines asked breathlessly, turning to squires.

"No, sir. I saw the message and called you, then stepped back."

"Okay. Go and get yourself a coffee."

"But, sir, my login details—"

"—will be deleted if you are not gone in three seconds!"

Squires scrambled out of the room and went down to the canteen. He took his time, ordered a skinny latte and walked slowly back to his office. As he reached the door, Haines emerged. He looked just as rattled as he had when he'd arrived.

"False alarm," the DG said. "I dealt with that particular request for you. Carry on."

Squires suspected Haines wasn't being truthful. If it was indeed a false alarm, the DG would surely have calmed down a little, but that wasn't the case. Squires wasn't about to call him out on it, though. Careers had ended for less.

His monitors were clear, and the request list was one item shorter than when he'd left.

The communique from the Canadians had been deleted.

Chapter 26

"Sonofabitch!"

Jimenez turned to see Costa sitting on the ground, holding his ankle.

"What is it now?"

"I twisted it," Costa grimaced.

Jimenez wasn't surprised. "What idiot wears high heeled boots in this terrain?"

"I didn't know we'd be tracking them through the jungle," Costa growled.

You don't know anything, you moron.

"Can you walk?" Jimenez asked him.

Costa rose on his good leg and gingerly put the injured foot on the ground. He grimaced, but after a couple of tests steps, he nodded.

"Good. Twist it again, and we're leaving you behind."

Jimenez gestured for the man on point to continue. After fetching the two police officers, they'd introduced Jimenez to the local tracker. The man didn't speak Spanish, but one of the cops spoke the tracker's language. As well as the team of five, Jimenez had asked the police to round up twenty volunteers from the village and offered a five-hundred-dollar reward for whoever found the helicopter. Each of the men had a whistle to notify Jimenez when they spotted the wreckage.

So far, the only sounds were the animals and insects of the jungle.

The five men continued in the direction they had last seen the chopper heading, four hours earlier. Jimenez had been hoping to see a plume of smoke or hear an explosion to pinpoint their location, but there had been neither.

"I bet they didn't even go down," Costa moaned. "We'll be walking around for the next two weeks while they're sitting on a beach drinking tequila."

Though he wasn't a natural killer, Jimenez was sure he could muster the strength to shoot Costa. Once in the stomach, another through the head…

"It went down," was all he said, and prayed he was right. He'd called Hernandez with an update, and his boss wasn't best pleased at losing the air ambulance. Hernandez would have to pay for a replacement. While the money was a trifling amount to the head of the Soldado cartel, the fact that they still hadn't caught the gringos really pissed him off.

I've already prepared a grave, Hernandez had said, and Jimenez knew the message was: find them, or it's your body that goes in the ground.

They soldiered on for another hour before a faint whistle sounded through the trees. Jimenez wasn't sure at first if he'd heard correctly, but when it came again and again, he jogged toward the noise.

Ten minutes later, he was standing underneath the helicopter, which was lodged nose down in a tree. The rest of the search party had gathered at the scene, and one of them was beaming proudly at the thought of the great bounty coming his way.

Bandages had been twisted together and hung from a branch near the remains of the helicopter. That told Jimenez that the gringos were still alive.

"Which way did they go?" he asked the tracker.

One of the cops came up to Jimenez and reminded him about the reward. Jimenez took a roll of hundred-dollar bills from his pocket and counted off five. "You can send them home," Jimenez said. "We won't need them anymore."

The officer handed the lucky man his bounty and dismissed the group, who all headed back to town.

"This way," the tracker said through his translator. A short man in his late fifties, yet nimble and alert, he led the way, eyes roving from the ground to the thick vegetation all around them. He was obviously following signs, but Jimenez had no idea what they were. He couldn't see footprints or blood trails, but the local clearly could.

The little man set a relentless pace, and it wasn't long before Jimenez was blowing hard. Costa looked like he was ready to drop, sweat pouring from him as he stumbled on the uneven ground.

The guide suddenly stopped, then looked left and right. He said something, and Jimenez looked at the cop for a translation.

"He said they split up here, and not too long ago."

"Why would they do that?" Costa asked.

Jimenez was wondering the same thing. It wouldn't have been a lover's tiff, so they must have gone their separate ways for a reason. He could only think of one thing. "To divide us."

"So what do we do?"

"We disappoint them," Jimenez said.

His only choice was which path to follow, but a woman's cry suddenly rang out, making the decision for him.

* * *

Eva's CIA training hadn't prepared her for anything like this, but Sonny was a natural. He made trekking through the jungle look easy, while for Eva it was hard work. She knew that was down to his days in the SAS, but the CIA hadn't seen fit to add jungle warfare to their clandestine ops training.

"This looks like the ideal spot," Sonny said, testing the flexibility of a young sapling.

He'd come up with an idea soon after leaving the crash site, and along the way he'd been collecting vines and branches to prepare an ambush. They'd also stopped for twenty minutes to allow Sonny to fashion a crude bow and arrow. He reckoned they had a decent lead on any pursuers, but that wouldn't last long.

Both knew that Eva was slowing them down, but to Sonny's credit, he never mentioned it.

"Let's get to it," Eva said. She emptied the contents of the first aid box into the bag while Sonny bent back the sapling he'd found so that the tip was touching the ground, and used some hanging vine to tie it to an exposed tree root. He then set a trip wire by stripping down the electrical cord Eva had salvaged from the helicopter, placing it five yards in front of the sapling, three inches off the ground.

His part complete, Sonny watched Eva gently place the empty plastic box on the sapling, adjust it to the correct angle, then slowly empty one bottle of alcohol in. She poured the other onto the ground around the trip wire.

"You sure the tree's strong enough?" she asked as she stood back to admire the trap.

"We'll know soon enough," Sonny said. "I'll double back and wait for them. When you hear my call, it's all on you."

Sonny kissed her, long and hard, then winked and disappeared into the jungle.

Eva ran to the hiding place she'd scoped out, behind a fallen tree. When she lay on her stomach, she could see under the log to the place where the trip wire had been set. The loaded flare gun was in her hand. All she could do now was wait for Sonny's signal.

Eva wasn't comfortable waiting for the enemy to show. She'd suggested powering on, in the hope of finding another village where they could get on a boat, but Sonny's argument made sense: if Costa was there to kill them, he was unlikely to bring a huge crowd to witness it. Therefore, it was better to wait for him, neutralize him, then disappear into the jungle. By the time Costa's boss sent a replacement, they would be long gone.

The signal from Sonny came a couple of hours later. They'd come across a few red howler monkeys after the boat accident, and Sonny was able to mimic their calls perfectly. She'd teased Sonny that he was a natural because it sounded like someone belching violently. It wasn't ideal using it as the signal—a real monkey might choose that moment to call for a mate, or warn other males not to invade his territory. But without proper comms they had no other option.

As soon as the third guttural *whoop* reached her, Eva screamed with all her might.

* * *

"This way!"

The two cops ran toward the scream, but the guide stayed rooted to the spot. He shouted something after them, but Jimenez couldn't understand him and the cops clearly didn't hear him. Costa chased after the police, and Jimenez followed. When he looked back, he saw the guide waving his arms frantically.

"Wait!" Jimenez shouted. "Something's wrong."

When he looked to the officers once more, he saw one of them trip and go down on his face just as a green box flew into the air, spraying what looked like water in a wide arc. It covered both cops, but Costa had heeded Jimenez's shout and pulled up short. A moment later, a red flash appeared from nowhere and the standing police officer burst into flames. He let loose a primal scream and pitched forward, and the moment he hit the ground, the area around him erupted in a huge fireball.

* * *

As soon as he saw the flames, Sonny broke from cover and ran toward the fire. In his hands was the bow he'd fashioned from a branch and the cord Eva had taken from the chopper. He'd only found enough suitable branches to make four crude arrows for it, and he knew he'd have to make every shot count, which was why he wanted to get as close as possible before loosing. Although a few practice shots had been somewhat successful, there was no telling where the arrows might end up.

There had been five people when he'd given Eva the signal, but now he could only see one, a local. He had no idea if the man was armed, but he wasn't taking any chances. When he got to within ten yards, the man turned at the sound of Sonny crashing through the undergrowth, his eyes wide with shock. The arrow flew from the bow, and though Sonny went for the biggest target—center mass—he hit the man in the right eye.

Sonny had another arrow on the string before the first kill hit the ground. He pushed on, searching for his next target, and saw a tall, skinny figure. Sonny let fly as he ran, but the arrow flew harmlessly wide of the mark. As he readied another, his opponent drew a revolver from the small of his back and pulled it up into a firing position. Sonny jinked to the left and threw himself behind a tree just as the weapon barked, but he wasn't quick enough. The bullet struck him just below the shoulder, flipping him in midair. He landed heavily on his back, the wind knocked out of him, and the initial shock of being shot wore off quickly as a wave of pain radiated from his injury.

Sonny's instinct was to survive at all costs. He grimaced as he used his good arm to draw the knife from his waistband, but it was too late. The tall gunman was already standing three yards from him, his weapon trained on Sonny's head.

"Drop it."

Sonny had no choice. He couldn't throw the knife from his supine position, not without telegraphing the move and inviting a quick death, and if the man wanted him dead, he'd have pulled the trigger already.

Sonny tossed the blade to the side and slapped the ground in frustration.

He could only hope that Eva was faring better than he was.

* * *

Eva watched the alcohol-filled box leap into the air and empty its contents over the two uniformed police officers. Before they could understand what was happening, she fired the flare gun at the one who was standing, and the effect was devastating. He became a human torch in seconds. As Eva reloaded the flare gun, the flaming cop fell forward, and as he hit the ground the jungle around him went up in a fireball. The other cop, the one who had tripped the wire, was immediately engulfed.

Eva ignored their screams. She wanted Costa. She'd seen the giant running after the police, then he'd stopped just before she fired. She tried to see through the roaring fire to spot him, but the blaze was too intense.

It was time to move positions. Costa would have seen where the flare came from, and he could be closing in on her. She backed up on her belly, then stood at a crouch and skirted the fire, hoping to flank him.

When she was able to see the area where Costa had been standing, she silently cursed. He was gone. He was out there somewhere, with a magazine full of lead. All she had was one extra flare, and it would take at least three seconds to reload. He could empty half a dozen rounds into her in that time.

As she prepared to move again, she heard the familiar sound of gunfire. It had come from the direction Sonny had run earlier, and as he didn't have a gun, it could only mean one thing.

He was in trouble.

Eva broke from cover, looking to go to his aid, but she only got a few steps before Costa stepped out from behind a tree. The cannon he was holding looked like a toy in his giant hand, but she knew it would do some serious damage if she took one of his bullets.

"Drop it!" Costa shouted.

For a brief moment she considered firing at him, but the flare gun was down by her side. By the time she raised it, she'd be dead. Reluctantly, she dropped her weapon.

"Hands in the air and turn around."

Eva swore to herself. She'd been hoping to get close enough to use the knife tucked into her waistband, but that chance was about to disappear.

"And the knife," Costa said as she slowly turned.

She took it out and tossed it aside.

Costa gestured with his pistol, and Eva started walking.

She started running when she saw Sonny lying on the ground, blood pouring from a chest wound.

A tall, bald man halted her run by sticking a revolver in her face.

She jerked to a stop five yards from Sonny. "Are you okay?" she asked him.

"I'll live," Sonny winced.

"Unfortunately for you," the bald man said in English. "My boss has plans for you, and they won't be pleasant." He turned to Costa. "Keep an eye on them while I call Felix."

Eva watched her captor hold up his phone as if searching for a signal, then he thrust it in his pocket.

"We'll have to take them back to the village. I can call from there."

"I've got a better idea," Costa said. He turned his gun on his companion and shot him through the head.

Eva watched the bald man fall, a surprised expression forever etched on his dead face.

"Am I supposed to thank you for that?" she asked Costa.

He gave her an evil grin. "I did that for pleasure." He turned and spat on the corpse. "Arrogant prick."

"So now what?" Eva asked. The longer she could keep him talking, the greater the chance she or Sonny could come up with a way out of this mess.

"Now, I take you back to Tingo Maria. Señor Diaz and I have some unfinished business with you."

"Then let me help him up," Eva said, moving toward Sonny.

"Not him," Costa said, raising his weapon and pointing it at Sonny. "Just you."

Eva leaped to get between the bullet and Sonny, but when the shot came she didn't feel a thing. No sensation of being kicked by a horse, no lancing pain, nothing. She landed on the ground and immediately looked at Sonny to see if he'd been hit, but he was just staring at Costa with a surprised look on his face. Eva looked to the giant, too, and saw that half of his face was missing. He stood statue-still for a couple of seconds, then collapsed to the ground.

Eva had no idea who'd shot Costa, but there was now a spare gun in play, and she wanted it. She scrambled to her feet and ran toward the corpse, but a burst of automatic fire chewed up the ground in front of her.

"Don't move!"

Eva turned to where the voice had come from and saw nothing. Then, like ghosts, two figures in camouflage detached themselves from the foliage and walked toward her, automatic rifles aimed at her head. Eva heard the crunch of feet on vegetation and turned to see two more figures, also dressed in U.S. army combat gear. These two had their weapons trained on Sonny.

She had no idea who they were, but Eva was sure pleased to see them.

One of the soldiers let his rifle go, and it swung from his chest. "Take the bodies," he said to one of his men, "and dump them in the river. The crocs can have them."

"And just who the hell are you?" Sonny asked, pulling himself to a sitting position.

"It's okay," Eva smiled. "They're the good guys."

The soldier pulled a pistol from a side holster and shot Sonny. Before Eva could react, he turned the gun on her and fired, hitting her in the belly.

"I'm afraid not."

Chapter 27

"Okay, any other business?" May asked.

"Just one," Ben Scott said. "We got a call from the British. MI5 to be exact. Someone we know just resurfaced."

"Who?" May asked.

"Tom Gray."

"Should we be worried?" Butler asked.

"No, he hasn't got his sights on us as far as we can tell. He's been living in Canada for the last couple of years, keeping himself to himself. I just thought that if we're ever gonna tie up that loose end, now's the time."

Again, the trio looked to May for guidance.

"How did they find him?" the head of the ESO asked.

"An immigration query was sent by the Canadian security service to MI5 asking for a full work-up on Graham Masters. That's the name Gray has been using. I looked into it and Gray has been renewing his tourist visa every six months. The last time was six weeks ago, so there would be no reason to send a request at this time. Also included in the file was his DNA profile and fingerprints. That seemed a little strange, so I had my people look into it. CSIS didn't sanction the request or have any knowledge of it. It appears to have been conducted by one of their operatives, Peter Walton."

"Why would he be interested in an immigration matter?" May asked. "Has Gray committed a crime in Canada?"

"Not that we know of. I'd like to send someone to Calgary to speak to Walton and find out what's going on."

"Do it," May said. He sat in thought for a few moments, then added, "Does CSIS know that Masters is Tom Gray?"

"No," Scott said. "The DG of MI5 sent a reply that simply said they had no criminal history for Graham Masters."

"Good," May said. "We don't want them spooking Gray. For now, grill Walton and find out who's interested in Gray. I want that line of enquiry closed down, by any means necessary. And send someone to keep an eye on Gray, but keep it discreet."

"I'm on it," Scott said.

May looked around the room. "Is that the last of the surprises?"

"There's a rumor that POTUS is going to announce a new gun control bill," Carter said.

"Again?" May sighed. He turned to Scott. "Ben, have a word with him."

Chapter 28

Mitch Engels walked to the entrance to the building just as Peter Walton stepped out of his car. Mitch was dressed as a courier, and he pretended to look at the address on the small box he was carrying as he reached the door at the same time as his target. He smiled at Peter, who offered a fleeting smile in return and started entering a code into the entry system.

"Who's that for?" Peter asked.

"You," Mitch said, his smile still in place. He took a silenced pistol from the box and pressed it into Peter's ribs. "Let's go have a chat."

Peter froze, but Mitch nudged the door open with his foot and pushed Peter inside.

"I think there's been some kind of mistake," Peter eventually managed to say, his voice filled with fear.

"Really? Then let's go straighten it out."

Mitch moved Peter to the elevator and pressed the button. When the doors opened, Mitch gestured with his gun and Peter stepped inside.

"All the way to the back," Mitch said as he followed him in.

They rode to the top floor in silence, and as the doors opened, Mitch got behind Peter and stuck the gun in his ribs once more. "I'm here for information. Don't make me have to shoot you."

Peter nodded so quickly that Mitch thought the man's head was about to come off.

They got to Peter's apartment. "Is there an alarm? Mitch asked.

"Yes."

"Honesty. I like that. In you go, disable it."

Peter unlocked the door and opened it. A faint intermittent beeping reached Mitch, and Peter punched some numbers into a keypad to silence it. Mitch followed him into the room and closed the door behind him.

"If you didn't silence the alarm and people turn up, you get the first bullet. Understand?"

Peter nodded.

"Do you need to properly cancel the alarm?" Mitch asked.

Peter shook his head.

"Good. Take a seat."

Peter slumped into an armchair and Mitch took in his environment. They were in the living room, with an archway at one end. Mitch backed up to the arch and peered through. He saw a hallway with three closed doors along the walls. "Anyone else here?" he asked Peter.

"No."

Trust wasn't high on Mitch's list of virtues. He checked each door, always keeping one eye on Peter and the gun trained in his direction. The three rooms—kitchen, bedroom and bathroom—were all empty. Mitch returned to the living room and locked the front door before standing in front of Peter.

"Tell me about Graham Masters."

Peter swallowed hard. "Who?"

Mitch gave him a look of disappointment, then shot the armchair an inch from Peter's head. "Just know that I have another nine bullets, and I only ever miss intentionally. Now, Graham Masters. Why did you send a request for information to MI5?"

A wet stain formed in Peter's crotch. "Who are you?"

Mitch raised the gun and pointed at Peter's chest. "Wrong answer."

Peter thrust his hands out. "Wait! Wait!" He took in deep breaths, then wiped sweat from his head. "My brother-in-law, Nat Kane. He asked me to find out about Masters. I have no idea why, I swear!"

Mitch lowered his weapon. "How does Nat get in touch with you?"

A shaky arm extended and pointed to a cell phone. "He calls me on that number."

"And do you ever call him?" Mitch asked. If he asked Peter to initiate a conversation and that was against protocol, it would be a red flag to Kane.

"Sometimes. If I can't get him information right away, he asks me to call him when it's ready."

"And what did you tell him about Graham Masters?"

"Nothing yet," Peter said. "I was going to call him when I got home from work."

"Do you give him the information over the phone?"

Peter shook his head vigorously. "Never. He always comes here."

Mitch picked up the phone and tossed it to Peter. "No time like the present."

* * *

Nat Kane drove to Peter's apartment as fast as the law allowed. The conversation had been brief but intriguing: *The results are in, and you wanna see this.*

Maybe Nat had stumbled across a wanted felon, and a huge reward was awaiting him. Nat just hoped it was worth abandoning his dinner.

He knocked on Peter's door and it opened. His brother-in-law looked like he was in shock.

This must be huge!

Nat stepped into the room, his pulse racing. He took a bundle of notes from his pocket and held them out, but before he could hand them over, a figure stepped out of the archway. He was dressed like a courier, but the silenced pistol in his hand told Nat that wasn't the case.

Nat turned back toward Peter. "What the fuck is this?"

"On the couch," the courier said. "Both of you."

He appeared to be mid-thirties, with ultra-short hair and a razor-thin mouth.

"Not before you tell me what the fuck is—"

The courier shot Nat in the knee, and he collapsed to the floor, howling in pain.

"Or lie there, it's all the same to me." The gunman turned to Peter. "I'm done with you." He raised the pistol, put a round into Peter's forehead and watched him slump to the carpet.

"Now, Nat. Can I call you Nat? Good. Nat, tell me why you were so interested in Graham Masters."

"Fuck you!" Nat grimaced. His entire leg was on fire, pain he'd never known the likes of.

"No thanks." The gunman backed up to the door and locked it, then returned to stand in front of Nat. "That has to hurt. Tell me about Masters, or I'll put one in the other leg."

"Why should I tell you? You're gonna kill me anyway." Nat looked over at Peter's corpse to reinforce his point.

"True," the gunman said, "but it's all about how you spend your last few minutes—or hours, I haven't decided yet."

Nat wanted to fight back. It was in his nature, his DNA. He'd never quit anything in his life. This battle, however, was unwinnable. He was injured and unarmed against a killer with a gun. Whichever way he looked at it, he was going to die. The only thing he had control of was how it was going to happen. A bullet to the head like Peter, or shot in each limb, possibly the stomach—he'd read in novels how that was a slow and painful death. And for what? To protect the asshole who destroyed people on a whim?

To refuse to talk would be a big *fuck you* to the man standing in front of him, but he already owed one of those to the man who'd put him in this position in the first place.

"I'll give you a name," Nat said through clenched teeth, "but first, tell me who Graham Masters really is. You could at least do that for me."

"Sorry, buddy. Can't help you. I was hired to kill anyone asking questions about Masters. I'd have to be pretty stupid to ask them myself."

That brought an incongruous smile to Nat's face. "Yeah, that makes sense. But at least do me one favor. When you go pay him a visit, shoot him in the balls. At least once."

The gunman smiled, a genuine show of pleasure. "Sure. I can do that."

Nat Kane closed his eyes, satisfied that the gratifying vision in his head would be his last. "His name is Luke Fraser. He's a lawyer, works at Goldstein, Fraser and Monk."

Chapter 29

Tom Gray took his phone from his pocket and woke up the screen.

"Damn!"

"What's wrong?" Joel Grant asked from the driver's seat.

"I've got three percent left. I forgot to charge it."

"You can borrow mine if you need it," Joel offered.

Gray turned his phone off and put it back in his pocket. "No, I was just gonna check the news anyway."

Joel tuned the radio to a local station. "These guys have bulletins every half hour."

A country song was finishing, and after an ad for a local car dealership, they heard the news headlines. The first one immediately set Gray's nerves on high alert.

"Okotoks police chief Oswald Crane say they are not looking for anyone else in connection with the death of local lawyer Luke Fraser, who was found unconscious at home this morning. Police say his wife found him covered in blood and called an ambulance, but by the time they made it to hospital, Mr. Fraser was pronounced dead. It is thought he was cleaning a pistol when there was an accidental discharge. Tributes to Mr. Fraser have been pouring in all day."

Gray had never believed in coincidence. For Fraser to suddenly die in an accident so soon after their confrontation…

"I've got a friend on the force who was part of that investigation," Joel said. "We were in high school together. Apparently, Fraser shot himself in the balls while cleaning his handgun."

"Did he?" Gray asked absently. He was more concerned with the timing of the death than the manner.

"Yeah. Blood everywhere. I can see someone discharging accidentally, sure, but to hit yourself there?" Joel shook his head. "Sounds icky to me."

Now Gray was *convinced* it wasn't self-inflicted. "Maybe," he said. "He was a lawyer. Those guys have lots of enemies."

"They sure do," Joel agreed. "My buddy said they'd drawn up a list of over forty people of interest before it was ruled an accident."

Gray was barely listening. He decided the time had come to ditch Okotoks and move on.

From now on, he and Melissa would travel light. Only one suitcase each. No need for a U-Haul, just throw their things in the back of the car and go. He would leave Joel enough to pay the rent on the house for another year so that his studies weren't interrupted, plus a little extra to keep him going. Gray had more money than he and Melissa could spend in a lifetime, and it wasn't Joel's fault that they had to split.

Gray sighed as he thought about breaking the news to Melissa. She would have to go through the upheaval of moving once more. New town, new school, new friends.

She wouldn't like it, but the alternative was to sit around and wait to see if there was indeed anything sinister behind Fraser's death.

"Something wrong?" Joel asked, looking at Gray in the mirror.

"What? No, just thinking about Melissa's science project. I have to help her build a working model of a volcano."

"She'll enjoy that," Joel said. "I did it as a kid. Lots of fun."

"Yeah, she's really looking forward to it."

And I'm going to disappoint her. Again.

They arrived at the school to find Melissa waiting in the usual place, under the oak tree. She said goodbye to her friends and ran to the car.

"Don't forget we're going to the mall to get a plastic cup, baking soda and vinegar," she told her dad excitedly.

"I know, darling. We're heading there now."

"Jane Marneur is *soooo* lucky. She got a puppy for her birthday. Can we get a puppy?"

Gray thought about it. On the face of it, it wasn't such a bad idea. She would have someone to play with after school, and it wouldn't take up too much space if they had to uproot in a hurry.

Like tonight.

"That sounds like a great idea," Gray beamed. "Let's wait until the weekend and then go look for one."

"Really? Oh, daddy, thank you! Thank you!" She threw her arms around him, then dug into her school bag and took out her phone. "I'll check the local shelters and see if they have a golden lab. That's the one I want."

Gray didn't have the heart to tell her that they wouldn't be shopping for one in Okotoks. He'd leave that for when they got home.

At the mall, Melissa wanted to go into the nearest pet store and get everything they would need for the new puppy. "We need a lead, a—"

"A leash," Gray corrected her. "They say "leash" here."

"Oh, right. A leash, a collar, a bowl, a bed, toys, food…"

"How about we wait until we've got the dog, then get all the stuff?"

"Because if we get the stuff first, you can't change your mind."

You can't argue with that logic, Gray told himself. At least it would show his commitment to getting a mutt when he broke the bad news. "Okay, go wild."

Melissa beamed and ran into the store. Gray followed her in to find she'd already picked out a plastic bone and a food bowl. He got a shopping cart and followed her around, never questioning her selections.

"Don't forget the ball. You'll need something for him to fetch."

"Her," Melissa said. "I want a girl."

Of course you do. "Sorry, her."

An hour—and three hundred dollars—later, they left the store laden with bags. Melissa had forgotten all about her science project, and Gray didn't remind her. As she wouldn't be doing it, there was no point.

"What do you want for dinner tonight?" Gray asked.

"Ice cream!" she squealed, still buzzing from her shopping spree.

"You can't just have ice cream for dinner," he said and noted her disappointment. "How about pizza, *then* ice cream?"

Melissa looked shocked. "Really?"

"Really truly," Gray smiled. Inside, he was hurting. This would, hopefully, soften the blow that would come when they got home. "Come on, let's go get some mint choc chip."

* * *

When they arrived at the house, Gray put the ice cream in the freezer and ordered pizza, then went to his room to get some money for Joel. He locked his bedroom door, then lifted the loose floorboard next to his bed and took out the bag containing cash and passports. He counted off thirty grand for the rent for one year, plus another twelve grand for Joel's living expenses. If Joel chose to move into cheaper accommodation and pocket the difference, that was up to him. He would leave the money with a brief note explaining that they had to leave at short notice. For now, he put the money in his sock drawer and went back downstairs.

Melissa was watching a TV show about some girls who had found a magical cookbook.

"Darling, I need to tell you something."

Melissa paused the TV. "What?"

Gray sat down next to her. There was no easy way to say it, so he just blurted it out. "We have to move again."

Her eyes began welling up. "Why?"

"Those men I told you about. I think they found us again." He wouldn't tell her about his suspicions, as that would mean having to explain Luke Fraser's dubious demise.

"But what if you're wrong this time?" Melissa said. "You always say you think they found us, but nothing ever happens. Maybe you're overreacting."

Gray was impressed that she knew such a big word, but he didn't commend her on it. It wasn't the time. "It's better to be safe than sorry," he told his daughter. "I'd rather move and be wrong a hundred times than be right and not move. You know what will happen if they find us."

A single tear fell as she nodded slowly.

Gray put his arm around Melissa and pulled her close, swallowing hard. It broke his heart to see her like this. "I'm so sorry, darling. I wish I could make it all go away, but there's nothing I can do. I just want you to be safe, you know that."

She nodded again, then looked up at him. "Does that mean we're not getting a puppy?"

"Of course we are," Gray smiled. "Just as soon as we find somewhere new, we'll go doggy shopping."

"First thing?"

"Before we even unpack," Gray promised.

She perked up a little, and the doorbell signaled the end of the conversation.

After paying cash for the pizza, Gray put it on plates for Melissa and him, and brought them to the sofa.

"So, what are we watching?"

Chapter 30

Eva woke to a pounding headache and the taste of metal in her parched mouth. Her throat ached, as if she was trying to swallow an apple whole. She sat up gingerly and tried to get her bearings. The last thing she remembered was being in the jungle…Sonny…the gun going off…

She clasped her stomach, then lifted an unfamiliar T-shirt to inspect her belly. There was no bullet wound, just a small red spot like an insect bite, and a dull ache in her abdomen.

Eva swung her bare feet onto cold, gunmetal grey tiles, stood warily and then took a few gentle steps to make sure her legs would support her weight. They seemed okay.

She looked around. She was in a room with white walls and ceiling. Furniture consisted of the bed she'd being lying on, nothing else. There were no windows either, just a metal door facing her.

She tried to push it open and was not surprised to find it locked. Eva banged on it, then stepped back and looked for another way out.

There were none. No air vents, but there was a camera recessed into the wall with a red light to show that it was active.

She sat back on the bed wondering what had happened to Sonny. She'd obviously been shot with a tranquilizer dart rather than a bullet. Had they done the same to Sonny? If so, where was he?

There was one question she didn't have to ask: who was behind it?

The troops who had killed Costa and his friend were not there by accident. They could only have been sent on the orders of one organization.

Eva wondered how the ESO could have found them, and she could only think of the ID she'd left at Diaz's house. She cursed herself for being so careless. The least she could have done was make an effort to find it before they'd left.

But the damage was done, and self-recrimination wouldn't solve her problem. She forced herself instead to focus on a way out.

Eva tossed the mattress off the bed, hoping to find wooden slats to use as a weapon, but she only found a solid sheet of steel. There was nothing on the frame that she could remove and use to defend herself—or attack anyone.

Frustrated, she slumped to the floor and put her head on her knees.

Moments later, she heard a key turning in the lock. Eva scrambled to her feet and ran to the door, standing to one side and pressing herself against the wall, ready to pounce on whoever entered.

"Go and stand by the bed," a booming voice said.

Eva looked around for a speaker system, but there didn't appear to be any. All she saw was the camera pointing at her.

"Do it now, Eva."

Reluctantly, Eva retreated to stand by the bed. The door opened and a figure dressed in black combat gear rushed in, an automatic rifle pointing at Eva. He was quickly followed by another, and they spaced themselves out so that she couldn't attack them both at the same time.

A third man strode in, but this one was wearing an expensive suit. He was in his forties, with short black hair.

"Hello, Eva. You're looking well...for someone who's supposed to be dead. Care to tell me how you pulled that off?"

She said nothing, but stood poised, ready to strike at the first opportunity.

"I didn't think so," he said, then appeared to notice the mess Eva had made. "I see you killed your bed."

Eva ignored his pitiful attempt at humor. "Where's Sonny?" she snarled.

"He's...somewhere else. And before you ask, he's fine. Sends his regards, in fact."

"I know who you are, which means I don't trust a word you say. I want to see him."

"All in good time," the suit said. "I'm Johnson, by the way."

Eva wanted to leap at the man's throat and rip it out with her teeth, but the two guards looked like they were itching to pull the trigger. She restrained herself—for now.

"What do you want from us?" Eva asked. They could have killed her and Sonny, but they hadn't. She suspected she knew why.

"I have a job for you." Johnson said.

I thought so. "Not interested."

"You might be when I tell you who the target is. Felix Hernandez."

"Never heard of him," Eva said.

"Maybe not, but you do know someone who works for him. Jose Diaz?"

That name she wasn't likely to forget soon, and it must have shown on her face.

"Yes, the very same," Johnson said. "It was Hernandez who sent those men to find you. I don't know why they turned on each other, but word is, Hernandez has a real hard-on for you and Sonny right now. He's an international player, so no matter where you go, there's always a chance he'll find you."

"If you didn't find us first," Eva growled.

Johnson grinned. "There is that. However, I thought I'd offer you the chance to strike first."

"You want me to kill Hernandez?"

Johnson clasped his hands together. "Exactly!"

Eva knew they weren't offering her this opportunity out of altruism. They must have another agenda.

"I think I'll pass."

Johnson's pleasant façade disappeared. "I don't think you appreciate the situation."

"I know exactly what the situation is. You need Hernandez dead for some reason, and knowing the ESO, it's financial. Well, you can go do your own dirty work. I'm not interested in lining your pockets any further."

"Not even if it means seeing Sonny alive again?"

Eva's hands balled into fists, and she saw the two guards tense in response.

"The only thing keeping you two alive," Johnson pressed, "is our desire—our *mutual* desire—to rid the world of Felix Hernandez. If you're not interested, there's no point having you around."

Work for your enemy, or die. It wasn't much of a choice. "Then I guess I'm in." Eva said. She would do the job, if only to get Hernandez off her own back, but she would spend as much time thinking about how she and Sonny could disappear again as she would planning the hit. They'd done it before, and they could do it again.

"Excellent!" Johnson smiled again, and Eva pictured him grinning while she rammed his teeth down his throat with a rifle butt before shooting him in the head.

"But I want to see Sonny first."

"No problem. I'll send him in."

Johnson walked out of the room and the two guards backed out after him. The door slammed shut and Eva heard the lock turn.

She only had to wait a couple of minutes before the door opened again, which meant he wasn't being held far away. That was good to know.

Sonny rushed in and the door slammed closed behind him. He was dressed the same as Eva, in black jeans and a plain white T-shirt. Like hers, his feet were bare. He swept her up in his arms and kissed her. "I thought you were dead," he said, cupping her face in his hands.

"That's happened a lot lately." There would be time for catching up later. For now, Eva wanted a way out of this place. She put the mattress back on the bed frame and they sat down. "How's the shoulder?"

Sonny pulled the neck of his T-Shirt aside to reveal a large dressing. "Healing nicely."

Eva dropped her voice. "Any idea where we are?" she whispered.

"Not a clue. I've seen my room, the hallway, and this room, that's it. We could be anywhere from Kansas to Moon Base Alpha."

That didn't help. She'd hoped he might have seen an exit at the very least.

"They want me to kill Felix Hernandez," she said to Sonny, loud enough for eavesdroppers to hear.

"Who's that?"

"The boss of Jose Diaz."

"Ah," said Sonny. "Any idea why?"

"With the ESO, it has to have something to do with money."

Sonny took her hand in his. "Are you going to do it?"

"I have no choice. If I don't, we both die." She leaned in closer and dropped her voice to a whisper as she pretended to kiss him. "I'm going to insist that it's a two-man job so that you can come with me. Once we're out of here, we'll find a way to escape."

Sonny's only response was to squeeze her hand.

"Time's up," Johnson's voice boomed over the hidden speakers.

Sonny stood as the door opened, then he leaned in and kissed her again. "Good luck."

A few moments after he left, Johnson reappeared along with his two bodyguards.

"Let's get this over with," Eva said. "I need overhead shots of his home, details of his personal security and a picture of Hernandez."

"No need to get ahead of ourselves," Johnson said. "Hernandez is our ultimate goal, but first we need to take out his likely successor. If we leave him in place, he slips into the top job and we're back where we started. What we

228

need is a fractured organization, with factions fighting among themselves as they try to salvage what's left of the cartel."

"And who's his successor?"

Johnson smiled. "Jose Diaz."

* * *

Eva allowed herself to be cuffed and taken to a room with a table in the center and two computers on a desk to her right. One of the guards stood in a corner of the room while the other remained outside. Like her own cell, there were no windows.

Johnson pointed to a chair and Eva took a seat. He placed a folder in front of her.

"This is what we have on Jose Diaz," he said.

"I know all about him," Eva told him, pushing the file away. "I've been inside his house and know the layout. Tell me about Hernandez."

Johnson replaced the folder with another one. "This is what we have on him," the ESO man said.

Eva opened it. The first page showed a head shot of Felix Hernandez. According to the bio underneath the photo he was sixty-seven, but there wasn't the slightest sign of grey in his black hair. He had bushy eyebrows and a bulbous nose over a thick black mustache.

The next page was his history. Eva skimmed through it, noting several murders he was suspected of either carrying out or sanctioning. No criminal charges had been filed.

A series of satellite photos showed the house Hernandez lived in. It was a sprawling estate surrounded on all sides by a thick wall. There was no cover within at least fifty yards of the building.

Eva spent an hour going through the rest of the file, then asked to see a map of the surrounding landscape. Johnson took Eva to one of the computer terminals and brought up a three-dimensional rendering of the area. He hovered behind her to keep a close eye on what she was doing.

Eva flattened out the view so that she was looking at the house from a height of around a hundred yards. She panned around until she spotted what she was looking for. Zooming in to the crest of a hill, she turned the image to face the building and checked the range. It was just over a mile.

Perfect.

She manipulated the screen until she was back at the house, scanning it from several angles. It was set over two floors, with a tiled terracotta roof. A balcony jutted from the eastern aspect, and she suspected that would be off the master bedroom.

"I don't suppose you have a blueprint of the building?" she asked Johnson.

"I'm afraid not."

"Then I've seen enough," she said, standing. "What support will I have?"

"We'll insert you by air five miles from the villa a few nights from now. He always spends the weekend at his home. Once the job is done, we'll fly you back out from a point two miles north of the landing zone. As for weapons, let me know what you need."

Eva thought about it for a moment. "Grenades. Six stun, six fragmentation. Two Glock 17s with suppressor, two knives, a HK 416 for me and a HK G36 for Sonny."

"Nice try," Johnson said, "but he's our insurance."

Eva narrowed her eyes. "This is just a hunch, but I suspect you've tried to kill Hernandez before, and failed."

Johnson said nothing, but his face betrayed him.

"I thought so. How many men did you send?"

Johnson deliberated, then said, "Six."

"Six. And you expect me to go in alone? This is a two-man job at the very least, and don't bother offering me one of your men. It has to be someone I've worked with before, someone I trust, someone who understands how I operate. That's Sonny."

Johnson chewed it over for a while. "Someone you trust," he muttered to himself. "Someone you've worked with before."

"Yes."

Johnson nodded slowly. "Okay."

"There's one other thing." Eva explained what she wanted.

Johnson frowned. "They exist?"

Eva nodded.

"I'll look into it," Johnson said. He walked to the door and gestured for the armed guard to open it. "Take her back to her room."

Chapter 31

Tom Gray woke to the sound of his alarm. He silenced it and looked at the time through weary eyes.

Two o'clock.

Remembering the reason for setting it so early, he got up and took a quick shower, then dressed and went downstairs. The bags were already by the door. The night before, Gray and Melissa had packed their clothes into two large suitcases, and the dog paraphernalia into a duffel bag. There were a couple of boxes of Melissa's belongings, too, and Gray had left her fully charged iPad on top so that she could play on it when she woke.

It would be a long drive. Gray had searched the internet for a new place to live while Melissa slept. He'd settled on a town called Portage La Prairie, an hour outside Winnipeg and just a few miles from Lake Manitoba. There were several rental properties listed, plus a private school that he could enroll Melissa in.

Gray left a note outside the door that connected Joel's apartment to the rest of the house, along with the bundle of cash he'd prepared the night before. His last job was to load the SUV, which he did using the spare key. Once their entire lives were in the back of the Expedition, he went back inside the house and up to his daughter's room.

Melissa was sleeping soundly. He wrapped her in a blanket and carried her to the car, placing her on the back seat. She stirred while he was buckling her seat belt, but soon dropped back into a deep sleep.

Gray locked the door to the house and dropped the keys into the mailbox. Without looking back, he got behind the wheel and set off. With any luck he'd be halfway to their new home by the time Melissa woke. They would then have to stop for food and a toilet break, but Gray hoped to reach their destination by six in the evening, traffic permitting.

Those hopes were dashed ten minutes from the house.

Gray cursed as the red and blue lights of a squad car lit up his rearview mirror. The last thing he needed was to be pulled over and taken into custody.

Calm down, he told himself. He'd checked the lights on the vehicle the evening before, and they were all in working order. He hadn't been going over the speed limit, either. Probably just a bored cop wondering what he was doing out at three in the morning.

Gray pulled over and the cop car stopped ten yards behind him. The lights continued to flash as the passenger got out and approached Gray's car. Gray wound down the window.

"Evening," the uniform said. He glanced in the back and saw Melissa fast asleep. "Bit late to be driving around, mister…?"

"Masters," Gray said. He had his license ready, and he handed it to the cop. "Did I do something wrong, officer?"

The cop handed his license back. "Step out of the vehicle, please."

"I wasn't speeding," Gray said.

The cop's hand rested on the butt of his pistol, the threat clear. "I said step out of the vehicle. Now."

Something was definitely wrong, but Gray could only comply with the cop's demands. He had no weapon to defend himself, and from his side mirror he could see another officer approaching from the rear.

Gray turned the engine off and took off his seat belt. The cops stood back to allow him to get out, then spun Gray around and forced him against the car.

"Spread your legs."

Gray did as he was told, placing his hands on the roof of the Expedition. Rough hands patted him down and emptied his pockets.

"He's clean."

Gray made to turn around, but he was pushed back against the car. "Just stay there."

"Can you at least tell me what this is about?" Gray asked, but the only response was a sharp prick in his neck. Gray reached up to stop it, but a strong hand clasped his arm and held it out straight. Gray struggled, but with each breath he could feel his strength draining away. The last thing he saw before darkness took him was his innocent daughter, who had slept through the entire thing.

* * *

"Any news?" Felix Hernandez asked his lieutenant.

"Nothing, Jefe. I've been trying Romeo's phone all morning. It goes straight to voicemail. It's either out of coverage or turned off."

It wasn't like Jimenez to ignore his calls. Or anyone else, for that matter.

The last update Jimenez had sent said the gringos were in some no-name town on the banks of a river. That had been over twenty-four hours ago. Perhaps his lieutenant was right, and the phone had either run out of battery or there was no signal that deep in the jungle.

"Call the people we leased the helicopter from. Find out where it is."

The lieutenant ran back inside, and Hernandez wondered what could have happened to Jimenez. Surely the gringos couldn't have got the better of him, could they? Jimenez had said they'd lost all of their possessions, so they weren't armed. Besides, Jimenez had the local cops on his side, as well as that brute Costa. There was no way two people—one of them a woman—could possibly have got the better of them.

Unless they had escaped, and Jimenez was too frightened to report it.

That must be it. More than anyone, Jimenez knows the punishment for failure.

The lieutenant returned, and it didn't look like he had good news.

"Jefe, the helicopter crashed. The pilot reported that he was forced out by the gringos and they took off. Shots were fired and smoke was seen coming from the engine. A search team is out looking for the wreckage."

"What about Jimenez? Do they know where he is?"

"They had no information on him. All they were concerned about was their helicopter…and who was going to pay for it."

"Deal with it," Hernandez said, dismissing the man with a wave of his hand. He had more important things to sort out than worry about a trifling few million for an old chopper.

"Yes, Jefe, of course."

Hernandez had no idea how long it would take to find the downed chopper, but he was sure Jimenez would throw every local resource at the task. He decided to give the man another day to report in with good news. If Jimenez couldn't find them by then, his usefulness would be at an end.

* * *

Eva rubbed her belly, trying to relieve the dull ache that had been plaguing her all day. She thought at first it might be food poisoning, but not even the ESO would be stupid enough to do that just before a mission. Maybe it was the after-effects of her time in the jungle and the raw fish she'd eaten. Whatever it was, trips to the toilet hadn't cured it.

Speaking of big shits, she hadn't seen Johnson for almost a day. She'd expected to be put with Sonny so that they could work up a plan for the assault on the Hernandez residence, but apart from the trays of finger food every four hours, she'd been left alone. The insertion time was getting closer, and every second of prep time was vital.

She heard the key turn in the lock and jumped off the bed. The door opened and Johnson followed the two armed guards inside.

"It's about time," she said. "These missions don't plan themselves. We need to get working on it right now if we're gonna pull it off."

"I agree," Johnson said. He held out the cuffs and Eva stepped forward with her hands out. He placed them on her wrists, then took her arm and led her out of the cell and down the corridor to the room she'd been in the day before.

Johnson opened the door. "Now that you've got your partner, I hope there are no more excuses."

"There won't be," Eva said. She walked in the room and had to do a double take. "Tom?"

Tom Gray leapt from his seat. Like Eva, he was cuffed, which was just as well. He looked ready to kill.

"What the hell are you doing here?" Gray asked.

"Long story," Eva said. She turned to Johnson. "Is this some kind of joke?"

Johnson smiled. "You said you needed someone you've worked with before, someone you trust. Here he is."

"I was talking about Sonny, you asshole. Tom's too old for this shit."

"I know, but you can't have Sonny. As I said, he's our insurance, just as Melissa will provide Tom with all the incentive he needs to complete the mission."

Gray lunged at Johnson, but the guard was alert and crashed the butt of his rifle into Gray's temple. He went down hard.

"Nice work, jackass," Eva scowled at the guard.

"I'll leave you two to work out the details," Johnson said, heading to the door.

"Not so fast," Eva said. "The reason I need Sonny is because a mile from the house there's a crest overlooking Hernandez's bedroom. Sonny can hit that. Tom can't."

Johnson looked deep in thought. "I'll have a word, see what I can pull."

He closed the door before Eva could push him further.

She turned back to the table just as Gray rose groggily to his feet. She tried to help him into a chair, but he pushed her away.

"I'm okay," he said, holding the side of his head.

"Yeah, you look it." She took his arm regardless and got him fully upright.

"What the hell is going on?" Gray asked her, sinking into his seat. "One minute I'm driving, the next I'm pulled over by the cops and *poof!* the lights go out. I woke up about half an hour ago and they brought me in here, no explanation or anything."

Eva sat opposite him. "I don't think I need to tell you who they are."

Gray shook his head. His expression said he immediately regretted it. "You said Sonny's with you?"

"Yeah. We've been together for a while now. They found us a few days ago," Eva told him. "We'd got into an altercation with some drug lord. While he was looking for us, he must have tipped these guys off. They want me to kill the drug lord and his boss."

"So why am I here, and what have they done with Melissa?"

"I'm sure Melissa will be fine. As for you…that might be my fault."

"Yours?" Gray asked. "How?"

"When Johnson—that's the asshole who just left—told me about the hit, I said it was a two-man job, and I needed someone I trusted. I was expecting him to let Sonny come with me. I never dreamed he would choose you instead. Believe me, Tom, I wasn't even sure if you were still alive. If I'd known you'd be dragged into this, I would have gone in alone."

"You can still go in alone. I'm not doing it." Gray touched his temple and winced.

"Remember who you're dealing with," Eva said. "These guys bombed a school just to flush me out into the open.

238

You think they'll hesitate to kill Melissa if you don't do as they say?"

"They'll probably kill us all afterwards, anyway."

Eva had thought the same, too. Sitting alone in her cell for almost a day, all she could do was think. She took his hand in hers and leaned in. "They won't, trust me."

Chapter 32

"...and that's why you're hemorrhaging money," Jed Baker said.

Travis Burke looked at the figures on the screen. The amount he was paying to the leasing company seemed like a good deal, but after taking into account fuel, payroll taxes and insurance, it was more than he was making per month per vehicle. Travis had been looking at each outgoing in solitude, not realizing that as activity increased, so did his spending.

Jed had only been with the company for one day, and already seemed a godsend. He'd worked in the industry for over thirty years and knew the trucking business inside-out. With him as office manager, Travis was sure his venture would thrive.

"It's common practice for leasing companies to charge what they can, especially with startups who don't know the ins and outs of the business. I'll set up a meeting with them this afternoon and renegotiate the contract. If they don't want to do that, we'll hand back the rigs and find someone else. I've worked with other companies that will charge you thirty percent less than these crooks."

240

Travis was impressed. He'd never considered asking his creditors to lower their demands, yet as Jed had pointed out, that alone would dramatically improve his financial situation. Jed was quickly turning out to be the best investment Travis had ever made.

There was a knock on the door, and Travis looked up to see a familiar figure through the glass.

What the hell is he doing here?

He got up and let Johnson in.

"Travis," the visitor said, shaking his hand. "Good to see you." He looked at the new office manager. "And you must be Jed. Hi, I'm Johnson."

"Just Johnson?" Jed asked.

"I was given a geeky first name, so I insist everyone just call me Johnson."

Travis felt compelled to break the awkward silence that followed. "So, what brings you around here?"

"Ah, yes. I need a word. It won't take long." Johnson looked at Jed.

Jed took the hint. "I'll go and grab a coffee."

When he left, Travis sat behind his desk. "How do you know Jed?"

"You'd be surprised at what I know about you."

Travis didn't doubt it. On his first visit, Johnson had known his intimate financial dealings. Knowing the name of an employee made sense. "I didn't expect to see you again. At least, not so soon."

"I didn't expect to be back, either," Johnson said. "but something's come up. We need you again."

Travis folded his arms across his chest. "What do you mean?"

"I mean there's another mission."

Travis shook his head. "No. Na-a. I did what you asked, but I'm not doing it again. That was a one-off. I'm through."

Johnson sighed. "If only it were that simple." He took a cell phone from his pocket, touched the screen a few times, then put it on the desk.

Travis saw a video ready to play. He hesitated, then hit the center of the screen and saw himself and Danny in the hut in Malundi. The camera looked to have been placed high up on the wall, and Travis knew it must have been hidden in the clock that had looked so out of place.

"Where does Evergood live?" Travis heard himself ask.

"Here," Danny said, "in his palace, but it is better if you take him on his way to the parade. His palace is heavily guarded. I've marked three potential sites along his route. Any of them should give you a decent shot at him."

Johnson picked up the phone and stopped the video. "It goes on, as you know." He put the device back in his pocket. "If that video were to reach the new president of Bulasi, he would surely demand your extradition. As we just signed such an agreement yesterday, we would be hard pressed to refuse."

Travis was stunned. "This is blackmail!"

"That's such an ugly word," Johnson said. "Pertinent, but ugly nonetheless. The thing is, once you accepted our coin, you became ours, and we need you in Colombia."

Colombia! Africa was bad enough, but some real bad shit went down in Colombia.

"If it makes you feel any better," Johnson said, "you won't be going in alone this time. There'll be three of you, and you're only there to provide support. You'll be on a hill a mile from the action."

"I was a mile from the action in Bulasi and nearly died."

"Oh yeah, how's the ass?"

"Sore," Travis said truthfully. He'd had it cleaned and dressed when he got back home, and while it was healing nicely, it was still tender. "It would hamper my escape if things got hairy."

"I'm sure that if you do your job right, it won't come to that."

"And how the hell would you know?" Travis growled. "You ever see combat?"

Johnson laughed. "I saw *Full Metal Jacket* once. Does that count?"

"Didn't think so. People like you are always happy to throw men into wars, but you don't have the balls to fight them yourself."

"That's where you're wrong," Johnson said, the annoying grin still on his face. "I don't make the decisions. That goes way above my pay grade. Like you, I'm a cog. Your specialty is killing people at long distances, mine is convincing the likes of you to pull the trigger."

"What if I call your bluff? You send that video to Bulasi, I'll tell them you sent me."

Johnson raised one eyebrow. "Really? 'A man called Johnson told me to do it'? Is that going to be your defense? What about all the money you recently came into, money that originated from a bank in Malundi? Did you think about that?"

"What? But you never said…" Travis slumped in his chair. Johnson—or whoever was controlling him—had thought this through. A lot more thoroughly than Travis had.

He'd sold his soul to the devil, and Lucifer had come to collect.

"How many more times will I have to do this?" he asked Johnson, not sure he wanted to hear the answer.

"Not many, I should imagine. We have other snipers, but they're indisposed right now. You should expect me or my replacement to come calling every…I don't know…two years? We really don't perform that many assassinations these days. Little call for it, to be honest."

Every two years! He was thirty-seven now. A kill very two years meant eleven more missions by the time he was sixty. Would they still expect him to perform when he was that old? "Do I ever get to retire?" Travis wondered, then realized he'd said it aloud.

"Sure. Given your age now, I'd say we could probably get three, maybe four more missions from you. After that, you won't be much good to us."

Travis had a feeling he knew what happened when assets became liabilities. He would literally know where the bodies were buried.

If he was going to do this, he needed an out, a way to ensure he didn't die before he was good and ready.

In the meantime, he would have to dance to the tune his greed had orchestrated.

"What's the mission?" Travis asked with a note of resignation.

"As I said, Colombia. Oh, and Peru. It's kind of a double-header. I'll give you half an hour to get Jed up to speed and leave him to run things while you're away. It shouldn't take more than three days. Once you've done that, I'll take you to meet your teammates."

Chapter 33

The journey wasn't as straightforward as Travis had expected. He'd hoped to learn something about his new paymasters from the get-go, but the car he'd ridden in had no plates. They'd driven to a nearby airfield where a chopper had been waiting, and the moment he climbed aboard a black hood was placed over his head.

The flight was a long one. Travis thought it might have been three hours, but he couldn't be sure; Johnson removed Travis' watch and phone during the flight.

When they landed, the hood stayed on through another short car ride, then Travis was led into a building. After an elevator ride down, he was taken through a series of doors that sounded like they were activated by a punch code.

The hood was suddenly pulled from his head as a door slammed behind him. Travis blinked as bright lights assaulted his senses.

"Sorry about the cloak and dagger stuff," Johnson said, "but this location is rather sensitive. Can't have the whole world knowing about it."

Especially me, Travis thought.

Johnson led him to a room with a steel door and an armed guard outside. The uniformed trooper opened it as they approached and Johnson stood aside to let Travis in.

Inside, there were three people. One was another guard dressed in black, who stood in one corner. At a table in the center of the room were a man and woman. There was something familiar about them, but Travis couldn't nail it down.

"Eva, Tom, meet Travis. He's your sniper."

Eva stood, glaring daggers at Johnson. "You said I could have Sonny."

"No, I said I'd see what I could do. The plan was for you to go in alone, but no, you said you needed a second man. You got Tom. Then you needed a sniper. You've got Travis. Are you now going to tell me you need someone who's slightly taller than you with blond hair for some bizarre operational reason? Because if you are, I'll get you someone like that." He moved in closer to Eva. "But you don't...get...Sonny."

Travis thought the woman was going to rip Johnson's head off—he almost wished she would—but she somehow retrained herself and sat back down.

"We'll be inserting you in twenty-four hours, so I suggest you get your heads together."

Johnson turned and left the room, leaving the three of them to get acquainted. If Travis was going to work with them, he might depend on them to save his life, and vice versa. It would help if they got off to a good start.

"What's your story?" he asked Eva. "I mean, call me crazy, but something tells me you didn't volunteer for this, either."

She looked at Travis as if he was something she'd inadvertently stepped in, but after a few moments, her features softened. "Me and the ESO go way back. Same for Tom."

"ESO?" Travis asked. It sounded familiar, but he couldn't quite place it.

"The people you work for," Tom said.

Travis shook his head slowly. "To be honest, I don't know who I'm working for. One minute he's offering to save my business, then next I find out I've signed up to some lifetime deal. He basically blackmailed me into doing this."

"Welcome to the club," Eva said. "He's holding my boyfriend hostage as well as Tom's daughter. If we don't complete the mission…" She made a gesture across her throat.

"Doesn't strike me as the best way to put a team together," he said. "Why don't they just use professionals? Send in the SEALs?"

"Apparently, they tried that," Eva told him. "It wasn't pretty."

That did Travis' confidence no good. If an active SEAL team couldn't pull off the job, what chance did these three have? It wasn't as though he had his choice of assignments, but this was already looking like a suicide mission. If he was going to come through it alive, it was best to know what he was working with.

"I'm ex-navy," Travis said. "SEAL Team Three. What about you guys?"

"Classified," Eva said. "I could tell you but then I'd just bore you. Let's just say I can handle myself."

Travis didn't push it. "What about you, Tom?" The man looked to be about fifty, and Travis hoped Johnson wouldn't be calling him into action at that age.

"Ex-SAS," Tom said. "Very ex."

Something clicked in Travis' head. He knew where he'd seen them before. "You're Tom Gray!" He turned to Eva. "And you. You're Eva...Eva Driscoll! I knew I'd seen you somewhere before!"

That somewhere had been on the TV news, right after some billionaire had got himself blown up by an Apache chopper and his father was sent to prison for life. The story had played for weeks.

"Guilty as charged," Gray said.

"Holy shit!"

"So, you happy with our credentials?" Eva asked.

Travis was too full of questions to hear hers. "I thought you guys went to prison."

"Long story," Eva said. "For now, we should concentrate on our mission."

Travis nodded. It was a long way to Colombia. Plenty of time to hear their side of things. It also reminded him that he didn't know who the target was.

"What exactly is the mission?" he asked.

Eva held up the face of another man who had been in the news recently. Travis could only think of one word.

"Shit."

Chapter 34

"Shouldn't be much longer," Sergeant Dana Sorrell said as she watched Melissa on the screen. The drug they'd put in her food had already made her drowsy, and the girl was now sitting on the edge of her bed, her head slowly drooping before she jerked herself awake.

"She's fighting it," Johnson said.

"That's because she's nine. Not many nine-year-olds want a nap in the afternoon."

The medication finally won. Melissa slumped sideways, her head landing just below the pillow. Sorrell picked up an oxygen bottle and rushed into the room along with a couple of medics, who wheeled a gurney in. Sorrell made sure the girl's airway was clear. Under normal circumstances, the anesthetic would have been administered in the pre-op room, but Johnson had insisted that the girl not know she was going into surgery. She placed a mask over Melissa's face and signaled for the medical assistants.

Sorrell had been an anesthetist in the Medical Corps for over twenty years, but it was only in the last few days that she'd been told to prep people for surgery without their consent. The other three had been adults, two men and a woman. It went against all of Sorrell's training and Hippocratic oath, but she'd been assured it was in the interest of national security. Sorrell wasn't one to question her superiors, and thankfully the girl was the last of them.

She and the medics stripped Melissa and covered her in a surgical gown, then wheeled her down the corridor, through three sets of doors and down two floors in the elevator to the OR. The surgeon was waiting, scrubbed and ready, and he watched as Melissa was transferred to the operating table. Sorrell took a seat by her head, monitoring her vitals.

"Good to go," she said, and the surgeon inserted a tube into Melissa's mouth, down her throat and farther. He then inserted two more tubes inside the first, one of them a camera, the other the instrument that would perform the surgery.

Sorrell's eyes alternated between monitoring Melissa's vital signs and the surgeon's monitor. When the camera and remote instrument were in place in the girl's stomach, the surgeon added a third tube to the mix. At the end of this one was a tiny transmitter that was encased in a material that would withstand the acidic properties of the stomach for at least five years.

Over the next two hours, the surgeon used the minuscule remote-control arm to attach the device to the roof of the stomach. A subcutaneous insertion under the skin would have been the normal procedure, but his superiors had insisted that it be undetectable. This way, the patient would feel some initial discomfort, but after a few days, they would have no further issues.

Once the operation was complete, Sorrell accompanied Melissa to the recovery room to monitor her. After forty minutes, she was stable enough to return to her cell, where she was dressed in her own clothes and placed on the bed to wake up in her own time.

* * *

Johnson watched the sleeping girl through the camera, then glanced down at his cell phone. The app connected to the transmitter's signal showed a green dot in the correct location. Johnson tapped the marker and her bio appeared in a side menu, with her name and the co-ordinates of her current position.

Johnson hit the menu and chose another name from the list: Eva Driscoll. Her marker showed her to be in her cell, as did those for Tom Gray and Simon "Sonny" Baines.

Driscoll might have fooled them into thinking she was dead once, but it wouldn't happen again.

Chapter 35

Eva had no idea what time it was. The constant bright light of her cell and lack of exterior reference made it impossible to distinguish between day and night, and her sleep pattern was totally screwed. All she knew was that Johnson said the mission would kick off soon.

She planned to jump into action a lot sooner than that. The moment she and Gray were handed their weapons, they would fight their way to Sonny's cell, then Melissa's, and then they would fight their way out. After that she had no idea what they would do, but at least they would be together and free.

The door opened and two guards walked in. One had his rifle trained on Eva while the other put a pile of clothes on the floor. They both retreated and the door slammed closed once more.

"Dress please," a voice said over the speaker.

Eva picked up the clothes and took them over to the bed. Everything was black. Pants, sweater, Kevlar jacket and boots. There was no sign of any of the weapons she'd asked Johnson for. She was disappointed, but not overly so. It would have been near impossible to fight her way out of the

252

cell anyway. As long as she got them before they left the facility, her plan was still good.

She dressed, not surprised that everything fit perfectly. Even the boots felt like they'd been worn-in. That would save her a few blisters during the long walks from the landing zones to the targets.

Ten minutes later, the door opened. Johnson held it open while the two guards entered. One had cuffs, the other a black hood.

"What the hell is this?" she asked, angry at the deviation from her plan.

"Precautions," Johnson said. "I know you'd like nothing more than to get your hands on some weapons and fight your way out of here, but I'm not as stupid as you think. You'll get everything you asked for on the transport, not before."

Frustrated, Eva thrust out her hands. The cuffs snapped on and the hood was placed over her head. Plan A was shot, but there was always plan B. Unfortunately, she would only be able to execute it if the mission was a success. Failure would mean death sentences for Melissa and Sonny.

Rough hands took her by the biceps and led her down corridors and through doors, and Eva memorized every turn, every doorway. It was a few minutes before she felt a breeze that told her she was outside. That suggested the facility was big, but she was confident she could navigate her way back to Sonny's cell.

The guards pulled her to a vehicle, and Eva heard a door slide open.

"Step up," one of them said, helping her inside. Once he had her seated, he strapped her in.

Eva waited for them to take the hood off, but the door slammed shut and she was left in silence. She decided to take it off herself, but the moment her hands went to her face she felt the barrel of a pistol on the back of her head.

"Leave it on," a voice said.

"I was told I'd get my gear on the transport. Where is it?"

"We'll be going to the transport in the next few minutes. We're just waiting for the others."

Gray arrived a few minutes later, cursing as he knocked his shin on the way into the vehicle, and Travis soon after that. Once they were in, the van started, and they drove for ten minutes. When they stopped, Eva was helped out of the vehicle and marched a short distance. She could hear the others close behind her.

Not long now, she told herself.

She heard the sound of helicopter rotors begin to whirl and felt the downwash as hands helped her aboard. Once again, she was strapped in tight, but before she could even think of making a move, a voice spoke.

"This bird will take you to the transport chopper. There you will be given the gear you asked for. You'll have time to eat and make any last-minute arrangements. While on this flight, do not remove your hood. If you do, you go out the door. Do I make myself understood?"

Eva fought back her anger. Johnson had anticipated her every move. By the time they landed, she would have no idea how to get back to Sonny.

She wasn't ready to give up yet. The moment she was on board the flight to Tingo Maria for the Diaz phase of the mission, she would force the pilots to fly back to the facility and would rescue Melissa and Sonny. She would also scour the place for Johnson and give him what he deserved.

254

The chopper took off and flew in a long curving arc, then straightened up for a while before tilting in the opposite direction. Eva suspected it was to throw off their sense of direction so that they couldn't trace their way back to the facility, but it was overkill. She had no idea which direction the bird had been facing when it took off, so the maneuvers were pointless.

Eva didn't bother trying to work out the elapsed flight time. It would do them no good. Instead, she thought about the mission ahead of them.

She had no problem with the hit on Diaz, but Hernandez would be an entirely different proposition. It wasn't going to be easy. After the failed mission by the SEAL unit the previous year, she expected Hernandez would have beefed up his security. That could mean anything from tripling his guard detail to deploying motion sensors in the surrounding jungle. They would have to be wary every step of the way.

If it ever got that far.

The flight was over three hours by Eva's guesstimate. When they landed, they were helped off the helicopter. Seconds after their feet hit the ground, they heard the chopper lift off again.

They stepped inside a building, where their hoods were removed and they saw two men in pilot uniforms. Eva blinked as her handcuffs were unlocked.

They were inside a hangar, and before them was a white Lear jet. Against one wall was a table loaded with weapons. Another bore a variety of food, from sandwiches to cold meats and cheese.

There was no one else in the hangar apart from Team Eva and the two pilots. One of them, with grey hair cropped close to his skull, introduced himself as Captain Hooper. The other was Franklin.

"We'll be wheels up in forty-five. That should be enough time to check your gear and take some food on."

Eva focused on the weapons. She found the HK she'd requested. She stripped it in seconds, checked the working parts, then put it back together and slammed a magazine home. Chambering a round, she turned and aimed it at Hooper.

"Take us back to the facility," she ordered the pilot.

"Johnson said you might try this," Hooper said, his hands in plain sight. A cell phone rang, and Hooper pointed to his pocket. "That's for you."

Eva gestured with her gun for him to answer it, and he took the device from his pocket slowly.

"Hello…yeah, one moment." Hooper held out the phone and Eva took it.

"Oh, Eva, so predictable," Johnson said. "And to be honest, I'm rather insulted. Did you really think I'd let you loose with such firepower?"

Eva said nothing, but she gripped the phone hard enough to crack the screen.

"Look up and to the right, in the corner of the room," Johnson said.

Eva did, and saw the camera pointing at her. She gave it the bird.

"Not very ladylike," Johnson said. "Just know that if at any point you deviate from the mission, Sonny and Melissa will die. As for Captain Hooper, he has no idea where I am, so there's no point pressing him on it. Just get yourself ready and do your job. If he doesn't call in on the hour, every hour, you know what happens."

256

"I got it," Eva said. "Just make sure the other items I asked for are here before we hit Hernandez."

"They will be."

The phone went dead. Eva looked at the cracked screen, then tossed it back to the pilot. "Sorry about that. Get yourself a new one and send the bill to Johnson."

"What was that all about?" Travis asked as the three of them returned to the task of checking their weapons and gear. They had all been issued watches, night vision gear, GPS devices, comms equipment, the weapons they'd requested and enough ammunition to see them through a dozen battles. There was also a camera to confirm the kills.

"Just Johnson reminding us that there's no backing down."

* * *

As promised, the flight took off three quarters of an hour later. Night had already fallen, so Eva wasn't able to make out where they were, but it didn't look like they were in the United States. What houses she could see were ramshackle, clumped together almost randomly, and no two roofs were alike. She suspected they were in Mexico, but it could have been any Central American country.

"What's our flight time?" she asked the co-pilot, Franklin.

"Five hours. You might as well get some sleep."

"Can you at least tell us where we're going? As we didn't bring parachutes, I assume we're not jumping over the target."

"Apiay, Colombia," Hooper broke in. "You'll be met there, that's all I know."

It was a bit of an anticlimax. Getting her game-head on had been for nothing. At least she knew that the facility where Sonny and Melissa were being held was probably somewhere in the U.S. The jet could travel at about 560 miles per hour, so they would be traveling about 2,800 miles. Her geographical knowledge was very good, so she suspected they'd taken off from Mexico. Sonny would be a three-hour helicopter ride from there. Those calculations didn't narrow down the possibilities much.

She went back into the cabin and took her seat. Tom and Travis were nibbling on snacks they'd found in the galley, and there was a bag of nuts on the table next to her.

"Aw, one of you bought me dinner. How thoughtful." She opened the snack and popped a few cashews in her mouth. "Five hours, then we switch planes," she told the others.

"I just wish I knew what day it is," Gray said.

"It's Friday," Eva told him. "I looked at Hooper's phone when I took the call from Johnson."

"So we hit Diaz tomorrow and Hernandez on Sunday," Travis said.

"That's the plan," Eva told him. "Just make sure we take Diaz without him raising the alarm. We don't want Hernandez on his guard."

They'd gone over this several times, but she didn't see the harm in making the point again. When they went in, it would have to be hard and fast, with no time for indecision.

Gray put his snack down and rubbed his stomach. "I don't know what they were feeding us, but my gut's been playing up for days."

"Mine, too," Eva said. "I thought it was some bad sushi, or after-effects from the dart they hit me with."

Gray looked miserable, and Eva knew it wasn't just from his upset stomach. He was worried about Melissa, and rightly so. The poor girl had been through so much already, and now she was separated from her father once more. It was one thing for the ESO to subject her, Sonny and Gray to this treatment, but not a little girl who should be enjoying her childhood, who was right now probably wondering if she would ever see her daddy again.

During the initial planning, before Travis arrived, Gray had told Eva about his last few years on the run. Always wary, never letting anyone get close to them, minimizing friendships, no sleepovers. That was no way for a child to grow up. She needed companionship, and not just from an old man.

"So what happened after you went to jail?" Travis asked, crumpling up his empty bag and stuffing it in a plastic cup. "Did you escape?"

"It's a long story," Eva said.

"Yeah, you already said that, and now we've got five hours to kill."

Eva wasn't sure she wanted to share her life story with the new guy. They'd only known each other for a few hours, and for all she knew he could be an ESO plant. On the other hand, she didn't want to piss the guy off as he'd be the one backing her up over the next couple of days.

"We were pardoned," she told him. That little bit of information wasn't going to hurt. If he started asking about where she got her fake IDs, though, she'd know he wasn't on the level.

"And then what?"

"We went on the run. Hiding out, trying to live a normal life, but the ESO wouldn't let us. They'll never let us. We hurt them too much, and now they think they own us."

"So how do you make it stop?" Travis asked.

"You don't," Gray said. "Once you're in their sights, that's it."

The news appeared to dampen Travis' mood. He looked down at his feet, then started shaking his head slowly. "It's gotta be hard for you, man, with a little girl and everything."

Gray didn't contradict him.

"Did they let you see her before we set off?"

Gray nodded solemnly. "I got a few minutes with her."

Eva could tell Gray was tearing himself apart just thinking back to that brief encounter, so she tried to change the subject. "You got family?" She asked Travis.

"Just my parents. Mom almost died having me, so they didn't bother trying for a little brother or sister. Just as well, I guess. Don't wanna give the ESO more leverage."

"How did you get mixed up in all of this?" Gray asked.

Travis told his story, from his first meeting with Johnson to getting shot in the ass and roped in for a second mission.

"Can't say I blame you for accepting that first job," Gray said. "Hard to pass up a million bucks when you're that deep in the hole."

"If I'd known it would lead to this, I would have opted for bankruptcy."

"Hindsight is a wonderful thing." Eva had often wondered what her life would be like if she hadn't tried to avenge her brother's murder, but always came to the same conclusion: she'd do it again in a heartbeat.

She reclined her seat and closed her eyes.

Chapter 36

Eva woke with a start to find Gray shaking her gently. "We're coming in to land."

She rubbed her eyes and stretched. Outside it was still dark, and the lights below were slowly getting bigger through the window.

She went to the galley for a bottle of water and sipped it as the plane descended, eventually landing with a soft bump and taxiing to a hangar. When Franklin opened the door and secured the retractable steps in place, they carried their gear onto Colombian soil.

A man in aviator gear met them at the bottom of the stairs. "I'm Major Willard. This way."

The trio followed Willard across the tarmac to the hangar. Inside was a Bell Boeing V-22, better known as an Osprey. The tilt-rotor aircraft had engine nacelles that were able to rotate ninety degrees to allow vertical take-off, then transition into conventional flight. It gave them the advantages of a helicopter, but with a much greater range.

"We've set up some bunks in the hangar," Willard told them, "and there's food and drink available. We'll be heading out in eighteen hours."

*　*　*

They were ready an hour early, so used the remaining time to check their gear again. Once that was done, they sat in silence, each dealing with the pre-mission nerves in their own way. For Eva, that meant thinking of what Diaz had planned to do to her. That was all the incentive she needed.

The major approached with half an hour to go to discuss ETAs and comms, and Willard gave them a couple of radios so that they could keep in contact with him.

"You know where to drop us?" Travis asked.

Willard produced a map and pointed to a marked location. "Here. It's about seven klicks west of the target." His finger moved four kilometers across the map. "We'll pick you up here six hours later." Willard gave them the exact co-ordinates and Gray entered them into the GPS device.

Eva was used to working in miles, not kilometers, but the military had to use the metric measurement to ensure interoperability with their allies, especially NATO forces.

"Don't be late," Willard warned them. "If you're not there when we arrive, I won't have the fuel to hang around and wait for you."

"We'll be there," Eva said. They had to travel a total of eleven klicks—almost seven miles—on foot, but even if each kilometer took them half an hour, that still left thirty minutes to kill Diaz. Plenty of time.

At eight PM on the dot, Willard whirled an arm as a signal to the co-pilot. The tail gate descended, and the giant rotors began to wind up. As they climbed inside, Eva said, "I thought it would be bigger."

The major pointed to a huge black plastic shape that took up most of the space inside. "We had to bring along extra fuel. The LZ is about a hundred klicks outside our max range. Once we drop you, we'll rendezvous with a tanker off the west coast, then come back and pick you up. We'll be in the air for three hours."

Willard squeezed around the fuel bowser and headed for the cockpit, while the trio stowed their gear and took their seats.

Eva didn't know about the others, but she was glad to finally be on her way.

* * *

The Osprey was the noisiest ride Eva had ever known, but then it hadn't been built for comfort. Travis had the worst of it, constantly shifting his position to relieve the pressure on his injured butt. Eva just hoped his wound wouldn't slow them down.

They were flying just a few hundred feet above the ground by this point, which meant they were close to the landing zone. When the air speed dropped as the nacelles tilted upwards, they knew it was game time. They all locked their NVGs into position and stood, waiting for the ramp to descend.

Gray was the first off as soon as the bird touched down. He ran twenty yards and took a knee, looking for threats. Eva came next. The moment Travis' foot touched the ground, the Osprey roared into the sky.

Gray checked his GPS, found a heading and started in that direction. The others followed, ten yards apart, with Travis bringing up the rear.

Eva had hoped to cover the five miles in two hours, but they did it in just over one. Shortly after midnight, Diaz's house came into view, the straight line of its roof just standing out against the treetops. It was half a klick away, and Eva planned to use the extra time to scope it out. She already knew the layout, but wanted to see whether Diaz had improved security.

The surrounding area was flat, so there no ideal vantage point for Travis. That meant he'd have to go into monkey mode.

"Travis, up this tree. It'll let you cover the front entrance. Once things kick off, kill anyone you see coming out. We'll radio you before we leave the house."

They had decided that Gray would go in with Eva. She'd drawn a map of the interior and they'd gone over it in detail, deciding which rooms they would clear first. At two in the morning, they expected Diaz to be asleep, so the guards' quarters would be the first target.

Gray helped Travis reach the lower branches of a tall tree and the ex-SEAL slowly made his way upwards, cautious not to draw attention to himself. After ten minutes, he let the others know over comms that he was in position and could see the front door. It was all clear, with just two lights on downstairs, none upstairs. No sign of any cameras, but two men were patrolling the grounds.

"You ready for this?" Eva asked Gray.

"No, but let's do it."

They pushed left for two hundred yards so that they could cross the road and approach the house from the side. They planned to scale the outer wall and drop into the garden, then make an entry at the rear, just as Sonny had done when he'd rescued Eva.

They managed the first part, with Eva easily grabbing the top of the wall with a running jump and pulling herself up. She leaned down and took Gray's hand, dragging him until he had a firm grip and foothold. He got himself on top of the wall, lying flat and listening for signs that they'd been spotted.

There was nothing, just the occasional sound of a nocturnal creature.

Things turned bad when they dropped into the garden.

Floodlights bathed the entire area in blinding white light, causing Eva and Tom to rip off their NVGs. A klaxon also sounded, and Travis' voice shouted in Eva's ear.

"Two coming from the front of the house!"

"Take them out!" Eva told him, trying to remain calm despite the shitstorm they'd wandered in to.

"We gotta move!" Gray said, a lot less composed. He was up and running before Eva had a chance to process his words. She sprinted after him as he headed for the rear corner of the house just as a guard with an assault rifle stepped into view from the back of the building. Gray fired as he ran, sending a burst that hit the man in the legs. He fell, his rifle chattering until Gray took proper aim and put a bullet in his head.

A burst of lead flew past Eva's head, and she turned and moved at the same time. One of the bodyguards from the front of the house was aiming for a second shot when a puff of crimson erupted from his head and he dropped to the ground. Eva expected his companion to appear, but Travis came over comms.

"Two down."

Eva ran to the corner, where Gray crouched. She peeked around the corner and saw that it was clear. She ran past Gray, who followed her a few steps behind.

The door to the back of the house burst open and a man ran out, straight into a burst from Eva's rifle. Gray leapfrogged her and sprinted toward the open door, pulling the pin from a fragmentation grenade as he ran. When he reached the entrance, he released the priming handle, waited one second, then tossed it inside, pressing himself against the wall for cover. The explosion shook the ground, but it didn't deter Gray. Once the shrapnel had done its work, he ran inside, with Eva on his six.

There was one dead local, or at least, what was left of him. Gray stepped over the upper half of the body and to the kitchen door, a stun grenade ready. The door was closed, so Gray emptied half a magazine into it to deter anyone on the other side, then kicked it open and threw the grenade in. As soon as he heard the blast, he ran into the hallway and across to the room where Eva had indicated the guards were quartered. A hail of bullets forced him to change path, and he ducked behind a marble table as more rounds smacked into the furniture around him. Another gun barked, then there was silence.

"Go!" Eva shouted.

Gray readied another frag and threw it inside the open door, running left toward the stairs as the explosion ripped through the room. He bounded upwards and stopped at the top, waiting for Eva to join him.

She tapped him on the shoulder and took the lead, heading to the left. Diaz's room was at the far end, through a set of double doors. Gray let her go and ran into the bedroom at the top of the stairs.

"Coming out on the balcony," he said to Travis, just to make sure he wasn't mistaken for a bad guy. He kicked open the French doors and ran along the balcony to the windows outside Diaz's room.

"On three," he told Eva, then started counting.

The moment he heard her strafe the door and gunfire erupt from inside the bedroom, Gray fired his own blast through the window and followed it up with a stun grenade. He was inside the room a second after it detonated, and Eva kicked the door in a moment later. In the light from the hallway, Gray could see three figures in various states of disorientation. He took one out while Eva dispatched another.

That just left Diaz.

He was on his knees, shaking his head to clear it. Eva didn't give him the chance. She lashed out with her foot and caught him in the face, shattering his nose and sending him flying backwards.

"Travis, watch the front, especially the balcony," she said into comms. To Gray she said, "Guard the hallway. We don't know if there are any left."

Gray was blowing hard from his exertions. "Just do him so we can get the fuck out of here."

"I need two minutes with him. I've got unfinished business."

Gray looked like he wanted to say something, but instead spat on the floor, then took a position by the splintered bedroom doors.

Eva dropped on Diaz, pinning his biceps under her knees. He howled in pain, but she grabbed his throat. "Remember me?"

Diaz focused his eyes, then his face registered first recognition, then fear.

"That's right, *puto*. Costa's dead, and so is the other guy you sent. Now it's your turn."

"I…I didn't send them. Hernandez did."

"Felix Hernandez?"

Diaz nodded. "That's right."

"Good, because he's next."

Before Diaz could say anything else, Eva punched him in the throat with all her strength. Diaz's eyes went big and he tried to speak, but his crushed voice box wouldn't obey his commands. He bucked as he fought for breath, but it was no good. Eva waited until he fell still, then climbed off and shot him in the head. She took the camera from a pouch and snapped off a couple of pictures, then ran to the door and tapped Gray on the shoulder. "Let's go."

She took point, weapon up and searching for targets, but the house was clear.

"We're coming out," she said over comms.

"Roger that," Travis said. "Got you covered."

They ran outside, where light still bathed the entire house and garden. The klaxon was still howling, too. Eva ran around the exterior of the house looking for it, and when she found it hidden underneath an eave, she blasted it with her rifle. The annoying sound stopped, and all they could do was hope it wasn't connected to the local police station. She would prefer the kill to remain undiscovered for the next twenty-four hours.

Long enough to kill Felix Hernandez.

Chapter 37

"There's no sign of them, Jefe. It's as if they dropped off the face of the earth."

Felix Hernandez slammed down the phone. It was over four days since he'd last heard from Romeo Jimenez, and now the two men he'd sent to the helicopter crash site had no positive news to report. Jorge had been trying the ex-cop's cell phone constantly throughout the last three days, but with no success.

Hernandez was about to order Jorge to send more people to the region to find out what the hell was going on when a name leapt into his head.

Jose Diaz.

He'd sent Costa to help Jimenez, so maybe he had some news. Hernandez picked up his phone and called.

It went straight to voicemail.

What the fuck is going on?

He tried again, but with the same result.

"Jorge!"

The lieutenant ran out of the house. "Jefe."

"Get me a burner cell and the landline number for Jose Diaz. He's not answering his cell."

269

Jorge disappeared and was back moments later. He handed Hernandez a slip of paper and the cartel boss dialed on the disposable phone.

It rang…and rang.

Hernandez cursed until he could hear his own blood pumping in his ears. The doctor had warned him about getting upset, but that was easy for a quack to suggest. He wasn't running a multi-billion-dollar business.

He did his breathing exercises until he was calm enough to think properly, and after weighing up the options he told Jorge to contact the local police and send a car around to the Diaz residence. They were to leave a message asking Diaz to call his uncle Felix urgently.

While Jorge ran off to carry out his orders, Hernandez pondered the severity of the situation. Jimenez's contacts had learned nothing about the woman. The address that had come back belonged to a rental apartment that was vacant, and no one matching her description had ever lived there, according to the neighbors. They had nothing else on her, which strengthened his belief that she was in fact DEA working undercover. If they'd stolen a helicopter, one of them must have known how to fly it, again dispelling the tourist angle.

The threat of the DEA was nothing new; they'd been a thorn in his ass for the last thirty years. They'd tried infiltrating his cartel, even direct assaults, but nothing had worked. The last attempt to capture him had been a colossal failure, and the six men his people had killed were still talked about in Bogotá. Their bodies had been strung up for everyone to see, especially the American media. He'd increased his security since that attack, but the Americans hadn't been foolish enough to try again.

If they ever did, they'd be wasting their time. His men would hold them off long enough for him to get to his tunnel, which ran for three miles underground. An electric vehicle would drive him to the other end, where he had men stationed around the clock. They would take him to a hideout in the jungle, and he would remain there until the heat died down.

Jorge ran to Hernandez, holding a cell phone. "Jefe, it's Jose Diaz!"

Finally. "Let me speak to him."

"No, I mean it's *about* Jose. He's dead."

Hernandez's breathing exercises were suddenly forgotten. "How?" he growled.

Jorge swallowed. "They're all dead. Everyone except the cook and the maid. They said the alarm went off and then there were explosions and gunfire. It only lasted a couple of minutes."

"Did they see who did it?" Hernandez asked, his anger growing.

"No, they hid under their beds until it was all over, then called the local police."

Hernandez was ready to explode, but he kept it in check. He would save it for the people responsible for messing with his organization.

"I want every cop we own down there today. I want to know who did this!"

Jorge wheeled away to relay the message, but Hernandez called him back. Something told him the hit on Diaz was just the beginning. "I want security tripled. Get twenty men from Bogotá. I want them here by sunset."

If anyone managed to get through the outer defenses, they wouldn't get inside his house, he'd make sure of it.

Chapter 38

The jog back to the rendezvous point was easier than the way in, purely because they were burning the adrenaline that had kicked in when the shooting started.

Willard arrived two minutes ahead of schedule to pick them up, and Eva even managed a snooze on the ride back to Apiay.

One down, one to go.

After a proper sleep and a decent meal, Eva was ready to go. Gray, though, didn't look as good. He appeared haggard, as if he'd aged ten years overnight.

"Couldn't sleep?" she asked him as they prepared drinks at the beverage station. Eva was drinking coffee while Gray opted for tea.

"No," he said, stirring sugar into his drink.

"Melissa?"

Gray's face gave her the answer.

Eva glanced around to make sure no one was within earshot. "When we complete this mission, I plan to bring a few extra weapons home," she said quietly. "Once we're back, we can fight our way to Sonny and Melissa and free them."

"And how does that stop them coming after us again?" Gray asked, not even slightly buoyed by her suggestion.

"It doesn't, but it's a start."

"You're assuming they'll take us back," Gray said. "What if they throw us out of the chopper on the way home, or just forget to pick us up again?"

He sipped his drink while Eva thought about his response. Gray had a point. If Johnson's plan was to get them to complete the job and then abandon them in country, there was no way they'd ever find Sonny and Melissa again. "I don't think that's his game plan," she said, thinking aloud. "He had the pick of any soldiers in the world and he chose us. He needs us."

"Maybe he needs you, but as you rightly said, I'm too old for this shit. Hell, I was too old ten years ago."

"Nonsense," Eva said. "You did okay out there."

"It was all muscle memory, my training kicking in, call it what you want. My mind knows what to do but my body just can't keep up anymore. By the time we got back on the Osprey, I felt like I'd been through a mincer. What really concerns me is that if they see I'm past it, they'll have no more use for me."

Eva could see his dilemma.

"I need to do what you and Sonny did," Gray continued. "Find a way to make them think I'm dead. I thought about a house fire or explosion, but I'd need to find—or create— two suitable bodies, and even then, they'd probably want DNA verification."

"Fires are no good," Eva agreed. "You need something where the bodies are unrecoverable. Plane crash over the Pacific—which they won't fall for again—or on a ship that sinks in the middle of the ocean, something along those lines."

"Or," Gray said, "get on a ship but go missing during the journey. Maybe jump over the side and get picked up by a submersible."

"That might work," Eva admitted, and it got her thinking about her own exit strategy. If she went missing again, the ESO would do everything within their power to verify her death, so it would have to be foolproof. There was time for that later, though. Right now, they had a mission to complete.

"Let's discuss it on the way back," she said. "For now, just make sure you grab an extra weapon once we've killed Hernandez. Even if it's just a knife, you can use it to disarm one of the guards and take their weapon."

"I will," Gray said. "Speaking of weapons, did Johnson send the other items you requested?"

"He did," Eva said. She picked up her coffee and walked over to a large metal container. She opened it and let Gray see the contents.

"What the hell are those?" he asked.

Travis walked over, still wet from the shower. "What we looking at?"

"These are Spikers," Eva said, lifting a metal tube from the container. It was fourteen inches long and an inch and a half in diameter. Near one end was a red switch guard. "They're made by an AI company called Beddoe Industries from North Carolina. These are prototypes."

"What do they do?" Travis asked.

Eva reached into the large container and picked up a square box. She opened it and took out one of ten discs, each the size of a dollar coin. "You peel off the backing here," she said, "and stick it to your helmet. That designates you as a friendly. Then, you raise the switch guard, point it skywards, then press and hold for three seconds."

"Then what happens?"

"Thirty tiny drones are released into the air. Within three seconds, they identify all humans within a hundred-yard range. Each chooses one as a target and destroys them by flying into them. Each drone carries a tiny amount of shaped explosive, and when it hits, it does the same damage as a fifty cal."

"Shit!" Gray exclaimed.

"Shit indeed. We've only got two of them, one each, so don't go wasting them if there's just a couple of bad guys in the area. If we're pinned down by a dozen or so, fine, but try to choose your moment."

"What if they all choose the same bad guy to kill?" Travis asked.

"They don't. They communicate like a hive mind. Once a target is identified and acquired, it passes that information on to the others. Once all targets are identified and assigned, they fly in for the kill. If there are fewer targets than drones, they double up. If there are more targets than they can handle, they go for the ones closest to the friendlies."

"I saw something similar on YouTube about ten years ago," Gray said, "but that one was used to destroy tanks. They'd fire a cluster of missiles above the battlefield and each one would identify an enemy tank and kill it."

"Yeah, same principle, only a lot smaller." Eva put the weapon back in the box but kept the discs out. "I suggest you stick three on your helmet instead of just one. You might duck after firing and cover it up inadvertently. Or it could fall off in battle. You never know."

"That wouldn't be good," Travis said.

"That's a slight understatement," Eva grinned.

Gray picked up a tube. "Lift, point, press, hold, pray you don't die. Got it."

"It's that simple," Eva said.

"How come our military hasn't got this already?" Travis asked. "And how the hell did you find out about it?"

"Something to do with ethics and collateral damage," Eva told him. "If you fire one of these when there are friendlies or civilians in the area, the drones can't differentiate. They need to eliminate that problem. As for your second question, you'll be surprised what you can find on the Internet if you look hard enough."

Travis opened a bottle of water and took a huge pull. "What else have you got for us? Iron Man suits? Invisibility cloaks?"

"Only this," Eva said, reaching into the container. She held up a small device that was made of light grey plastic, with a screen at one end.

"A Gameboy?" Travis laughed. "You wanna play Super Mario between firefights?"

"It's a radio frequency meter. It allows us to detect electromagnetic fields, extremely low-frequency fields and radio frequencies. When I was up against Henry Langton, he had sensors surrounding his house which sent electronic signals back to a control room. I brought this along just in case Hernandez has something similar. He could have motion sensors, CCTV cameras, anything. I'd rather have it and not need it than walk into a trap. Once we set down, I need to pair all of our electrical devices to it so they can be ignored, otherwise we'll just get false positives."

Travis looked at Gray. "The lady's thought of everything."

"I hope so. I promised my little girl I'd be back."

* * *

Eva checked her watch. It was approaching midnight, and they would be at their destination soon. She took the remaining time to check her gear once more, ensuring her three markers were in place on her helmet and her rifle had a round chambered.

"Comms check," she said. "Check one."

"Check two," Gray replied.

"Check three," Travis said.

Eva stood and made sure none of her equipment rattled or was about to fall out. Her pockets were crammed with ammunition, grenades hung from her black webbing, and the Spiker was strapped across her abdomen for easy reach. Coupled with the sidearm and six-inch knife, she was as prepared for battle as she'd ever been.

Eva had chosen the landing zone herself. It was in a valley, which meant their transport could fly in under the radar and the valley walls would mask the sound of their approach.

At least, she hoped so. The Osprey was such a noisy beast that she'd moved the LZ to eight miles from the Hernandez residence instead of the five she'd originally chosen. The extra distance would add over an hour to their journey, but they'd all agreed it was better to be cautious.

The aircraft slowed. Travis and Gray got to their feet and did their own final checks, then brought down their NVGs and waited for landing. When the ramp fell, they piled out and took their positions until the bird was gone.

Eva took the lead. In her hand was the GPS rather than the radio frequency meter. She didn't expect Hernandez to have any early warning systems this far out, but once they got to within a mile of his home, she would switch devices and slow the pace.

They made good time, stopping just once to take on water. At three in the morning, they reached the point where Travis would set up.

The hill overlooked the Hernandez place at an elevation of roughly a hundred feet. Travis got himself settled, preparing his hide and readying his water and spare magazines.

"How does it look?" Eva asked.

Travis peered through his scope. "I can see the front and east side of the house. Sixteen hundred yards, no wind, clear line of sight. Just like a day on the range."

Eva tapped her boot against his. "Watch our backs. We're counting on you."

Travis gave them a thumbs up, and Eva and Gray set off toward the target.

"You sure that thing works?" Gray asked her. She was now carrying the frequency detector, holding it out in front of her and sweeping it slowly from side to side.

"We'll soon find out. If it beeps and we find something, then yes. If not, and we walk into hell, then I guess not."

"Good talk," Gray muttered. "In next week's edition of *How to Inspire Confidence*, Eva explains that the Spikers were only ever tested on mannequins and the friendly markers are not a hundred percent effective."

"You read their latest test report, too?" Eva asked.

Gray's face dropped. "What? Are you serious? Was I right?"

"Nope," she grinned, "but no one likes a smartass."

Gray stared at her as she walked ahead, and couldn't help but smile.

* * *

Eva stopped and raised a clenched fist. Gray immediately froze.

"I got something," she said. She looked up from the device and scanned the area in front of her. Nothing looked out of place, but then that would defeat the purpose. She checked the scope again and moved it slowly from side to side until she had a bearing, then moved forward one small step at a time. It seemed like hours before she found two sensors, facing each other, set on thin metal spikes about a foot off the ground. Eva slowly bent down and scraped some dry soil into her hand, crushed it together until it was a fine powder, and threw it in the gap between the two devices. A thin red line briefly appeared.

Eva signaled that they should go around it. They skirted the area, and when the meter remained quiet, she switched to the GPS to get a bearing, then back to the frequency detector. They were three hundred yards from the house now, within touching distance.

The frequency detector found one more electronic trip wire, but that was the last obstacle before the trees ended and only fifty yards of open ground separated them from the outer wall of Hernandez's compound.

"How's it looking?" Eva asked Travis over comms.

"Clear where you are. There are four guards patrolling the grounds inside the wall, always one on each aspect. It won't be easy to get to the house unseen."

"If you take one out, how long have we got before the next one finds him?"

"Thirty seconds," Travis said, "no more."

The wall was ninety yards from the house. They would have to scale the wall and cover the distance in half a minute.

"Ready for a sprint, old man?"

"Go for it."

They jogged over the open ground to the wall, where Tom braced himself against it and cradled his hand so that Eva could get a step up.

"Wait!" Travis' voice exploded in her ear. "They're getting a message. Shit. One of them's pointing at your position! They're moving toward you!"

"We must have tripped another sensor," Eva said to Gray. "Let's move." To Travis she said, "We're gonna need a rolling commentary."

Eva sprinted to the right with Gray close on her heels.

"They're copying your movements. They must have a camera on you."

"Impossible," Eva replied. "I didn't detect anything."

"Then how are they…shit. Wait one."

"What?" Eva said. "What is it?"

She heard a *crack* from above, and when she looked up, she saw something flying toward her. Eva dodged as a two-foot-long drone crashed against the wall.

"Eye in the sky," Travis said. "You're welcome."

Eva signaled for Gray to about-face and run in the opposite direction. If the guards continued on the same heading, they might be able to flank them.

"Where are they now?" Eva asked as she ran.

"Still at your last known, but there's more of them. I count twelve."

280

Eva stopped and told Gray to make a cradle. She stepped into it and Gray heaved her upwards. She grabbed the top of the wall and told Travis to create a diversion.

"On three," he said.

Eva counted down, then pulled herself up so she was lying flat on top of the wall. Through green-tinted goggles, she saw one man lying on the grass, then another fell. Eva reached down and took Gray's hand, pulling him up. Once he had both hands on the wall, Eva brought her rifle around and got ready to drop down the other side.

The remaining guards were running for cover, some firing wildly into the air. Travis picked off another, but then half a dozen more burst from a set of French windows. There were too many for Eva to take out when she was in such an exposed position.

Time to see if this sci-fi shit really works, Eva told herself. She glanced at Gray's helmet and saw that his markers were clearly visible, then patted her own to make sure hers were still in place. She yanked the Spiker from its Velcro holder and flicked up the trigger guard.

"Spiker up!"

She pointed the tube in the direction of the Colombians and pressed down on the button, saying a silent prayer. As her count reached three, the end of the tube exploded like a party popper and a jet of tiny projectiles shot into the air. Eva watched in fascination as the outer casings fell away to reveal the drones inside. Each one was about the size of a hornet, just over an inch long, and they hovered in a cloud a hundred feet above the ground.

And they hovered…and hovered…

Just when Eva thought she'd fired a dud, the cloud dissipated, each drone zooming off in its own direction.

The result was instant and devastating. The fifteen men in the garden fell as one, as if someone had switched off their collective life force.

"Holy fuck!" Travis exclaimed. "Did you just see what I saw?"

"Never mind that, just form up on us," Eva told him. "We're going in." The rest of the fight was going to take place inside, so there was no point having Travis lying a mile away with his thumb up his ass.

Eva jumped down, and Gray landed next to her a moment later. "We go in there," Eva said, pointing to the open French windows on the ground floor.

They sprinted to the entrance, Eva firing a short burst through the opening to deter any shooters inside. They took positions on either side of the doors and Gray threw a flashbang inside. At the explosion, they ran inside and took down two of Hernandez's men before they could recover from the blast.

They were in a large sitting room, and an open door led out to a brightly lit hallway. Gray peeked around the side of the door and immediately drew back as automatic weapon fire splintered the oak near his head.

"Frags," he told Eva. They each threw a fragmentation grenade through the doorway at the same time and pushed themselves against the wall as red-hot shrapnel flew in a thousand directions at once. Gray was first through the door, but several guns chattered from the upper balcony. He jinked sideways and dove behind a couch that had been blown onto its back. Rounds slammed into the furniture as he held his rifle over the top to spray fire toward the upper floor.

Eva joined in, sending measured bursts upwards, but as one man fell, two more appeared. There were now six of them with the advantage of the high ground, and two more appeared from a doorway across the hall.

Much as she hated to do it, Eva knew they had to deploy the second Spiker. She'd really wanted to keep it until they got back so she could use it in the rescue, but that would only happen if they managed to survive the next few minutes.

"Tom! Spiker!"

* * *

Hernandez jerked awake as Jorge shook him.

"*Jefe*, the Americans are here! We must go!"

"What? Who is—"

An explosion cut him off, and Hernandez was wide awake. "How many are there?"

"We don't know. Two were spotted approaching the house, but the camera drone was shot down. It appears they have a team of snipers because there are at least seventeen men dead in the grounds."

"Seventeen?"

Jorge nodded. "Come, we must get you to safety."

Hernandez leapt out of bed and followed Jorge to the walk-in closet. Jorge pressed a wall tile inwards just as two blasts in quick succession rocked the house.

"That was closer!" Hernandez said. "Hurry!"

A door clicked and Jorge pushed it all the way open, then stood aside so Hernandez could go first. They were in a passageway lit only by floor lights, which they followed to another door. This one swished open as they reached it, and

283

Hernandez stepped into the elevator. It was powered by its own generator, so even if the electricity was cut to the rest of the house, he would still be able to escape.

Hernandez turned toward Jorge, just in time to see his lieutenant's head release a puff of blood before he collapsed to the ground.

* * *

Gray pulled the tube from his webbing and recalled the chant he'd been reciting on the flight: *Lift, point, press, hold.*

He flicked off the trigger guard, aimed at the ceiling and pressed the button. After what felt like an hour, the end popped and the drones flew upwards. They hovered above him, then darted away to dispense death.

The room fell silent, and Gray was up and running for the stairs a second later. He heard Eva chasing him up to the second floor, and when they reached the top Gray worked out that the room with the balcony was to their left.

"This way," he said. He peeked around a corner but saw no one, so he stepped out and to the side so that Eva could hug the other wall. There was just one room before they reached the double doors of the master bedroom. The single door opened outwards, suggesting it was a closet rather than a bedroom. Eva covered Gray as he swung it open. He'd guessed right. There was a variety of cleaning implements, but no bad guys.

Gray shifted his focus back to the main bedroom. The door was open a couple of inches. Gray stuck the barrel of his rifle inside, expecting a barrage of gunfire, but none came. He used the gun to push the door all the way open, and still the room remained silent. He signaled to Eva that he would go to the right and she should take the left. On three, they rushed into the room, weapons searching for threats, and saw no one.

But it wasn't quiet.

Gray followed the sound of hushed voices into a side room, and he saw that the wall was slightly open. It had to be some kind of secret passage. Indicating that he would go in, Gray pushed the door open slowly and saw two figures about ten yards away. One had his back to Gray, while the taller one was facing him. Gray could only see half of his face, but that was enough.

Felix Hernandez.

Gray fired at his principal target, but the round struck the first man in the head. He went down and Gray fired again, but Hernandez had ducked sideways and metal doors closed on him. Gray emptied his magazine and inserted another as he ran to the end of the passage, where he heard the sound of motors whirring.

"It's an elevator!" he told Eva, searching all around the door frame for a button to call it back. There was none. "Check back there, see if there's a control panel. There's nothing here."

* * *

Felix Hernandez threw himself to the side as bullets slammed into the back wall of the elevator. When the doors closed, he heard even more rounds pepper the doors, but the descent had already started.

How had they got past so many men so quickly? His security detail was supposed to slow down any attack to give him time to get away, but now they knew about his tunnel. There was nothing to stop them following him.

All he could do was buy himself some time.

When the doors opened, he dashed out into the tunnel that was three yards wide, with a semi-circular roof and strip lighting that ran the length of the ceiling. He grabbed his go-bag, but instead of taking it with him, he jammed it in the open elevator doors so that the car couldn't go back up.

Hernandez climbed onto his electric buggy and jammed his foot on the pedal. It wasn't the fastest conveyance, its top speed only twenty miles an hour, but that was as fast as Olympians could run one mile. For someone to catch him on foot over three miles would be impossible. By the time he got to the other end, his men would be ready and would hold off any pursuers until he was clear of the area.

Then it would be time to plan his revenge.

* * *

"There's nothing here!" Eva shouted.

"Then we'll have to pry it open."

Eva stabbed her knife between the doors, then pried them apart enough for Gray to get his fingers in the gap. He heaved the doors apart.

"I'm at the front door," Travis said over comms. "Where are you?"

"Second floor, turn left at the top of the stairs, through the double doors at the end," Eva replied.

Gray looked into the empty shaft. He could see the elevator at the bottom. "I'm going down," he said, swapping out his magazine for a full one.

"I'll go," Eva said, squeezing past him. "You wait for Travis, then come after me."

She grabbed the steel cable in the center of the shaft and swung out, then worked her way down hand over hand. Sliding would have stripped away her thin gloves and pared the skin from her palms and fingers.

Her feet touched the roof of the car, and she ripped the ventilation grille off. Sticking her head inside, she saw that the door had been wedged open, which explained why the car hadn't returned to the upper level.

Eva clicked her throat mic. "I'm going in," she said to Gray. "I'll send the car back up for you guys."

"Be careful."

Always.

Eva eased herself through the hole, kicked the bag to the side and stepped into a tunnel, looking for threats. There was nowhere for anyone to hide except straight ahead, and the only thing in that direction was moving away from her.

Eva started sprinting after the fleeing cartel boss, but soon saw she was wasting her time. Hernandez was increasing his advantage with every step she took. She fired a burst from her rifle, more in frustration than in hope of hitting him. He had to be a thousand yards away, well outside the range of her weapon.

She stopped to catch her breath and heard footsteps behind her. When she turned, she saw Gray and Travis running toward her.

"He's gone," she panted. "We missed him."

Travis put his rifle to his shoulder and peered through the scope. "Maybe not." He adjusted a dial, then adopted a stance with one foot slightly in front of the other.

Eva watched his breathing slow, and when he exhaled he squeezed the trigger. In the confines of the tunnel the retort was loud, even with the fitted suppressor. With Hernandez so far away, she couldn't see whether Travis' aim had been true.

"Did you get him?"

Travis lowered his weapon, looking dejected, and Eva cursed.

"I'm frankly insulted that you should even ask that." Travis' face suddenly brightened, "Of course I got him."

Eva slapped his chest with the back of her hand. "What is it about guns that turns men into assholes? Come on, we need a photo for Johnson as proof."

She jogged down the tunnel with the others close behind her. Five minutes later they were standing over the body of one of the most feared cartel bosses in South America. Eva snapped a dozen pictures of what was left of Hernandez. The bullet had blown half of his face off, but even without his right cheek and eye, he was still recognizable.

"I suggest we get the hell out of here," Gray said.

"I'm with you," Travis said. He pulled the corpse from the buggy and got behind the wheel. After executing a three-point turn he patted the battery compartment behind his seat. "All aboard. Next stop, anywhere that serves cold beer."

Chapter 39

The ride back would normally have been a chance to come down from a mission high, but for Eva and Gray, there was still work to be done.

Both had taken knives from some of the dead bodies lying in the grounds and had secreted them on their bodies, knowing they would have to hand in the equipment they'd been issued. Once they were back at the holding facility, they would strike on Eva's signal.

"Something wrong?" Eva asked Gray. While she was fired up for the confrontation ahead, Gray didn't appear so focused.

He fixed her in a cold gaze. "I'm ready," he said.

"But…?"

Gray sighed. "When does it end, Eva? Say we manage to rescue them. What then? We get away, and a few months down the line Johnson or whoever is knocking on our door again. 'Hey, Tom. Mind if we look after Melissa while you go kill someone for us?'"

"I've been thinking about that," Eva said, "and I have an idea."

"What?"

"I'll tell you once we've got them out. If we don't pull that off, it's moot."

They lapsed into silence. Gray looked across the aisle at Travis, who'd fallen asleep, his head resting on the vibrating bulkhead.

"It's a good job you pulled that sniper bullshit to try to get Sonny on the team," Gray said. "If it wasn't for Travis, we wouldn't be here."

Gray was right. The ex-SEAL had not only saved their lives—twice—but the mission would have been a failure if not for him. The sad thing was, his success had only made Travis more valuable to the ESO, and they would undoubtedly come calling again. Tragic as it was, Travis wasn't the first, and he wouldn't be the last.

That wasn't her concern, though. All she cared about right now was getting Sonny back.

When they arrived back at the air base in Apiay, there was no time to shower or eat. Willard checked in their gear and stuck the camera in his pocket, then Hooper ushered them aboard the waiting Lear jet and retracted the stairs.

"Welcome back," the captain said. "Hope the Air Force treated you well."

"Not as well as you guys," Eva smiled seductively. "So, where are we headed?"

"Wichita Falls."

Eva was surprised that her flirtatious move had worked. She'd expected some vague response, not an exact location. "And from there…?"

"There'll be a chopper waiting, that's all I know."

It was better than nothing.

"Take a seat," Hooper said, "we'll be on our way in a couple of minutes."

Hooper entered the cockpit and locked the door, and Eva turned to see the boys had already settled in for the flight. Travis had found a bottle of beer somewhere, but she was glad to see Gray was sipping on a bottle of water. The last thing she wanted was him drunk when she needed him most.

Eva got herself a diet soda from the galley, then took her seat and strapped herself in. She leaned across the aisle. "Something doesn't feel right," she said to Gray. "When we took this jet to Colombia, we flew from Central America. I'm sure of it. Now we're heading to Texas."

Gray frowned. "Why the sudden lack of secrecy?"

Eva could only think of one thing, and it wasn't good. "Maybe it doesn't matter if we discover the location, because Johnson plans to take us out."

She could see anger spreading across Gray's face, and she knew it wasn't because he was worried about his own fate. Men like Gray were not afraid of dying. He was concerned for his little girl.

Eva's hand caressed the trouser leg where she'd hidden her knife. "We won't let it come to that."

* * *

By the time they landed at Sheppard Air Force Base, Eva and Gray were wound tight as watch springs. Both had transferred their knives to their sleeves for ease of access, and as they climbed out of the jet their eyes darted everywhere to assess their surroundings. There were no threats. The helicopter sat fifty yards away and there were no armed units in sight.

As they walked toward the chopper, Eva leaned into Gray. "We'll be at our most vulnerable when they put on the hoods," she whispered, even though there was no one but Travis near them. "We can't let that happen. Our only chance is to take the pilot hostage and force him to take us back to the facility. Anyone else on the bird has to die."

Gray simply nodded.

Eva shook her arms as she walked, as if fighting off an early morning chill, but she was shifting the blade closer to her wrist. She felt the hilt just inside the cuff of her left sleeve.

As they reached the helicopter, Eva expected someone to step out and offer them black hoods, but she saw that the cabin was empty. The lone pilot hit a switch and the rotors began to turn slowly.

Confused, Eva looked at Gray, who simply shrugged and climbed aboard. Travis followed him, but Eva had one last look around in case it was an ambush. No one was paying them any interest.

She got in and closed the door, then strapped herself into her seat.

"Something's definitely wrong," she said to Gray above the noise of the rotors.

"Maybe this one's just a ferry. Maybe they'll try to hit us on the next leg of the journey."

That had to be it. She allowed herself to relax, but only a little.

The chopper took off and flew away from the rising sun. Eva put on the headset so that she could communicate with the pilot.

"What's our flight time?" she asked him.

"Eighty minutes."

Eva did a rough calculation. That would take them about two hundred miles, and as they were pointing west, their destination was somewhere in Texas. It was strange that they should take such a short hop. Perhaps the hit would take place when they landed, or maybe this was just another leg on a circuitous journey designed to disorientate them.

She would find out in just over an hour.

Eva closed her eyes and thought of Sonny. They'd been together for a couple of years now, and in that time they hadn't shared an angry word. Every moment with him had been a joy, and she wouldn't trade him for anyone. She certainly couldn't see herself living without him. He'd risked his life to save hers, and Eva was determined to repay that debt.

She jerked awake and realized she'd dozed off. Below them, fields stretched for mile upon mile, some fallow, others growing a variety of crops. She checked her watch and saw that the eighty minutes were almost up.

"Can you see an airport?" she asked Gray as she scanned her side.

"No, there's nothing down there."

What the hell is Johnson playing at? Eva wondered. Perhaps he was just messing with their heads, giving them hope before striking when they least suspected it.

"Wherever it is, we're near," Gray said, and Eva felt the chopper slowly descending, too.

"Maybe it's underground," she told Gray, but even then, she'd expect to see some kind of building above ground level. There had to be access somehow, and she didn't recall walking up any ramps when they had left a couple of days earlier.

"I see a couple of cars down there," Travis said as the chopper slowed.

Eva scooted over and looked out of his window. There was a black sedan and a silver SUV parked by the side of the road, but nothing else for miles in any direction.

"This must be where they plan to do it," she told Gray.

He took the knife from his sleeve. "Then we make sure we take some of them with us."

They touched down twenty yards from the vehicles, but Eva was in no hurry to get out. She first wanted to see what they were facing. If it was an overwhelming force, they could always force the pilot to take off and re-evaluate.

The rotors wound down, but there was still no movement from the cars. Eva decided the kill squad was waiting for them to leave the helicopter before showing their hand. She wasn't going to make it easy for them by making the first move.

"Melissa?" Gray said, with disbelief.

Eva saw her at the same time. The rear door of the SUV opened and Melissa ran out toward the helicopter.

Gray pushed his door open and met her halfway. He dropped to his knees and hugged her as the blades overhead came to rest.

"Daddy! I knew you'd come back."

Eva was furious. It was one thing to kill her and Gray, but to make Melissa watch was diabolical.

The other passenger door opened and Sonny stepped around the SUV. Unlike Melissa, he had a big smile on his face. The driver also stepped out and he tossed the keys to Sonny.

Eva got out, still wary. She could see another driver in the sedan, but apart from those two, there didn't appear to be anyone else.

"What's going on? " she asked Sonny. He said nothing, just picked her up and kissed her. Eva kissed him back, but she still had one eye on the SUV driver who was standing next to the sedan.

"Can we go now, Daddy? I'm so hungry my tummy hurts."

When Sonny put Eva down, she pushed him away at arms' length. "I'll ask you again, what the hell is going on?"

"We're free to go," Sonny smiled. "Johnson received the photos you took and he told me to thank you for a job well done."

"I hope you told him to go f—" Eva saw Melissa looking at her and changed tack. "—fly a kite."

"Those very words," Sonny laughed. "But seriously, the SUV is ours." He peeled off and went to greet Gray. "Long time, mate," Sonny said, giving him a bro hug. "How you been doing?"

"You know what it's like," Gray said. "Always looking over your shoulder, keeping to yourself."

"Tell me about it. The amount of times I've dreamed of having a beer with the guys…"

"You seem to be doing okay for yourself. So you snagged Driscoll, eh? How does a reprobate like you pull that off?"

"Long story."

"Then I think it's time we got that beer and you can tell it."

"Deal," Sonny said. He pointed at the SUV. "All your gear is in the back."

"Including a cloth bag?" Gray asked.

"Dunno. Johnson just said all your stuff."

Gray took Melissa's hand and walked to the car. In the back, he saw his bag containing his cash and passport, and when he opened it, everything appeared to be there.

The SUV driver walked over to them, holding out a phone. "It's for you," he said to Eva.

She took the handset and placed it next to her ear.

"I just wanted to thank you for clearing up our little problem," Johnson said. "I asked Sonny to convey a message, but let's just say he appeared reluctant."

"What do you expect me to say? You're welcome?"

"No, not really. That's not your style. What I would like is to know how the Spikers worked in the field."

Eva considered her answer. "Not great," she said. "Half of them flew into pictures hanging on the wall, some hit statues. Thankfully there were enough of them to help us out of a situation."

It was a lie. She'd been really impressed with the weapon, but she wanted to buy shares in the company before the ESO dived in and the price skyrocketed. The Spikers would undoubtedly be sanctioned for use by the military within a few years, making the creators—and any investors— extremely rich.

"That's a shame," Johnson said. "I had high hopes for them. Not to worry. I guess all that's left to say is have a good life. The SUV is yours, and we gave Sonny a little cash to keep you going for a few days."

"You really expect me to believe you won't come calling again?" Eva snarled.

"Oh, we will," Johnson said, "and as you've discovered, we'll always find you. You might as well just hang out and enjoy life instead of hiding and constantly looking over your shoulder. A job every year or so isn't so bad, is it?"

"It is when it's for people like you."

"That's why you and Sonny will never work together. I'll always need him as leverage when an op comes up. If only you'd change your mind and see what an opportunity we're offering, things would be much better. You could settle down, find a permanent home, make friends, work together, and you'd have us to fix any problems that might arise. IRS, police, you name it. All you have to do is say you'll come on board."

Eva wanted to explode on his sorry ass, but Melissa was too close and would hear everything. "Don't forget that it was the ESO who killed my brother. You think I could willingly work for you after that?"

"That was the old ESO," Johnson said. "Henry Langton was a renegade, too blinded by power to see the big picture. We've evolved."

"I don't care. We're through. If you send anyone to pick us up, we'll kill them."

"We'll see. For now, spend some time together, then think about it. I'll be in touch."

The phone went dead. Eva handed it back to the driver and told the others the bare bones of the conversation.

"He must think we're crazy," Gray said. "No way I'm working for them again."

"Me neither," Sonny added.

"Then we're in agreement," Eva said. "Now what?"

"Food!" Melissa said.

"Good idea." Eva turned to the driver. "Where's the nearest town?"

He pointed up the road. "Canyon is ten miles up that way."

She thanked him and got in the front passenger seat of the SUV. Sonny got in beside her and stuck the key in the ignition. When everyone was aboard, he set off.

"How was it?" Sonny asked Eva.

She glanced in the mirror and saw an attentive Melissa sitting between Travis and her dad. "I'll tell you later."

Chapter 40

Stopping at the first roadside diner they came across, they sat at a booth that accommodated them all. A waitress in a pink uniform appeared immediately. The four adults ordered coffee while Melissa let the woman run through a dozen milkshake flavors before choosing vanilla.

"Can I have a burger?" Melissa asked Gray.

"Anything you like, darling." To Eva he said, "I normally watch what she eats, but not any more."

"What about a cheeseburger?" Melissa pressed.

Gray looked at his own menu. "How about the triple decker cheeseburger with extra bacon and double paprika fries?"

"Really?"

"Sure. I'll have the same."

The waitress brought their drinks and took their order a few minutes later. Melissa slurped at a foaming mountain of cream and sprinkles.

"Where are you going from here?" Sonny asked Gray.

"Not sure. You heard what Johnson said. They'll find us if they want to. I think I'll just stop running for a while and spend some quality time with Melissa. Take in Disneyland, Universal Studios—"

"Really?" Melissa squealed. "We're going to Disneyland? When? When?"

"Not until you've eaten and I've had a good night's sleep," Gray smiled, ruffling her hair.

Melissa shook her head and put her bangs back in place. "And don't forget we're getting a dog, too."

"A dog?" Travis said, sipping his coffee. "What kind?"

"A golden retriever puppy, and she's gonna be called Snuffles."

"Snuffles?" Gray asked, making a horrified face. "Seriously?"

"Or maybe Jenna…yeah, I like Jenna better."

"Me too," Gray said, wiping imaginary sweat from his brow. "Imagine me walking the dog, it gets off the leash and I'm shouting, "Snuffles! Snuffles!'"

Melissa laughed. "That would be so cool."

"If you're getting a dog," Travis said, "make sure you get it chipped. I had a puppy a few years ago and it got out of the yard. Never saw it again. And there are new chips coming out that can track the animal wherever it is, just like you can track your phone. That way, you don't have to wait until someone takes your dog to the pound."

"Can we get that, daddy?" Melissa asked.

"Of course, we can."

The food arrived and they ate mostly in silence. It was the first hot meal for Gray, Eva and Travis in a few days. Sonny and Melissa were ravenous, too.

After they ate, Sonny drove them into Canyon. They looked for motels that had the layout they were looking for and found one at the fifth attempt. After renting a block of three rooms, they drove to an aqua park Gray had found online. They spent most of the day in the water, with Gray, Sonny and Eva doing laps in the pool while Melissa concentrated on the slides and Travis just chilled. At six they headed home, picking up pizza and wings on the way.

Back at the motel, they ate at a picnic table just fifteen yards from their rooms, and afterwards Gray put Melissa to bed while Sonny and Eva went to a local liquor store and bought two cases of beer. When Melissa fell asleep, Gray joined the others at the picnic table. Travis had wandered off and was talking on his phone.

"She's been through a lot," Eva said, taking a bottle from a cooler she'd bought and twisting the top off.

"More than any nine-year-old should have to go through," Gray agreed. "Hopefully I can make it up to her in the next few months."

"And what after that?" Sonny asked. "If Johnson comes calling…?"

Gray drank half the bottle in one go and smacked his lips. "What *can* we do?"

Eva looked at Sonny, who nodded. "When we were in the diner, Travis said something that got me thinking. From the moment we left the facility, all I could think about was tracing my way back to get to Sonny. What if we got ourselves chipped, like Travis said? Ones where we can track them on a phone. I did some research at the pool and there are some with nationwide coverage. You download an app and it can pinpoint your pet's location anywhere in the U.S. using satellite tracking. There's one that has worldwide coverage, but it's still in development."

"And you want to put one of those in yourself?" Gray asked.

"Why not? If we do get separated again, at least we'll know where the other one is. Same goes for Melissa. Wouldn't you want to know where she was if she went missing?"

"Of course…but…there are ethical questions. I mean, putting a tracker in a child? Surely you can get arrested for that."

"Maybe you should ask her," Eva suggested. "I know she's only nine, but kids grow up so fast. Discuss it with her, at least."

"And what about when she turns fifteen and wants her privacy?" Gray asked. "Do I just rip it out again?"

"There is that," Sonny said. "We just thought, you know, with everything that's going on…"

"I know," Gray said. "And thanks. It's a great idea, really, but rather than implant something, I'll just get her an amulet or ankle bracelet. I got one with a camera in it, so surely there'll be one with a tracking device."

"I thought of that," Eva said," but when I woke up in that place, they'd taken everything of mine, including jewelry. I want something they can't detect."

Gray finished his beer and reached for another. "Then something sewn into her clothes," he said. "I'll think about it."

Travis returned. "Just spoke to Jed, my new office manager. Things are running smoothly, so I think I'll take a couple of days to get my head around things."

Eva tossed him a beer. "First, get your head around that. We owe you."

"Yeah," Gray agreed, raising his own bottle in a toast. "You saved our asses out there. To the fish boys!"

"The fish boys!" Sonny and Eva echoed.

Travis laughed. "I'm used to people being jealous of the SEALs, but I never heard them called fish boys before."

"Jealous?!" Sonny exclaimed. "Pah! We *invented* special warfare."

"Says the man who fell out of a twenty-foot boat!"

Sonny looked at Eva. "You told him?"

"She told me," Travis laughed again.

"I can't believe you told him."

Eva feigned surprise. "It was a long flight. What else were we gonna discuss? Crochet patterns?"

The banter continued into the night. When Gray retired to his room, he was as content as he'd been in years, but one look at Melissa's sleeping form reminded him how close he'd come to losing her. If Travis hadn't been so alert, if one of those bullets had penetrated the couch he'd been taking cover behind, he wouldn't be here right now. She would be alone in the world. Well, not quite alone. She still had her grandparents, the Hatchers, and Sonny and Eva would surely look after her until a permanent arrangement was in place.

But Gray didn't want any of that. He was her daddy, and wanted to be there for her, forever.

He thought about the idea Eva had floated. It would be wise to have a way to track his daughter, even if it wasn't something as permanent as an implant. In the morning, he would look to see what solutions were available on the internet.

That would solve one problem, but a bigger one remained. The ESO. They wouldn't stop, not until he was either dead or too frail to be of any use.

There was no point trying to figure it out through a beer haze. He decided to sleep on it and see what ideas the new day brought.

Chapter 41

Two days after receiving their new-found freedom, Eva and Sonny drove into Dallas in their rental. They'd said their goodbyes to Gray and Melissa, who had taken the SUV and headed for Florida, and Travis had caught a flight back to Tennessee.

Sonny pulled up in the parking lot of the electronics manufacturer they'd found on a technology review website. The company was the forerunner in GPS tracking devices, and they had read about an ongoing trial to implant chips into animals.

Sonny and Eva planned to be their human Guinea pigs.

At the reception desk they asked for John Devereaux, a man they'd spoken with briefly on the phone. After waiting on a couch for a few minutes, Devereaux came to greet them. He was in his thirties, a lot younger than Eva had been expecting for a company boss.

"Miss Hayes, Mr. Wilson, I'm John Devereaux. A pleasure to meet you. Please, come this way."

Devereaux led them down a few corridors to a spacious office and offered them seats on a leather couch. He sat in an armchair opposite them.

"So, you're interested in our new KD10 chip, I understand."

Over the phone, Eva had said they represented a nationwide veterinary company and were interested in stocking Devereaux's latest product in all of their outlets. First, though, they wanted to know about its capabilities and limitations.

"Very much so," Eva told him. "Could you tell us why it stands out against the other products on the market?"

Devereaux launched into a rehearsed spiel, waxing lyrical about the KD10. He told them about its long life, the extensive range of coverage, and the compact design which minimized the trauma on the subject. "It also doubles as a standard chip, so if the animal is taken to a vet, he can determine who the owner is. The main feature that distinguishes it from its competitors, though, is its global coverage. Other manufacturers can offer nationwide tracking, but if your dog is stolen abroad, that's not much use. The KD10 is the only model that can find a pooch anywhere from Manhattan to Melbourne, Bismarck to Beijing."

It was exactly what they needed.

"Could we see a demonstration?" Sonny asked.

"Most certainly," Devereaux told him. "We don't have any animals at this facility, but I can show you the process, if that's okay."

"That's fine," Sonny assured him.

Devereaux went to a cabinet and took out what looked like a metal glue gun. He ejected a small capsule from one end and handed it to Eva. "That's your chip," he said.

It was cylindrical, about half an inch long.

Devereaux took it back and replaced it in the gun. "You push the nozzle up against the animal's hind leg at an angle and simply press the trigger. The chip is buried in the muscle and uses a tiny thermoelectric generator to power itself using the animal's own body heat."

"Sounds simple enough," Eva said. "Is there any pain involved for the subject?"

"Initially the area will be a little tender, but the entry wound soon heals and normal mobility is back within a day or two."

"And how long will it last?" Sonny asked.

"At the moment, about five years, but we're constantly updating the design of the generator and hope to have something that will last the lifetime of the animal within the next few months."

Eva smiled. "It sounds like just the thing we're looking for. What about tracking? How is that done?"

Devereaux took out his phone and opened an app. "Each chip has a unique identifier. You register that with the app, which is free to download, and that's it. On here, I've got some prototypes that we sent out over the last few months. We track all units constantly as the telemetry helps guide any future improvements." He handed Eva the screen, which had a few dozen green dots spread out all over the country.

"Impressive," she said. She used her thumb and forefinger to zoom in so that she could see how accurate the instrument was. She spotted a couple of markers in Dallas, their current location, and expanded that view as far as it would allow. She realized that it was showing the building they were in. "You said there were no animals in this facility," she said. "According to this, there are two."

Devereaux took the phone from her. "That can't be right. We've sent out a few samples to the Humane Society, ASPCA and a few government agencies, but that's it. We don't perform any field testing ourselves." He fiddled with the screen for a few moments, then looked baffled. "According to this, the signals are either directly above this office, or directly below us. That can't be. Unless…" Devereaux strode to the cabinet and took out a small box. He opened the lid and compared the data from the signal to the chips in his hand. "I thought we might have registered a couple of samples without sending them out, but that's not the case. Besides, they wouldn't work because they're powered by body heat. They have a tiny battery to kickstart the process, but that isn't activated until just before they're shipped out to customers." He put the box back in the cabinet. "I can only apologize for this. Something is causing a false reading. Though I suppose it's better to discover it now than a few months down the line. I'll look into it urgently."

Eva wasn't that concerned about phantom readings. All she wanted was to get her hands on two of the chips.

"Would it be possible to take a couple of samples with us?" she asked.

"I'm not sure," Devereaux said. "I'd rather wait until we fix this glitch."

It wasn't what Eva was hoping to hear. If they left empty handed, it could be months before they got their hands on them, and they didn't want to hang around in the USA for that long.

"It's more for the effect on the subjects than the tracking ability right now," she said, but Devereaux didn't seem to be listening. He was focused on his phone, his fingers deftly manipulating menus.

"Could we?" Sonny said. "We really want to make sure our customers' pets don't suffer. That's our real concern."

Devereaux looked up from his screen. "No, I'm sorry. Until I can get to the bottom of this, I won't be conducting any further field tests."

Eva was inwardly furious, but didn't let it show. They would get their hands on some chips somehow.

"Well, thank you for your time. If you change your mind, you have my number."

Sonny looked at her pleadingly, but she used her eyes to indicate that they should leave. Devereaux shook their hands, and Eva assured him they could make their own way out.

"Why didn't you fight harder?" Sonny asked as they walked back to the reception area.

"Because that would have made him suspicious. We can always come back."

They'd just reached the entrance when they heard Devereaux calling their assumed names. They turned to see him running their way.

"Miss Hayes, are you wearing anything electronic?" he asked.

Eva thought about it, then shook her head. "All I've got is my phone. Why?"

"As you left my office, the markers on my phone moved, too. I think the interference is coming from something you're carrying. Look."

He showed them the phone, and on the screen the two green dots had moved. They now appeared to be just inside the building.

"Could you take your phone and put it on that table over there?" Devereaux asked Eva.

"Sure," she said. If it solved the issue, she thought, Devereaux might change his mind and allow them to take the samples.

She walked to a reception area twenty yards away and put her phone down, then walked back.

"This doesn't make sense," Devereaux said. "I saw the marker move when you did, but now it's back here. The issue isn't your phone, it's something else on your body." He looked deep in thought for a moment. "Would you mind coming back to my office? I want to test something."

Eva retrieved her phone and they retraced their steps to Deveraux's office, where he took a metal wand from his cabinet. "This can detect the RFID signal from the chips. If something is causing an erroneous signal, this might pick it up."

He asked Eva and Sonny to place their phones on his desk, then waved the wand over Eva's body. When it reached her midriff, it beeped.

"Extraordinary." Devereaux moved the wand down to her feet, then all the way back to her head. It was only when it reached her stomach that it reacted. "This is very strange. Unless you have an electronic bra, the chip is registering from inside you."

"That can't be," Eva said. She looked at Sonny. "Try him."

Devereaux ran the detector over Sonny's body, and it beeped when it reached his abdomen. "Exactly the same place," Devereaux said, stunned.

Eva rubbed the area where the signal had come from. It had troubled her for a couple of days, from the moment she'd woke after being shot in the jungle. The dull ache was now gone.

It was now clear how it got inside her. "Johnson," she muttered.

"Who?" Devereaux asked.

"Never mind. Who did you register these chips to?"

"I'm afraid that's—"

Eva grabbed him by the neck and squeezed. "You tell me that's confidential and I'll rip your throat out. Someone put this in me and I want to know who it was."

Devereaux gurgled, and Eva released her grip so that he could answer.

"I...I can find out." He took his phone out and woke up the screen.

"Slowly," Eva warned him. "I want to see everything you do."

A terrified Devereaux nodded. He held the phone so that Eva could see his every movement and clicked on her marker. This brought up a menu and he selected one of the options.

"It's a government research facility," he said. "Located in Roswell, New Mexico. They requested four units last week."

"Two for us, two for Tom and Melissa," Sonny said.

"Who?" Devereaux asked. "What exactly is going on?"

"I'll tell you," Eva said. "You've stumbled onto a government secret, one that you don't want to be part of. If you breathe a word of this to anyone, you can count the rest of your life in hours, not years. If you disable the signal, they will kill you. If you refuse to provide more units, they will kill you. You mention that we were here, they'll kill you. In short, you carry on as if you know nothing and you'll be fine."

Devereaux looked like his entire world had caved in.

"Also," Eva added, "I need the identifiers for the four units as well as details on how to download the app."

Devereaux took a sheet of paper from a note pad and tried to write down the details she'd asked for, but his hands were shaking too much.

"Just read them out," Eva said, taking the pen from his grasp.

Devereaux did, and Eva asked him for the name and address of the government research building. Once she had that, she signaled to Sonny that it was time to leave.

"Remember," Eva said to Devereaux as they reached the door. "We were never here. If anyone asks why our signals were here, say it's a GPS alignment error or something. You don't want us to come back."

She closed his office door behind her and they calmly walked out of the building. Once outside, Sonny stopped her.

"So we're taking these things out, right?"

"Wrong," Eva said, and started walking to the car. Once in, she told Sonny to get them out of the area fast.

"But you can't seriously want to keep that thing inside you," he said as he swung into traffic.

"Why not? We were going to get them, anyway."

"I know, but Johnson can see where we are."

"Exactly," Eva said. "If we go off grid, he'll know something's wrong, and if he suspects that we know about the operation in Roswell, he'll close it down. As things stand, we know where he is. Remember a few days ago, sailing up some river in Peru, you said we should take the fight to them?"

"I remember," Sonny said, "but you told me it was impossible. We have no idea who they are."

"That's right." She patted her stomach. "But now we have a place to start."

THE END

Thank you for reading *When Death Strikes*. We hope you enjoyed it.

If you would like to be informed about new releases, simply send an email with "Driscoll" in the subject line to alanmac@ntlworld.com to be added to the mailing list. Alan only sends around three emails a year, so you won't be bombarded with spam. You can find all of Alan's books and the reading order at www.alanmcdermottbooks.co.uk.